The Interim of Olympus

Chantel Grayson

Chapter 1

Hera

Was this a dream? If so, she wanted to live in dreams forever.

Hera had just observed her husband blow himself up into dust. And not just any sort of dust, but that mushroom-cloud shaped, surrounded by sparkles and halos with the dissipating fritter of frayed electricity sort of dust. The kind that signified complete and utter destruction. As she stood in his bedchamber, observing the space her husband once occupied, the skeletal form of Death joined her—materializing in a manner that was in keeping with his punctual arrival for an appointment. The servant of the Underworld was wearing his standard attire of a vest and morning coat. He removed his top hat in the presence of the Queen. An inkwell pen peeked from behind the lapel of his pocket as he examined the clipboard with his ivory-boned fingers. Since his face was free of skin, the depth of his eye sockets and the practiced arch of his brow somehow reflected an expression of befuddlement. She blinked and waited for him to translate the findings on his manifest.

"There seems to be…a discrepancy…" he said in a well-mannered tone. Although polite, Death was never greeted with warmth and a welcome. He was the symbol of the end and therefore the most hated deity in the world. Arguably the universe. And currently, unhelpful.

"Discrepancy," he said again.

She blinked. Again.

Death cleared his throat and turned the manifest to the left. He turned it to the right. Finally, upside down. His vision was clearer than most and yet, she deduced that they were both novices today.

Slowly, she removed herself from the bedchamber and into the portrait-lined corridor where nothing was amiss. The servants were sticking to the edges of the path so as not to darken the runners, the windows near the stairs were being cleansed of pollen and the sky was the shade of a robin's egg. Two doors down, a recessed closet occupied by a wooden pedestal that supported the rotary. The handset was polished and arched and decorated with petite and humble cherubs. Her manner was calm as she lifted it from the clasp and waited for the voice of Iris to ask her where she wanted to be connected.

"The Underworld."

The switchboard made a few necessary clicks until a beep, followed by another, preceded a tired voice. Tired and annoyed.

"What is it?" The tone used by each recipient did not vary, and neither did the list of possible callers. Out of each of the rotaries in Olympus, this one was connected to only two others. Because of this, she needed not to introduce herself, but considering the morning had begun with such a questionable occurrence, she did so anyway.

"It's Hera. I was calling to ask if my husband was with you." She crossed an arm over her waist and listened as a yawn interrupted their silence. Death peeked his head from the doorframe and mouthed his employer's name inquisitively. She gave a terse nod, wondering who else she would be calling at a time like this.

"Why would Zeus be here?"

"I don't know."

"Well…" the voice on the rotary extended as if he were stretching his arms. "What *do* you know?"

"That he's not here." She lowered her lashes and hoped her curtness could be heard. She had better things planned for her morning, such as getting fitted for a new gown, walking the gardens and tending to her peacocks. She had little patience for the back and forth. "But Death is here."

"…alright."

2

"For Zeus?" She turned to Death whose knuckles were holding the door frame as his shoulders lifted. She heard shuffling over the headset, followed by a *click*. An affable voice asked her if she wanted to accept a transfer.

She set the phone down on the pedestal and stepped back as a faint blue light emerged from the mouthpiece. Hades had manifested before her, visibly robbed of his sleep. His mostly salt-colored hair was disheveled, and his narrow, dark eyes squinted. They had flecks of silver in them that reflected the shadows as much as the light. Like a coin belonging to the aged pockets of a wise traveler. Hades was the sort who always dressed impeccably, the epitome of a gentleman. But today Hera was surprised to see that he donned a pair of simple cotton trousers, a shirt without a collar and a sack jacket that must have been the closest garment near the rotary. Even half asleep and in his leisurewear, he was near perfection.

He cursed as their eyes followed one another to his bare feet.

"Long night?" she asked flatly.

"Yes." He placed his hands firmly in his pockets. Tall and reassuring, she concealed the comfort she always felt from being in his presence. "I was reading."

She wondered if undergarments were now being printed with passages as Hades was never without the attention of a young maiden. No matter. She gave a spiritless apology for disturbing him and pointed in the direction of her husband's bedchamber. As well as Death. The servant proceeded into the room, manifest in hand, as quick as possible and attempted to appear comfortable in the company of his employer. Although his probationary period was over, Death continued to feel as though he needed to prove himself. He even offered his master his shoes, seeing how Hades' brow shook with disgust as he refused to enter Zeus' bedchamber without proper protection from the floors. Death lifted his own boots. There was something sticky coating the marble…

In addition to that, Zeus' room was offensively ostentatious and there was a lingering scent of nudity in the air. Columns in the shapes of garden nymphs lined the walls. Collectively they supported the domed, mural painted ceiling that depicted additional bathing women. The mural was only interrupted by the golden coffers and

3

the opening at the center that was a double glass pane. The sky was still blue. A perfect morning for walking her peacocks, Hera thought. In the center of the chamber was Zeus' *bed*. It was conjured from dense cumulonimbus clouds with dramatic curves and soft crests. Before the three of them, they were tall and malleable aside from the vacant imprint of Zeus' large form that was still pressed into the folds.

Zeus rarely left his post unless it was in honor of himself. Parades and whatnot. As the Godking of Mount Olympus, everything was brought to him with a crook of his meaty finger. Food. Game. Women. Even arguments. Hera had arrived there today to put an end to the *rivalry* between Aphrodite and Persephone. Those two had been feuding over Adonis, a human of course. One that Hera had threatened to kill in an artistic fashion if the two did not get their heads on right. After Adonis declared Aphrodite the most beautiful, Persephone set her sights on Hades in order to acquire a title. A feat Aphrodite could not have. The pettiness was enough to make Hera get involved. As Queen of the gods, she wanted to avoid another Helen of Troy situation. They were still the hot topic of gossip during tea with the Norse.

Zeus had done as he did with most matters and discarded the feud as if they were children who would soon grow bored of their toys. She remembered his lecture, as she associated it with the vexatious grin he used while scratching himself. She had folded her arms, determined to remain until he settled things outright. Instead, he took his thumb and forefinger and massaged them together. Static flickered and a lightning bolt formed. One he twirled like a piece of thread and threw against the wall behind her.

The bolt had bounced from the surface, flew over her shoulder, and into his fingers again. He picked another point on the wall, one close enough to her person to let her know he was doing this to annoy her and tossed it again. The tempo was like that of unwanted rain. She lifted her own fingers to her temple and massaged the porcelain skin of her forehead.

"I told them to share Adonis," Zeus had said, growing more confident in his sporting abilities. Her husband could barely race a chariot, let alone throw a lightning bolt with purpose. Ever since

Athena had been plucked from the gardens, Zeus had become lazy in the art of combat and called it delegation.

"They are gods," Hera reminded him. "They don't know how to share."

He chuckled. "Then I shall command it."

The lightning bolt had bounced off the wall again. He caught it again. He examined it between his fingertips and bounced it off the floor near her feet. He made a gesture, as if beckoning her to disappear, only this time, when he tossed the lightning at an experimental angle, the bolt of electricity ricocheted from wall to wall until it landed at his chest and entered the area where his heart was housed. It disappeared into his flesh, as they both stared at his skin and then to each other with a blank and unwavering expression. He lifted a finger, as if to berate her again, and then *poof!*

He was gone.

Hades furrowed his brow as she explained her side of the story without urgency.

"You've finally found a way to get rid of him?" he grinned as he leaned his shoulder on the doorframe. He then thought the better of it, straightened his posture and brushed his sleeve.

"I didn't do it," she leered at him. "Although, I wish I had."

Hades held a finger to his lips, playfully warning her to not reveal anything condemning. But she matched his grin, knowing that most would have celebrated her accomplishment.

"How do we even know he is dead?" She gestured towards Death. As if on cue, he was once again analyzing his clipboard.

"Well," Hades rubbed his arm. "What does it say on your manifest, Death?"

"There is a discrepancy."

"And what is that?"

"That is what it says. See?"

As he extended his papers, Hades had to remind him that they could not see the words etched onto the parchment—names of those whose time was approaching them, a list of locations Death needed to be and his shopping list. The manifest was only for his eyes and those of his co-workers in the Underworld—Janus and Hecate. There needed to be at least one perk to the job, considering the holder of the position had to assume the uniform of a skeleton and have their eyes permanently removed in order to see better. Hades didn't even know if the first part was entirely true. Why did Death have to look like a skeleton?

Hera turned to Hades. "Did you not see him down there? Are you sure?"

"If Zeus came bellowing into the Underworld, landed on Charon's boat and kicked and screamed his way all the way down the Styx, I am sure my housekeeper would have notified me. That," he lifted a shoulder, "and I would simply know."

"But he's not here..." Hera placed a hand to her heart. "It is strange. It's as if I felt him...*die*. But...he's not...gone..."

"Death," Hades said with a snap of his finger. "Find me some sort of tong so that I may sift."

Death, eager to please, found the closest object to satisfy the needs of his employer. A broom. As Hades mentioned the irony to Hera, who did not lighten her mood, he accepted Death's shoes in order to move about the bedchamber. He began using the bristles to maneuver through the clouds. The white curls hummed and puffed as they were being rummaged and brushed aside. Hera and Death peered behind him, interested in the excursion. When Hades completed his circle, finding nothing, he stood upright, leaned the broom in the crook of his elbow and folded his arms. His fingers rested underneath his chin.

"Very interesting..."

"Gods almighty." Hera took a deep breath.

"Now, now, we all agreed it was tacky to pray to oneself."

"Can you not make jokes at a time like this?"

He held out his hands. "If I thought this was an antic, I wouldn't be here. Neither you nor Zeus are capable of humor, which is how I knew this was indeed puzzling."

She began to pace. "He *is* gone. I *know* that."

"But he's not in the Underworld. *I* know that."

"Then where could he be? A god doesn't simply disappear."

"Well...it is written that only a god can kill a god...but suicide...." Hades turned to Death. "Is there a precedent?"

Knowing that no one else could examine his clipboard, Death made a show of flipping through the pages. All two of them. Over and over again as if he were indeed a scholar. Hera massaged her brow as Hades snatched the documents away.

"We can tell there are only two pages, we just can't read the bloody words!"

"Oh, r-right…well…um…to my knowledge…no, Your Grace," Death stood upright. "There is no precedent. But there is—"

Without a sound, Hera communicated that she was mere seconds away from turning them both into boars and having Cook butcher and serve them to the villagers for a spontaneous stew. Sensing this, Hades and Death proceeded to back away slowly, but the cloud began to shift causing the three of them to turn at the sight of sudden movement. Hades, not one to wield a sword or volunteer for combat, withdrew himself behind Hera. If anything was more frightening in all the lands it was the Queen herself. Death followed until Hades gave him a look that said there wasn't enough room behind Hera's tall and lithe form for the two of them.

A soft moan, or a groan, came from the confines of Zeus' bed. Until the clouds began to part and out rolled something small and naked. It squirmed and fidgeted, like a newborn baby deer learning to walk. It had a head full of long, wavy white hair that fell to the nape of its back. The skin was the color of soft russet and the eyes looked like golden nuggets trimmed in darkness.

As the creature finally found its footing, no one lifting a finger to help, they realized they were looking at a girl. Simultaneously, she yelped at the sight of them. She also realized she was indecent and reached for the cloud to shield herself. She made a face as if she had inhaled something foul, lifted the layers to her nose and dropped it instantly. She allowed her hands and tangled hair to cover her form instead.

"What is that…?" Hades mumbled to Hera's ear. "What. Is. That?"

"Not…Zeus…" Hera angled her chin. She and Hades both turned to Death who was examining the manifest closely. He pointed to the page and then to the girl. His eyes widened with the relief of accuracy.

"The discrepancy."

The girl, whoever she was, was not one that Hera had seen before. And she was aware of many of Zeus' conquests. Perhaps all of them. Zeus had reserved the bedchambers in this wing for his lovers and mistresses. He kept them close until he tired of them, changing them out as one did their coats for the seasons. This girl, however, was new and unused despite her appearance. She had a small frame with healthy thighs and breasts. Her slender neck supported an innocent round face. Round, like a heart with full lips and wide eyes that reminded her of a sitting rabbit. She swallowed and took a step back as Hades nudged Hera forward.

Coward, Hera scoffed at him before addressing the girl and commanding she identify herself.

"I...," the girl said, blinking. "I am...I am..." She quickly shook her head. "I can't remember...I don't know my name...I don't know where I am. I don't know who I am..."

When the girl's voice began to tremble, so did their surroundings. As tears threatened her eyes, the blue sky beyond the chamber window began to grey. The sound of distant thunder filled their bellies, reminding them of Zeus' frequent tantrums. Hades stepped from behind Hera, broom in hand. He extended the bristled end to the girl's shoulder and bestowed upon her gentle taps.

"There, there. Do not cry little one."

The girl attempted to dry her eyes but appeared bashful about removing her hands from their duty of protecting her breasts and thighs. Hades removed his coat, placed it on the end of the broom, and extended it to her. Cautiously, she reached for it. When the light fabric was in her possession, she wove her arms through the sleeves and secured the buttons with shy relief. She pushed her hair from her face and stood patiently, as if awaiting instructions.

Hera, whose expression was cold and fixated, felt the tap of Hades finger on her shoulder. She looked into his silver eyes, opposite the endless despair of Death's sockets. Hades crossed his arms and said academically.

"It is a woman."

"I can see that," Hera gritted her teeth. "But how did she get here? Who is she? And why has my husband vanished?"

"Hera, how could I possibly know for sure?"

"How could I possibly know for sure that you don't?"

He blinked and nodded, accepting her point. He looked over his shoulder at the girl who attempted to wave at them, reluctantly, as if she were watching animals behind the glass panes of an exhibit. He held up two fingers to wave back and signaled for Hera and Death to join him in a huddle. Elevating the privacy of their conversation. He continued.

"Do you think she is a misplaced soul? From the Underworld?"

Death answered this time. His confidence had joined him now. "We would have known, my co-workers and I. She is the discrepancy."

Hades rolled his eyes and made a smooth attempt to insert his shoulder in Death's place. Elevating the privacy of his and Hera's conversation.

"Do you get the feeling she is at the very least, ichor?"

"Our blood?" Hera looked appalled. "I would have an easier time believing that Uranus' genitals burst and gave birth, again." He chuckled, although she didn't mean it to be funny. "No, this is another one of my husband's conquests."

"I am not sure about that."

"I am. It's the only explanation. He was sitting on her, keeping her warm for when he was ready—"

"Um…"

"She is nothing."

Hades flashed a look of concern that was foreign to the Queen. Hera and her husband had not been intimate in centuries, which corresponded with the length of time she had been incapable of feeling affection for anyone other than her animals. She was far past pity, even if Hades was convinced there was something more to the girl.

"Hera, I *feel* something…" he tried his hand again. "Something that I cannot explain but, in a way, I can. As if she is in fact one of us."

9

"The discrepancy—" Death had also tried again, but they both hissed at him to shut up. Hera broke away from their group and turned in a way that made her skirts glide across her waist. She folded her arms and faced the girl. Hera's decision was made. Her sentence, final.

With a snap of her fingers and her festering anger, Hera summoned her prized peacock, Robin. The bird unleashed a dreadful howl befitting of his malicious glare and determination. Robin knew his mission: Rid the girl of her eyes and have her stagger about the gardens with sockets as deep as Death's. And after, Hera would turn her into a bear. The girl would stumble through the woods, blind and hairy, until she fell off a cliff and broke her neck. That was unless the hunters did not get to her first.

At the sight of the ferocious peacock, the girl was quick to leap into a sprint, away from Robin's wings and angry beak. The bird launched from its talons and hovered as majestic as a winged horse. The girl tripped on the cloud as she ducked behind the folds of Zeus' bed. The chase had Hera grinning at the heart. Her only regret was that her husband would not be here to see the demise of the mistress that he would dare to hide from her. Wherever he was, the afterlife or oblivion, the girl could join him there. Zeus and all of his lovers could keep one another for eternity, as she and he had once promised in their vows.

Hades knew not to stand between Hera and an act of vengeance, but she could feel his uncertainty. Death was shooting glares between his manifest and the girl. He slowly held up a finger, as if he were wanting to speak. He stopped himself and eyed the manifest again.

The girl cried out in pain as Robin's sharp beak nicked her heel. She hopped on one foot, scrambling to get away, but then she fell to the floor. The peacock pounced onto the back of her, sinking its claws into her flesh. His beak pierced and stabbed at her hands and yanked at her hair. She screamed and cried as she curled herself into a ball. Meanwhile, Hades nudged Hera and gestured eagerly to the stained marble.

Blood.

Golden blood.

The only blood that shone as bright as the sun was blood that belonged to the gods. It was what made them gods, the fact that Gaia had birthed them from her gardens. Gold blood, immortal blood, was the result of being shaped from a Titan. It did not make them family, simply of the same race.

"Hera!" Hades gritted his teeth. "Call off the attack!"

She ignored him.

Although she was surprised by the revelation of golden blood, her anger was so deeply rooted that it often took a life of its own. All she wanted was solace for Zeus' unfaithfulness. Hera wanted to get rid of the girl or bring about a painful next few hours, or days, or millennia. If it hurt him, she would bring pain to the girl over and over again.

"Hera!"

Hades' grey eyes stared directly into her own as his hands held firm on her shoulders. He was shaking her, pleading with her for the girl's sake. His empathetic expression pinched her heart, but she had learned to never show weakness. Even if she had to carry out sentences that she did not want to.

She shoved him aside and was about to enact her curse when the sound of thunder and a flash of lightning pulsed before their eyes and startled them all. The smell of char and burning flesh filled their noses. It was unhappily married with the stench of old sex.

The girl was on her back, fizzing with electricity and panting heavily. Her wounds were in the process of suturing themselves as her fingers clutched the lifeless Robin. Hera's beautiful peacock, once the color of precious gems and pure juniper and spruce, had been burnt to a crisp. He reminded her of Icarus, only worse, because she did not mourn Icarus. She would mourn Robin. The bird twitched from the girl's fingers and crumbled into ashes. Everyone remained silent, stunned and still. Everyone, except for Death. He walked over to Robin, examined his clipboard and pointed happily.

"Right on schedule."

Chapter 2

Ares & Poseidon

"Did you know, I've seen his bare arse more as an adult than when he was a child?"

"Yes, Your Grace."

"It's actually quite disturbing, the more that I think about it."

"Yes, Your Grace."

"Do you usually leave him like this?"

"His lordship can become hostile when abruptly awoken. The staff, they have yet to move past the sudden departure of Mr. Winston, one of the footmen. He made the mistake of shaking Lord Ares to inform him of a letter, and then met the unfortunate end of one of his lordship's spears."

"Surely, he revived." Gods weren't allowed to kill humans. Not directly anyway.

"Be that as it may, Your Grace, Mr. Winston now suffers from post-traumatic stress disorder. He can only eat his meals with a spoon and prefers glue to needles when it comes to mending his lordship's clothing. No, we dare not wake him."

Poseidon removed a cheroot and a pack of matches from the inner pocket of his morning coat. Striking the head on the coarse strip, he held the flame to the end of the bark-colored husk and inhaled. If he allowed the fire the luxury of cleansing the scene before him, it would save him the task. He took another puff, considering this option strongly.

Ares lie planted on his stomach. Snoring. Lifeless, yet noisome. His knees were folded beneath him and his trousers were bunched around his ankles. Regardless of gender, someone beautiful must have accompanied him at some point during the night. Or, he was pissing out the window of his coach, hit a bump in the road and fell to the floor without the energy required to lift himself again.

Ares, a notorious rake who spent his evenings drinking and gambling at his own clubs, was so infamous that his actions were chronicled in the papers, yet frequent enough that they were just as quickly forgotten. Each week that the heat-pressed tabloids arrived through the post, Poseidon had felt as though he were reading a serial. Ares and his latest adventures were more entertaining than the races. Poseidon, the more responsible of the two, always had a laugh at the illustrations. One of Ares covered in his own sick was a holiday present he had hired a muralist to paint in Ares' drawing room. Poseidon unveiled the surprise at a holiday party. Ares had not yet painted over it.

Poseidon finished his cheroot before giving the order to the butler to prepare a bath for Ares and for the valet to lay out his clothing and pack his trunks. When it was just the two of them in the garden of the residence, Poseidon lifted his hands and conjured a funnel of wind and water. The adolescent tornado spun with vigor as it spiraled into the air and thrashed towards the open door of Ares' coach. It entered the confines and assaulted without pause. Poseidon knew Ares was awake by the spray of spears that were hurled in his direction with murderous intent.

Poseidon lowered his chin to avoid one of the attacks. His ichor, known for being one of the best warriors, was too impaired to stumble to the earth with grace. Ares was drenched and cursing. The playing cards he often used to cheat at the tables were half stuck to his face.

"Attack me when I am most vulnerable!? I will—"

Poseidon said nothing as Ares waved his arms and manifested more spears to come to his aid. He instead looked to the house as a sharp scream emerged from the residence. The butler, nonplused, approached them with a towel for his master and news of Mr. Winston's demise. One of the spears had flown through a window and stabbed the footman in the throat. His death was pardoned but painful.

***

Considering that Ares' coach was in the process of fumigation, they sent for a hansom to escort them to the train station. Once on board his private car, Ares finished his serving of coffee in two swallows. He placed the crystal on a tray, which was immediately retrieved by a servant. He extended his fingers for another as he leaned back in his chair and allowed a handmaiden to stroke his forehead with a cool compress. She gently brushed aside his earthy brown curls and gave his jawline extra attention. Another maiden was set to task on his fingers.

Poseidon did not ask why a man who did not bother to toss his own garbage in the bin would need to have his hands massaged. Instead, he remained firm in the settee across from Ares. One leg rested over the knee of the other. He held two fingers of whiskey on the armrest and kept his gaze fixated out the window.

"I grant permission for you to speak your opinions." Ares peered at Poseidon when the maiden repositioned herself. He mocked dramatically, "Tell me, what hast thou brooding on such a fine day?"

"I am not brooding."

"You look as though you are about to murder someone."

"That's just how my face is."

"I've seen you smile. Once." Ares' deeply tanned skin absorbed the shine of the finger bowl that was being placed before him. Completing her chore of washing his hands, the handmaiden dabbed them gently with a towel. He examined his freshly cleaned nails and nodded his approval, but before she was excused, he gestured for her to lean down so he could whisper something in her ear. Her pale skin turned crimson as she giggled and escorted the second maiden back to the servant's car.

Poseidon was birthed centuries before Ares, and therefore lived long enough to see his early beginnings in the philandering ichor. Poseidon was once quick to anger, quicker to judge and distastefully arrogant. He invented the talent for saying just the right thing to start a tryst, careless of the consequences. When one lived as long as the gods, personalities came in waves. Some as treacherous and everlasting as the storms he created.

Currently, he was in a tolerant mood when it came to Ares. He was also of a ruling mind when it came to Oceanus, his realm. As the Ocean King, his goal was for the people of his realm to live long and prosper. Unfortunately, they were still feeling the effects of Zeus' hypocrisy. Hence, his transparent mood.

Zeus, the Godking, had a reputation for leading the world to war, if and when opportunity had suited him. Poseidon's involvement in the most recent scuffle was a bitter taste that coated his tongue like dark chocolate. He despised dark chocolate. Having once been in love, he learned how foolish it was to succumb to such an inexplicable ailment. It was an invisible contract where man signed over his body, his heart and his mind to another to do as they pleased. It turned scholars into circus performers and sharks into minnows. So, when he heard that the battle of Troy was over a woman, he refrained from rolling his eyes. But he couldn't help his outburst when he learned it was also because of his ichor. Them and a damned apple.

The story, he vaguely remembered, involved Zeus instigating Paris who was the judge at the Winter Ball's Apple of Discord Pageant. The usual participants stood on a stage in their most beautiful of gowns—Hera, Athena, Persephone, Aphrodite, a few angels, a few humans. Paris, in his first year of moderating the ballots, was susceptible to bribes. Aphrodite, arguably the most beautiful, knew how to persuade a man as vain as Paris. She offered him the love of Helen, debatably the most beautiful human in the world, if she received his vote, initiating a series of events that ruined the Winter Holiday for some, made them the laughing stock of others and put an end to the pageants. Everyone was more concerned about the pageants.

Poseidon didn't see the logic of getting involved, but Zeus demanded he do his part. Ships. One thousand to be exact. His realm was in charge of building, staffing and navigating the vessels that launched towards the city. Poseidon was still paying the bills, salaries and overtime for his laborers that Zeus should have reimbursed him for.

As if reading his mind, Ares smiled at him as he continued to sip his coffee. "It's the Godking, yes? Are you still quibbling over the war?"

It was centuries ago, and Poseidon wanted to move past this as much as anyone. His next endeavor, with Ares as his business partner, was sure to bring the profits his realm needed.

Pleasure yachts.

Pompous ships that could trap people in the middle of the ocean and force them to eat, spend and gamble without escape. It was opposite the ship of war and trade that he was used to. This creation would be a portable prison for fun and leisure. Poseidon and Ares, having the knowledge of business and vices, approached the project with equal enthusiasm. Poseidon was in charge of the planning, building and logistics, while Ares oversaw the aesthetics, food and game.

It was a prime idea, but also expensive. The initial investment, patent and construction was hefty even for a god. His coffers weren't empty, but they weren't healthy either. He had paid all of the expenses from the war first, leaving him little room to spend unwisely. He needed Zeus' reimbursement and also his agreement when it came to Oceanus. Poseidon's realm was hidden under the waves, but there was an assortment of islands that bordered the opening like a mother's embrace. Islands that Poseidon managed but Zeus failed to grant under his jurisdiction—making Poseidon the glorified landlord of Milos, Icaria, Rhodes and Cythera. A landlord who was not granted any of the island's profits. It was only fair to allow him to absorb the islands into Oceanus. The Godking denied him.

What had weakened Poseidon's control of the islands had strengthened the strife between himself and his ichor. If he could help it, Poseidon wanted nothing to do with them.

When their train came to its stop, they descended the platform and headed for the array of decorated servants who were already managing their trunks. The vessel had the palace crest of an eagle plastered on the side and a pair of clean, white Thoroughbreds that waited patiently. It had been some time since he visited Olympus and when he did, his method of transportation was a transfer through the rotary. But this was an *emergency*, as Iris' call had implied. One of astronomical potential. Out of familiarity with Ares' behavior regarding palace correspondence, he knew he would be punished for not taking the time to retrieve him along the way. That, and he considered Ares a friend.

"I do wonder what this is all about." Ares ran his fingers through his curls and examined his appearance in the reflection of the coach. He had matching brown eyes with hints of red. He was wearing one of his better suits of course, considering the company they were more likely to cross. "Just because we all agreed to try our hands at this *familial meeting...thing,* doesn't give her the right to abuse the power. We just saw one another one...two decades ago?"

Poseidon shrugged and caught a glimpse of himself in the reflection next to Ares. His attire was more casual and relaxed, although they were going to the same place. His tailored coat was unbuttoned to reveal a shirt with a flat collar. His trousers were decorated by the chain of his pocket watch and not the studs of jewels that Ares preferred. Further contrasting, Poseidon was a bit taller and leaner than Ares. His stature and broad shoulders came from working alongside the builders who birthed ships. His blue eyes were almost hidden under his short but shabby black hair. He ran his fingers over the stubble along his cheeks and jaw. He would soon be due for a shave.

It took additional time to get settled into the coach. Ares did not pack lightly. Each of his dress coats required their own confine and Poseidon had to deny him the request of bringing a few maidens along for company. Besides, time alone gave them an opportunity to speak more freely and discuss the details of Iris' cryptic message. Iris operated the switchboard at the palace and was responsible for transferring calls. She also oversaw the mailrooms. Needless to say, she was knee-deep in invitations and a heavy smoker. She had the front-line of gossip because she often eavesdropped when she shouldn't have.

But not even she could offer more information. She simply told Poseidon to return to the palace as soon as possible. That he and Ares were among the small selection of ichor who were asked to attend. Poseidon, Ares as well, knew that if there was any trouble facing the palace, Hera was the type to handle it herself. Although her methods were questionable, she was consistent in her independence when it came to ruling and managing her realm, ichor and husband. If not, defiant. Meetings were only called to settle disputes or to *catch-up*. It was something new they were trying, instead of throwing each other from cliffs or mutilating one another's favorite humans.

As the two pondered what the *emergency* could entail, Ares shook his head and pouted. "If this is another trap where one is to gaze upon their beauty and decide who is the fairest—"

"I don't think that's the case."

"Good. I for one am smart enough to know that there is never a correct answer. One might believe they should only fear their Queen, but I fear all of them."

Poseidon smirked. Although he was at the mercy of the hierarchy of ichor, he did not fear anyone. Not even Zeus. He did however wonder why Zeus did not call this meeting. Hera was usually in attendance unless he made a show of dismissing her so that he, Poseidon and Hades—kings of Olympus, Oceanus and the Underworld—could speak frankly. Or argue without witnesses.

As they traveled along the groomed roads, they knew that they were nearing their destination due to the overwhelming scent of flowers. The gardens were full of anemones, hydrangeas, spring roses and palms. Wild animals grazed, horses were exercised by the stable boys and lakes and rivers became organized garden features with stone walls. Oversized vases and marble statues were being cleaned and polished.

They passed through the village first. Ares took stock of any maidens he felt would be in need of his company later. The homes were in uneven rows and lined with trees and beloved gardens. The walls were made of stucco, wood and lightly washed stone. Communal baths were filled with pure, cobalt blue waters where the people bathed and cleansed with a fortitude that accompanied life on the mountain. A forest that was very much alive, swayed in the distance.

Ares, whose sightseeing became more objective, lowered the glass partition of his window and squinted. With an eager grin, he extended his hand towards Poseidon.

"Hand me one of those heating stones."

"No."

Ares turned to him and frowned. "Come now Sai, they're on your side. Just there, under your boot."

He lowered his chin and emphasized. "They are for keeping the coach warm."

Ares relaxed his face into a small grin. "I preferred a hot one," he reached into his pocket and withdrew a coal-colored pebble. "But this will do."

Poseidon leaned his head back, not interested in bearing witness to what would happen next. He did imagine it, however. The flower-picking Adonis frolicking through the gardens with a basket over his arm and wearing a sliver of fabric. The man was always semi-naked, and mortal, and annoying. He spoke in one of those sing-song voices that made everything seem fuzzy. Poseidon avoided him, but Ares loathed him to distraction.

If there were ever a contest between the three most handsome ichor—Poseidon, Ares and Hades—the outcome would be debatable. Of course, if *Adonis* were encouraged to insert himself, he would win without qualm. Not because he was beautiful, but because he was desirable among all the women who crossed him.

"Careful." Poseidon felt he would do his duty by warning Ares once. "You'll be as jealous as Hera."

"I am not jealous of that chubby bastard," Ares growled. "And, I can have any woman who wants me." He gripped the stone in his clutches, turning it to dust. He then corrected himself by withdrawing a second from his pocket and taking aim.

Ares would not admit that perhaps he was a little envious. Adonis was the preferred dance partner at balls. Maidens would wave their handkerchiefs at the man as he pranced down the paths of Olympus. They touched his leg underneath the dinner table and offered him their breasts for comfort. He had two of the loveliest gods feuding over him and instead of putting an end to the quarrel by choosing a side, he would say in a lulling tone that *the beauty of love is that there is always enough of it to go around.*

Adonis was an idiot.

Winding his arm, Ares hurled the stone out the window and watched as it hit its zenith and plunked onto Adonis' skull. The only god to match Athena in combat, his aim was impeccable. Ares was convinced that today, the man's choice to wear leaves in his hair was enough to earn him a punch or two. But a stone to the head, one that made his flowers spill high into the sky and his basket tumble along with his body, was solace. Ares quickly lifted the glass of the window and lowered himself in his seat. He held his hand to his mouth and snickered.

Chapter 3

Zeus?

They were talking amongst themselves. Whispering and shrugging. For her, there was waiting. A lot of waiting. She was tucked behind a curtain of the amphitheater and asked to remain until she was called upon. She had watched as shadows emerged from the doors that disappeared beneath the mezzanine, until a small group formed and hung loosely in a circle. Personalities, and sometimes voices, were as large as the room itself. Her eyes scanned her surroundings, and once again were amazed by the most spectacular room she had ever seen.

Maybe she had seen better.

Maybe, she had not.

The theater was a perfectly shaped dome. The seats were trimmed in gold and lined with velvet cushions the shade of eggplants. The murals of nymphs on the ceiling were illuminated softly by countless chandeliers and crystal cut wall sconces. She imagined ballerinas gliding across the lacquered floors like skaters kissing the ice. She imagined opera singers standing with their fingers intertwined with one another and creating music with the unique and heavy instrument that was their voice.

Maybe she had been an opera singer.

Maybe she had been a ballerina.

Maybe, she had not.

She tried to close her eyes and picture a life before. There had to have been a life before. *She* had to have been. She wondered if she had a home that was made of stone or clay. If there was a kitchen that always smelled of bread. Perhaps it was crowded with plants that she sprinkled with water. Maybe her furniture was chipped on the corners. Maybe her windows were deeply smudged with the debris of a bustling city.

Whenever she strained too hard, she felt a migraine knock at her temples. Her memory, even her name, was difficult to recall. It was like a secret buried beneath the floorboards of the amphitheater. *Discrepancy* is what they called her. It was whispered and questioned as she remained hidden behind the curtains.

After the incident with the peacock—she felt horrible for the animal but was more alarmed at how quickly her wounds were healing—the next thing she remembered was the angry woman storming from the room and the skeleton man giving her a bow as the broom man shuffled her down the corridor with the pointy end of his tool. She could keep his coat, he had told her. He was polite, if not determined to keep his distance. As if she had been swimming in something septic. When they entered a room that was heavy with steam and floral scented oils, multiple hands assaulted her at once. They were tugging, pulling, attempting to remove the very clothing—the only clothing—she currently owned.

In her mind, the fingers of these servants had morphed into talons that belonged to a vicious bird. Their noses had sunken into their lips and formed a single beak that lunged and shrieked at her. Once again, her fear had erupted into a wave of harsh lightning. She was unaware of how she was able to conjure such power. She appreciated, however, that it made her attackers flee in the opposite direction.

That, and it felt absolutely delightful.

She had been overcome with the notion of something remarkable, the fact that she could burn the place to the ground if she chose.

She remembered how she had cackled insanely as the electricity surged from her fingertips, and when she rolled the currents into a ball, which she had hurled at the priceless artwork that hung on the walls, leaving behind only charred squares. She began to feel confident and showy, like a star athlete in the colosseum. In her naked state, she did not feel vulnerable, but like a god among gods. Like the bringer of wrath or the conqueror of the heavens. As if she were invincible. That, or her mind had completely lost her.

Some of the servants leapt out the windows, while others hid behind the furniture in fear. All the while, the broom man barked.

"Ambrosia!" he commanded. "Quickly!"

A bowl was suddenly presented before her by a cowering servant. In it, a serving of perfectly diced fruits, lounging and lining the rims of a delicate cloud of white. As if the shape of the dish were a winding road and the fruit formed a little caravan. A tempting caravan. The white was pure and light and fluffy. It smelled sweet and comforting. There was a slight char on the tip, as if it had been roasted before the final presentation. Like marshmallows. Delicious, pure marshmallows. It was calling to her. The smell, the sight, the warmth it provided had calmed the storm within her chest and brought about a sense of longing. A longing to eat.

"What is it?" she asked, lowering her deadly fingers.

"A delicious treat. Befitting gods." The broom man took it from the servant and waved it to her in a zig-zag pattern. Her eyes followed obediently. His smirk need not try so hard. "Would you like a taste, little one?"

To prove his sincerity, he had taken a spoon, dipped it into the crystal bowl and lifted it to his lips. She watched as his throat massaged the treat until it settled in his belly. He was about to take another helping when she reached for it. As she took her first bite, she closed her eyes and pictured the bliss of being everywhere and nowhere all at once. Her shoulders relaxed and her body's warmth increased ten-fold, stemming from the muscles of her heart like tree branches induced with concentrated sugar.

With the ambrosia in hand, she was easily guided to the bath. The handmaidens did not struggle as they detangled her hair. They washed, combed and braided her tresses into two sections that began at her crown. Her hair wove into an intricate knot that allowed the remaining thick strands to cascade like a waterfall down her back. Her second serving was given to her to coax her onto a platform where seamstresses worked to find a gown. Compared to the angry woman who snorted in her direction, she was a head shorter and a little fuller in her hips and breasts, so the seamstresses had to chop and release multiple inches of fabric to make her presentable.

When they finished, and she was on her third serving of ambrosia, she had a moment to glance at herself in the mirror. The gown was the color of gold, like most things in the palace, and had an empire waist and ribbons that wove through pieces of eyelet lace. It felt expensive and soft.

Maybe she had been a princess.

Maybe, she had not.

Now, looking at the floor of the amphitheater, her bowl sat empty once again. With nothing in it, it was a useless piece of crystal she tapped gently with her foot. She liked the sound of the curve of glass rolling about on a hard surface. With nothing else to distract her, she was unsure of what to do. She could attempt to count the chandeliers again, and the wall sconces or the number of nude women that were painted on the murals. She could wander backstage and explore. She wanted to explore. But the broom man asked her to stay here. And, he had given her four servings of ambrosia with a promise of more. The least she could do was comply.

She removed her gloves and eyed her fingertips. She felt a pulse of static emitting from them like fizz from freshly opened soda water. As she increased the intensity, ever so slightly, she noticed that a loose strand of hair was floating towards her hands. She smiled. Like the broom man, waving the ambrosia, she waved her hand to make her hair follow suit. A budding snake charmer, her hair chased her fingers up, down and around.

She giggled, a little louder this time.

"Enjoying yourself?" the broom man asked. He had returned and was standing before her, tall and clean and with shoes.

"No," she quickly lowered her hands and placed them behind her back like a dutiful student. "I mean yes, I mean…I am patiently content, Mr. Broom Man."

"Broom ma—" he chuckled. It was at that moment she determined that she had nothing to fear from him. That she liked him. It was as if trustworthiness, with hints of a carefree perspective, pulsed from him like the static in her fingers. It wasn't simply because he had given her ambrosia, she told herself. "My name is Hades. Come, I want to introduce you to my ichor."

"Ichor?" she asked, walking beside him and wondering why on earth his mother would call him "Hades." He looked like an Edwards or Harrisons or Sebastians. Yes, a Sebastians. Intelligent, cunning and never without the silent command of respect. His smile was kind and she wondered if the flicker of silver in his eyes reflected a mischievous youth. Maybe, "Hades" had been a pet name for trouble. Her mind settled on that with a surprising ease.

"It's what we call our race. Or, anyone who bleeds gold, as you do."

She pointed to herself. "I am ichor?"

"So it seems."

"Ichor, the Discrepancy." She nodded with attempted dignity. "That is who I am."

When she looked up at him, proud to form this conclusion about herself, his jaw twitched as he averted his gaze. He was withholding a laugh that would have shaken the amphitheater to its core. Opposite the angry woman from earlier, who stood facing them, still with a scowl on her face.

Her name was Hera, and she was quite stunning. If he were the moon—pale and grey—her features would have made her the night sky that embraced it. Her hair was twilight black with subtle notes of blue. Her eyes were the color of a penguin's tuxedo. She had long lashes, pale and creamy skin. She was tall and thin, and her hair was curled, pinned and secured with expensive hairpins shaped into leaves. Everything about her was affluent and *more*. She was more beautiful than the rest. More important. More frightening.

"I apologize for the mess I made of your peacock." She bowed. When in doubt, bow to all.

Hades cleared his throat and ushered the conversation away from the deceased bird. He gestured to the rest in the circle, beginning with Ares. Another handsome sort who had deeply tanned skin, brown hair and beautiful, volcanic red eyes. He also appeared to be snickering. His shoulders bounced as he tried to keep himself together.

Athena was glaring at him. Tall and strong and very pretty, she might have been close to slapping poor Ares. Either that, or she was ready to slap the discrepancy. Demeter stood next to her. The worrisome sort. She was twisting her handkerchief so hard between her fingers that her knuckles were beginning to turn purple. Hestia, dressed in a conservative habit that only showed the skin of her face, appeared to be concerned for all involved. The one called Aphrodite, rivaling Hera in beauty, was glaring, sizing up the discrepancy, unhappy with the results and ready to issue a challenge. Persephone possessed a beauty that made one look twice, otherwise they might have missed it. Persephone was the only one who bowed back, out of politeness. And finally, there was Poseidon.

His allure was threatening. His gaze was dangerous. The brown of her skin fought hard to not betray her, but she could feel the rush of heat into her neck and cheeks. The blood in her body was off course, making her feel as though her physiology had taken a holiday. Her breathing had ceased. Her heart was no longer beating. The moisture abandoned her throat and her tongue was as dry as a frayed rope.

Leaving only the electricity within her veins to keep her alive.

Electricity that was uncontrollably pulsing at her fingertips, causing her to keep her hands behind her back and pray no one could feel her intensity. Her power was a toy magnet compared to his pull. She swore she saw the lights flicker, but that could have been in her mind.

He was so handsome. Tall, lean with broad shoulders. Black layered hair that looked as if he had just rolled out of bed. His piercing blue eyes rivaled the vibrancy of the peacock's breast that had assaulted her. She looked at him again and then quickly looked away.

"Alright there, little one?" Hades reached to place his hand on her shoulder. She shook her head and playfully took a step away.

"Me? Oh yes, sir, I am fine. I am…" She stopped. The return of her blood flow had brought with it her wit. She blinked and shook her head again as she scanned the group before her. "Each of you are…named after the Olympians? Greek gods?"

They exchanged glances among themselves. Some of them cruel, but mostly entertained. Especially Ares, who had to keep his hand to his lips as Athena gave him a hard slap on the shoulder. Hades made an elongated vowel sound while scratching hair.

"We *are* the Olympians," slowly he added. "And gods."

She couldn't help herself. She didn't know where it came from, but as if she were riding Ares' coattails she began snickering behind her fingers. Chortling. Giggling. Until the two of them were laughing uncontrollably and no one was able to explain to a jury the source of their inappropriate humor. She took a breath and heaved so hard that electricity pulsed from her body like a magnetic wave. Each of the chandeliers flickered until she hiccupped. And then, the lights went out.

***

Considering there was no electricity within the entire palace, and she could feel her lack of support from the ichor as much as she could feel her power surging through her bones, she decided to take Hades' advice and walk herself through the gardens while he and the others continued to chat. They had moved to the conservatory, a room full of windows with a domed roof. She understood the need for separation, even if she preferred not to be alone.

Because Olympus was settled in the mountains, it was accustomed to strong winds and the former Godking's lightning storms. Therefore, nothing was built over three stories tall, not even the palace. This did not compromise the extensive reach of the estate. It stretched well over 2,000 acres. The majority of the grounds were occupied by gardens and baths. Clusters of oriental lilies, brightly colored tulips, roses and white camellias spotted the horizon like flecks of paint. Blades of grass created a ripple effect as the wind pushed through them. Topiaries styled to perfection lined stoned pathways. There were no unique rivers. The waters were all confined in glass-tiled holes that wove through the gardens like a spider's web. They were decorated with waterfalls and oil-burning lanterns. Horses grazed in the distance and columns, molested by ivy, supported pergolas that reminded her of cake toppers.

People bathed. In the waters, in the sun, in the flowers. Clothing was optional here, no matter the shape of one's body, and for reasons she could not explain, she did not mind. She simply nodded and waved at anyone who smiled in her direction. She was so lost in the surrounding beauty that she nearly collided with someone who was kneeling in the grass near a rose bush.

"Oh, I'm so sorry sir."

"No worries," a chipper voice caught her. Given how strange the morning had been so far, she could use a bit of chipper. A man with cherubic features, a plump form and a basket full of flowers smiled broadly at her. He smelled like a dream and he looked as though he felt like a pillow. She suddenly had the urge to hug him. Just being in his presence had corrected her as she realized the waves and smiles that she had earlier received were not meant for her.

"You're a new sight," he said in a lovely tone.

"I am new...I believe."

"Ah, welcome to Olympus." As he reached into his basket, his fingertips brushed a rose that he then withdrew. He examined the petals and held it up to her face. He shook his head, mumbled to himself and placed it back into the basket. It took only a second for his smile to return as he nodded at his assortment. He came across a yellow chrysanthemum with hints of ochre. With care, he broke off the stem and placed it in her hair.

"Yes," he said with a prayer's clap. "That is the one."

"You are very kind. Thank you, sir."

"Adonis." When he bowed at the waist, she could see a few flakes of red in his otherwise golden curls. As if he had been hit with a bucket of paint. Or...blood. "And you?"

"Dis...crepency..."

He made a face, as if her name were, in fact, the most unusual. More so than Hades, Persephone and Aphrodite. He was about to speak when a trickle of blood escaped his hair and crawled down his forehead. She leapt back as he placed his fingers to his temple.

"Oh darn," he moaned politely. "You must forgive me, as a stone fell from the sky and collided with my head earlier."

"You need a doctor."

He waved his hand. "I will heal. As I usually do when it happens. It is my luck, you see, but also fortunate that it is in fact me and no one else that is the victim of the falling rocks. Now tell me, what brings you to Olympus? Did you come for work? Marriage? Are you a traveling songstress?"

"I am not entirely sure." She did not know how to explain memory loss. If she had forgotten something, how did she know what it was she once remembered? She could only tell him what she could, which did not deter him. He listened with visible surprise as she explained her sudden appearance in Zeus' room. How she possessed Zeus' power.

"But you remember how to speak. What is that thing, over there?" Her eyes followed to where his finger pointed.

"A statue…"

"There!" he said with a grin. "Not all is lost."

Her ability to recall basic objects did not ease her mind. It did not compare to what was missing. Turning points, momentous life experiences, secrets, a first kiss, a first dance, a family, or being a god. She had the powers of Zeus flourishing through her body and golden blood giving her life. And no one could explain who she was. No one could explain Zeus' absence.

Adonis, much to her delight, did have a plan. He suggested that he accompany her on a tour of the village and that maybe someone would recognize her. If not, a smell or a sound could bring about the return of her memory. He introduced her to villagers, there were so many, and she knew that she wouldn't be able to recall most of their names. But they all seemed to know of him. Men scowled and maidens abandoned their tasks of washing or reading to be by his side. He handed each of them a flower. Something befitting and unique. She saw the jealousy in their eyes when two women were bestowed the same breed. However, Adonis made sure to match them with the appropriate color as well.

No chrysanthemums.

Her flower was so aggressive looking in its girth and mass and abundance of petals, and as they explored the grounds of Olympus it only became a clearer reflection of how out of place she felt. It was a flower for her. Different from all the rest.

"Adonis…" she waited for him to return to her. He was being handed a pie to fit into his basket. He had been given plenty of food—from breads to fruit—and the items somehow sat snugly in his magical vessel. He was even able to swing it gently as he pranced.

They were walking by the baths near the palace again. The sun was high in the sky and the weather was uncertain.

Maybe it would rain.

Maybe, it would not.

It reflected her mood perfectly. Puzzling and dubious. She was walking beside Adonis on top of Mount Olympus. She could conjure electricity. If she said so out loud, she would think herself mad.

"Yes, my lady?"

"What if I told you this was all a dream and you weren't real?"

He seemed to give her question some thought before he extended an apple to her, "Then I shall hope you never wake as I do not want this life to end." She bit into the fruit and hummed as her tongue touched the coarse and sweet exterior. The fruit here was delicious. "I was going to visit Iris at the post. Would you like to come? We can see if there has been an obituary or an advertisement for a missing person. Someone fitting of your description."

"What a great idea!"

Without hurry, they reached a section of the palace that was tucked in the rear, she noticed that it was busy with servants and working-class people entering a set of large double doors. Through the portal was a small corridor that led to a set of stairs that brought them deep underground. When they reached the landing, she gasped.

It was as if she had arrived in an entirely different city. Conveniences that were available in congested cities across the world. A network of hallways was cramped with restaurants and market stands. Merchants sold produce and vegetables as well as canteens stacked with today's lunch of roast beef soaked in onion soup and fresh bread sliced and sprinkled with dried tomatoes and feta. Women carried burlap sacks as they exited tea shops. Men, with their pocket watches and whiskers, left the milliners with repaired hats. Little girls decorated in ribbons enthused over the button-made dolls in the windows of the haberdashery.

Carts were pulled by the waist of strong young drivers, carrying people in pairs. A small boy stood on a crate waving gossip sheets for sale. His shorts and stockings were clean from being in an environment free from the grime of a contaminated city. She recognized Ares on the cover. Him and, she supposed, his rear.

"Where are we?" she asked Adonis. It was as if she were wedged between traditions. Some stuck with the old—dressed in wraps and sheer silks. Others were moving forward—in tweed, leathers and furs.

The European charm colored their cheeks. Husband and wife walked arm in arm. Sons sat on the safety of their father's shoulders while an inbred dog wobbled close behind. She had to dodge a pram that slowed for her to peep inside. A baby, the color of freshly creamed coffee cooed inside. She goggled over it as the mother gave her attention to Adonis.

"We are still in Olympus," he said, gently placing his hand on her shoulder and leading her past the laundry. "This is the mountain."

"These people live here?"

"Not really," he smirked. "This place was always under the palace. It was an old servant's quarters. But considering Olympus is so secluded and the gods do like their amenities, space was carved to make room for small shops and larger workstations. The opening of shops brought shoppers, and shoppers meant jobs, which meant an increase in the population. You've only been inside the gates and not past the village. Further down the mountain, the capital stretches far. These tunnels are simply a faster way to travel. You see those stairs there? And that lift? They go deeper into the rock. You can come out at the other end of the kingdom."

"So, anyone could enter the palace?"

"No. When we return, we will need special credentials to get past the guards. I will gladly show you later. But for now…"

Two cast iron gates stood before them. The metal wove to form the shape of Acanthus scrolls and grapevines. Little cherubs sat in the curves and eyed one another with their short wings and empty pots. Through the gaps, she could see movement among soft yellow lighting. Someone on the other side approached, gave them a look and opened the door fully.

"You leave your postage there," the man said, gesturing to a window across the hall. A young couple happily walked by with stacks of letters secured with ribbon. The woman held onto the arm of her partner as they lowered a lever and dropped the stack of vellum inside. They walked away very much in love.

"We are also here to see Iris," Adonis beamed.

The man grunted and gestured for them to come inside.

Tobacco-laced clouds hovered towards the tall ceilings. Between the deep mahogany coffers, delicate pendant lights hung overhead. The air was so thick, the tip of her tongue was beginning to feel numb. There were rows of long desks—essentially, pieces of wood without divides. Men, but mostly women, sat among them in self-made spaces. Some hovered over colored copies of advertisements. Others stood in the corner and smoked. Sounds of clicks from the onslaught of fingers to keys made her pause. She hurried over to one of the desks and hovered.

"What is that?" she asked.

The woman looked up from her chair that swiveled. She held a stick in one hand that contained a slim cigarette. Her nails were freshly manicured, and her lips were painted. Her hair was pinned in tight curls and her dress was dropped at the waist. In addition to her Greek styled headdress, she had a feather behind her ear. She looked very stylish.

"A typewriter," she grinned. "It's very new and very efficient."

"A typewriter? How does it work?"

As the woman demonstrated, another walked by with her arms heavy in parchment. She made a comment about the machine and how it could not replace beautiful, hand crafted lettering. The woman at the typewriter rolled her eyes and winked before she resumed her task.

"What are they doing?" she asked Adonis, excited about her discoveries. Every inch of Olympus delighted her.

"This is the mailroom. Also, the room for correspondence. Many letters, laws and invitations leave the palace and circulate through Olympus, the Underworld and Oceanus. For the important missives, a draft is scribbled and sent here. The writer's proof, edit, construct the copy, take a vow of secrecy bound by blood and the sacrifice of their first-born, until it is finalized. Then, they hand write the names, pen the addresses and seal it shut. They dust it in gold, a few flecks of rose water and add the ornaments. Presentation is key."

Adonis pointed to the maps of the realms that hung along the walls. She admired them as if they were fine pieces of art. She hoped to visit the Underworld and Oceanus one day.

"They make stamps over here," Adonis said, further entertaining her. He showed her a machine where scrolls and dramatic curls were turned into metal presses. She watched as one of the women dipped the address of the palace into a well of ink and carefully pressed it on an envelope and allowed it time to dry. An assortment of waxes for seals were above the station. The variety reminded her of colored charcoal pencils.

At the back of the room, a wooden door with a frosted glass window was engraved with the symbol of an eye. Adonis knocked joyfully. A grunt from the other side beckoned them to enter. Inside, her eyes began to water at the aggressive charge of smoke. Iris, another ichor, was gazing out a tiny window that was pressed to the top of her sunken office. She took one look at them and grinned. As if she were in the beginning pages of a book and so far, had been enticed to read on.

"So, this is the discrepancy." At their alarm, she waved her hand. "I've heard all about it by now."

Iris lowered her thick-rimmed glasses so that they freed up her nose and dangled under her chin by a diamond studded chain. She was wearing a day skirt of muslin and lace and looked the part of a proper lady. Only it wasn't a skirt. They were wide trousers. The discrepancy approached Iris, wide-eyed over the sight of individual legs on a woman. She beamed, hoping she could wear trousers someday.

Adonis placed a pair of geraniums on the corner of her workstation—not even the most beautiful of blossoms would occupy the real estate of the cigarette she kept behind her ear. She leaned her rear on her desk, allowing the discrepancy to travel the small confines of the room. Iris' space was packed and messy. She had day-old bread resting on newspaper, coffee in a sticky tankard, piles of parchment that was burnt at the edges and a switchboard in the corner that remained dormant. It had a few holes for transfers and connecting lines. On the corner, a headset dangled from one of the pegs.

After making proper introductions, Adonis explained the nature of their visit. Iris lit her cigarette with a golden lighter. She nodded when they were done and scratched her temple with her thumb.

"Unfortunately, Hera has kept things quiet at the palace and hushed the rumors that were spreading through the paper mills."

"All the papers?" Adonis tilted his chin.

Iris grinned. "It is one of my many talents."

She went to the mound that was her desk and withdrew a golden quill. Her cigarette still between her lips, she gave the quill a flick of her finger, as if awakening it from a slumber. She placed it on a blank piece of parchment and whispered the name—*Zeus*. When she did, the quill went mad along the old, stained sheets. Adonis and the discrepancy leaned over the desk and saw that it was creating an index. A list of references to Zeus and recent accountings of his name. Running her finger along the lines of ink, Iris closed her eyes, furrowed her brow and shook her head.

"Everyone knows better than to defy their Queen and leak a scandal. She will turn them into ants. And then, she will make them attend a school for ants."

"What do you think, Iris?" Adonis held his basket before him with two hands. He knew that Iris was the intellectual sort. The *thinking* woman. He would be surprised if she had not compiled her own theories regarding the incident that has befallen the gods.

Each of them looked around for somewhere to plant themselves when Iris gestured for them to sit. In the end, Adonis settled for a small stack of unsteady books while the discrepancy took to the rug made of old papers. She spread her dress and placed her hands firmly in her lap, as if they were two children awaiting a story. Iris told the best stories.

"All ichor are birthed from Gaia's garden."

"Who is Gaia?" the discrepancy raised her hand and asked.

"Gaia is a Titan who watches over the Earth. Using a special clay, she molds us with her fingers, threads us with essence and plants us in her nourished soil that she waters with milk from her bosom. Seeds form within our molds and roots escape into the soil and we grow. Some quicker than others. Some late. When we become of *child* age, we uproot and continue our development until we reach a certain point."

"What point?"

"The point in which we remain stagnant." Iris gestured to herself. "It is how Gaia pictured us. Very rarely do we use our strength to veer from her vision. Fighting with her is…" Iris released a sigh and skipped her internal conversation. "But you were not born from the soil. You suddenly appeared as Zeus disappeared. In a way, it's as if you've taken his place. As if you were reincarnated."

"A reincarnation of Zeus," she leaned forward. "Is that what I am?"

Iris lifted a shoulder and wrapped a single arm around her waist. She searched her mess for a cigarette holder that she found without trouble. She inserted her shortened bud and continued smoking. From this angle, with her long features and limbs, she looked as if she were holding a fairy wand. Her golden quill still scribbled behind her until she looked at it, remembered it was on, and told it to shoo back into her desk.

"So…I am Zeus?"

"Not sure. In a way, you have his essence. We can all feel it a bit. I can also feel…something else. But I do not think he is fully gone. And even if he was, we cannot say. It would cause panic. Reincarnation sounds better."

"What a lovely dream then." Adonis gave them an assuring nod. "You are the almighty Zeus, but opposite in every way." He turned to Iris. "She can create thunder and electricity."

"Yes," Iris grinned. "And murder peacocks and inhale ambrosia. But I am afraid that is as far as I can help you. Anything else would be hearsay."

"Where is this Gaia," the discrepancy asked.

Adonis nodded. "My question, as well. We should pay her a visit. The woman who grew the gods and created this beautiful world would have the answers."

"I am afraid she is indisposed," Iris said with a grunt.

"Dead!?" they both exclaimed.

"No! She's on vacation with her boyfriend." Iris finished her cigarette and tapped it out on the side of her desk. Ash fell to the floor. "And before you ask, no one knows when she will return or where she is exactly. But I am sure Hera and the others will do the legwork and try to make contact. Which means they will leave the task to me. Speaking of which."

The switchboard was lighting up. Iris strode over, picked up the headset, said very few words and authorized a transfer. When she ended the call, she turned to them. "You'd best be off. I need to get back to work."

Adonis could see the sadness of the discrepancy. Gaia was like a physician—always on holiday when you needed them most. He gave her a pat on her shoulder and helped her to her feet. He brushed her skirts for her as she withheld a sigh.

Iris stood between them, a tender smile on her face as she lifted the chin of the discrepancy with her fingers.

"Do you know much about reincarnation, luv? No? In essence, we return to this world with a rare, yet much needed second chance."

"But, if this is my second life, then why can't I remember anything? And why am I here?"

Iris wrapped her arm around her shoulder and led her out of her office. The air of the common room was fresh compared to Iris' chamber. "Usually, the past life is so dreadful that we don't want to remember. Forgetting is a gift. We are gods, but even we surround ourselves with unanswered questions and the mistakes of our past. If not for you, this could be for the benefit of others."

"Of…others…"

"We cannot ignore the possibility that you could have been placed on this world to make our lives easier. Did you ever think of that? That *because* you are without your memories, you might help the rest of us find deliverance from the former Godking?"

"Um…no…"

"Just a thought."

Chapter 4

Hades & Death

Death dodged the mass of hankering porters. He didn't have luggage, but they offered to carry his clipboard and pocket watch for a coin. He held onto his items, including the manifest that had gotten him into a pickle, and the pocket watch that held the spirit of a deceased peacock. The absence of either would have damned him for all eternity.

He maneuvered through the crowded docks that rest near the entrance of the Underworld. A firework display gone wrong had caused over two hundred fatalities. Not that the fireworks were defective, they sparkled beautifully. The advancement in pyrotechnics and steam powered hydraulics was impressive for the usually slow developing human race. Apparently, two boating captains had thought the same thing.

Their gazes, along with those of their passengers, had been fixated on the colorful sky. The boats collided, head-on, and erupted into a display of smoke and fire that people on the shores believed to be a surprise second showing. What a treat, they thought.

He pushed his way through the line, remembering the faces of all he collected. They remembered him as well and made obscene gestures with their tongues and fingers, evidence that Death was, indeed, the most hated deity in the universe. Normally he could manifest to his destination. He would have bypassed the crowds and been in his office by now, but his transportation allowance, managed by Mrs. Janus, must have gone overlooked. She must have forgotten to replenish his credits, and he wanted to assume it was because she was busy dealing with the discrepancy.

"Mr. Death!" He turned at the rare sound of his name being preceded by a title. It was Mr. Winston, one of Ares' footmen. Twice before the man had been stabbed in the heart with a spear and, judging by the look of him, had once again met a similar fate. So much so that Mr. Winston did not require Death to collect him. He knew the path to the Underworld and entered cooperatively. Gods weren't allowed to dispose of humans directly, hence whenever they needed to get rid of them, they would have to resort to some sort of elaborately creative scheme. But poor Mr. Winston still had to go through the process of admittance and paperwork. Poor Mr. Winston.

There was a hole in his livery, and the apparition of how he died kept flashing over his person, like the cloak of a ghost. At the very least, Death could offer the man a ride. He, too, needed to get back to work.

"Oh, thank you kind sir." Mr. Winston trembled as he followed Death through the crowd. When they arrived at the row of boats, Death flagged down Mr. Charon. He was the managerial guide on the River Styx. Although overworked, he enjoyed the responsibility. He patiently escorted people to the eyes of judgement--an office where souls were given their welcome packets—with a friendly demeanor and fun facts about the Underworld. Mr. Charon's underlings were called the River Styx First Impression Brand and Hospitality Associates—RSFIBHA for short. FIBA for shorter.

"For Mr. Winston and I." Death gestured to Mr. Winston as he reached into his pocket and withdrew two coins.

Mr. Charon accepted the payment graciously and held the boat steady as they lowered themselves inside. People groaned at Death's audacity to skip the line. They cursed him, knowing he couldn't kill them twice. Death would have countered that he couldn't kill them the first time, but they wouldn't allow him the chance of a rebuttal.

"I have no problem giving a tour," Charon said as he pushed them away from the docks. His old and wrinkly face, underneath a boater hat and neckcloth, was cheery even though there was no sun here. Only sun imitations. A lantern hung from the end of his vessel, in an attempt to recreate the effect of a proper gondola. "But since you've both been here more often than not—"

Death and Mr. Winston knew how much the narrative of the Underworld meant to Mr. Charon. They smiled at one another and agreed to allow him to give them the full experience.

The River Styx was dark and grey and beautiful. It sparkled like a galaxy, carrying souls that traveled throughout the Underworld—perhaps on their way to visit friends and family across the various corners of the realm. Similar to a bypass. The sky was studded in souls that looked like stars—souls of those who either chose or asked to assume an eternal rest.

"And on ye left, you will see the house of Cerberus." A small beach with a cave was a safe distance away. Cerberus, the three-headed canine of Hades, was licking her paws and lounging peacefully. There was a sign posted that warned visitors to not feed the animal. Hades did not want to come down and separate the heads from fighting over a single bone. That, and he was very finicky about her diet. Her coat had to remain shiny and silky in order for her to win best in show.

When there was no food involved, Cerberus was a docile creature. She liked for her ears to be scratched and her belly rubbed. She also liked wearing Christmas sweaters. She would sit for hours while a team of people with a crane dressed her and her three heads. She would pose for photos and her portraits would be pressed on holiday cards and mailed to all of Olympus. Anyone with an address always received a holiday card from Hades.

"Overhead, we have the Hypnos," Mr. Charon continued. "Guardians of sleep."

Large stone epitaphs that were sculpted into faces with resting eyes hovered above them on wings of stone. They were the Underworld's equivalent of birds, but they also glided among the ever-resting souls. They hummed sweet lullabies as they flew past. A few, every now and again, would settle on the floppy ears of Cerberus. The animal twitched and shook her head to rid herself of them. If she were in a playful mood, she would have stood on her hind legs and attempted to capture them.

"And the sea nymphs. Don't get too close or they'll—"

"Mr. Charon, sir?" Death reminded him that they were approaching his destination.

Mr. Winston had about another third of the tour to go, but he wasn't in a hurry. And here, at the very least, he was safe from his master's home.

"Thank you again, Mr. Death." They shook hands before they parted.

"Good luck to you, Mr. Winston." *I'll be seeing you again, soon.*

Death departed at the docks of Cocytus. The district was made of stacked brick homes that were pressed together. Gardens and lawns were non-existent, considering the Underworld was shielded from the sun, but it didn't mean the efforts of residents went unnoticed and unrewarded. Fences and windows were lined with pots and troughs full of soil. They pressed seeds into the damp moisture and strategically incorporated sun lamps for a slow, but steady, growth of herbs and vegetables. Death admired a beautiful stalk of peppers. They would sell for a high dollar here, where the food was mostly imported.

Death tipped his hat at anyone he passed. Of course, they spat at him or crossed the road to walk on the other side. After progressing a few blocks, he arrived at 903 Cliff Street. He opened the cast iron gate and walked down the grey stone-pressed path. He ascended a few gently crooked stairs, withdrew his key and let himself inside.

"Your Grace," he stopped in an instant. Hades was sitting on one of the lounge chairs. Mrs. Federer was serving him tea. One of his legs was crossed over his knee. He flexed his foot at the tempo of the music emitting from the brass horn of the gramophone.

"Death. Finally, you've arrived."

Without going into an explanation regarding his inability to manifest, he apologized for the delay. Hades gestured to the stairs which led to the upper floor and Death's office. The Underworld was so congested, they had to take whatever real estate they could gain. People rarely moved or relocated, and offices doubled as living spaces that doubled as shops that doubled as tea rooms. The only zoning laws that were strongly enforced were industrial and adult entertainment. Hades did not want a factory next to a water tower or a brothel next to a playground.

Upstairs, the walls in between the rooms had been demolished to create one large workspace. There were four desks—two on the left wall, one on their right when they entered, and a last, wedged near the door of the bathing chambers and relief pot. Having already greeted his lordship, Mrs. Janus, his assistant and office manager, was bustling about with files and paperwork in hand. She often mumbled to herself, which was easy to do, considering that she had two faces—literal eyes in the back of her head. Her ability to perform double the duties made her qualified to sift through records as well as make travel arrangements for Death. She was also in charge of scheduling. She was an older ichor, and firmly set in her ways. She refused to modernize their system and preferred pushing paper. Their archives stretched underneath the house in an underground labyrinth.

The third employee was Mrs. Hecate. Her primary role was loss prevention. A ghost hunter, some had called her. In the case of magical beings or those who had the capabilities to evade Death's capture, she would intervene. She had a sharp, investigative mind, carried pistols under her skirts, had a foul mouth and was inherently rude. She also volunteered at the dead pets' animal shelter. Death would say the latter act of kindness created a balanced personality, but no...Hecate simply did not like him. She felt her job was only necessary because he failed to do his own. That, and she liked throwing things into his eye sockets.

"I'm glad you're all here now," Hades began. He still had his tea in his hands but only stirred. As if the rhythm assisted him with pacing his thoughts. "We need to discuss certain matters. But let me first begin by asking if the soul of Zeus has turned up anywhere?"

The room was silent as Mrs. Janus' neck rotated, allowing each of her faces to provide an answer. "I am afraid not, Your Grace," her faces came to their conclusion. "It is as if he never left the skies."

"Perhaps this discrepancy ate him," Hecate had the courage to speak nonchalantly and rest her boots on the edge of Death's desk. She was an ichor, of course, which gave her liberties to speak casually half the time. She excelled at her job, which granted her the other half. "It wouldn't be the first time a god was devoured or hid inside the belly of another."

"I've considered this," Hades appeared embarrassed to admit. "But I do not believe so. The girl, although an inconvenience, is not lying. She would have admitted if she swallowed Zeus or if she knew who she was. Do we truly know nothing of her? Is she an escaped soul, perhaps?"

That awarded him a daring glare from Hecate, but he had to be sure. The girl's soul could have been on the way to the Underworld and got intermixed with Zeus' before he had a chance to regenerate. If possible.

Hades went to the corner behind Janus' desk, observing the free-flowing quill that was scribbling into an open book. A diary so large that it required its very own pedestal. The quill worked without pause. Names of people, of beings, of animals were written in no particular order and with no definitive dates. It simply meant that their time was approaching.

This used to be a problem in the past—the golden quill at work. Once, their department was much bigger, occupying an entire warehouse that shared walls with the processing department, housing for souls and job placement services. But when people began seeing the names of their loved ones appear, leaks became frequent. Souls would try to warn their loved ones. Hence, Hecate's position. On the other hand, there were those who wrote the names of their enemies. Or tried to, if they could get the stubborn quill to cooperate.

There was so much power in a name, Death realized. His own brought an image of hatred and despair. And the discrepancy, to no fault of her own, was nameless. Without it, how could Mrs. Janus begin to know who or what she was?

Hades ran his fingers along his jaw before he sat aside his teacup. It was unfinished. It was unlike his lordship who accepted Mrs. Federer's offerings with modest angst. He passed each of them a serious look as he commanded Death to shut the door. "Listen to me, all of you," his tone serious. "You will continue to investigate and let me know if you learn anything new. Anything. Understood? And you will keep any discoveries between the people in this room.

No gossip. No rumors. I will be working with Hera to manage the discrepancy. Hecate, you will be in charge of looking for Zeus. Iris is in charge of looking for Gaia."

"And me, Your Grace?" Death pointed to himself.

A mutual nod rippled through them as Hades gestured for Death to follow him outside. The two exited the house and took a walk down the street. Going nowhere. Hades turned to Death, and Death understood. Whatever Hades was about to voice was to remain between them—the Soul King and him.

"I hope I don't have to explain, Death, what would happen if people began to believe that Zeus had met his end."

"The girl. Do you think—"

"The girl, she is one of us."

"And how does that affect his lordship, if I may ask?"

To Death's surprise, Hades smiled. "There have not been many surprises as of late and I am tempted to keep an eye on this one."

"Keep an eye on?"

"Oh," his lordship gestured to his eyes as if to remind himself that Death was not in possession of a pair of his own, in a traditional sense. Death hated *eye* jokes. He could see just fine. Although, a bit differently. "As much as it puzzles me to admit, Zeus' prized eagle answers only to her. She commands the skies and her powers are strong and natural. She can eat ambrosia and not die."

Death had met many souls who had consumed the gods' precious treat. Whether it was by accident or offered to them as a means to exterminate them, humans or anyone not born of Chaos, would meet their end. Very few could resist it's calling. In other literature, it was an apple in a garden or a siren's call or a beautiful face. To Death, it was fruit in a bowl of cow juices. All things he hated and the reasons why he had never grown over six feet when he roamed the land of the living.

But something in his lordship's tone perplexed Death. Hades sounded, if Death dared to speak out loud, entertained. As if this was in fact a pleasant surprise that he wasn't ready to rid them of. It made Death wonder if the Soul King knew more than he was letting on about Zeus' disappearance.

43

"Will she act as Zeus?" Death asked. "An heir presumptive, if you will?"

Hades chuckled lightly. Death couldn't see the humor of the situation. Afterall, if the girl were to sit on the throne, she was to manage the gods. A resistant bunch. And what of Hera? Was this her new husband? Could there be two queens?

They stopped at the edge of a lake of souls. Ahead was the correctional facility for violators of this realm. Those who had one more chance or otherwise, be forced into an eternal sleep. Both of them were straining their necks to peer into the windows, as if they expected to see lightning emitting from one of the small bedrooms. As if Zeus were damning those who told him that the time for reading and puzzles had passed. If Zeus was in there, if he were down here, they would know. They hoped.

"Is that Robin?" Hades asked, breaking their comfortable silence.

Death held up his pocket watch and placed it in his lordship's open fingers. Robin, along with other peacocks of Hera's horde, had a nice six-acre resort that was Hades' home. His lordship had taken it upon himself to tend to her peacocks personally. As he handed over the soul of the bird, Death saw a smile spread across Hades' face. It was small, faint and full of alleviation. Death's eyes were better than most and he could see it, a small flicker of relief. As if Hades felt this was all for the best. Death was thinking this, he did not say so out loud.

Chapter 5

Hera

"Would you stop doing that?"

The girl had been placing her fingertips together, generating static and pulling them apart again. The fizzy waves stretched slowly, as her objective was to not break their bond. Like chewing gum. The effect was causing Hera's hair to rise from the nape of her neck. That, and the sound was annoying.

"My husband killed himself by playing with lightning." Hera could feel the girl turn to Hades for confirmation. He must have given it, as she stopped immediately and hurried her pace to catch up with Hera.

It had been a few days since the discrepancy arrived, and the girl had filled her time by toying with her powers, eating ambrosia, taking walks with Adonis and visiting Iris in the mountain. She liked making friends and being outside and showing interest over any little thing. Additionally, the girl was the compliant sort. She was polite and playful, opposite her husband, and Hera didn't know which was worse. Zeus, although a domineering ass, was always sure of himself and could lead them from trouble if need be. Now, Hera was the one everyone turned to for answers. It was an unfamiliar feeling.

In his absence, Zeus would have appointed Hades or Poseidon to oversee his realm, but Poseidon wanted little to do with those matters, and Hades preferred that she, the Queen, issued commands. As if he expected no less. She was always strong and could handle her ichor, but it did not refrain her from swallowing her tension with full bottles of wine.

Hades had volunteered to assist her with the discrepancy. Of course, he could have been worried that Hera would attempt to enact another curse. Or unleash the wrath of her remaining

45

peacocks. She might have mentioned that they should convince the girl to try her hand at a lightning bolt to the heart. Just to see what would happen. With a sigh, he swayed her from it.

"Where are we going?" the discrepancy asked.

"Here," Hera said simply as they stopped at a door. Hades opened it for them, and the girl entered cautiously. "This is where you will be sleeping."

The bedchamber was not Zeus', which was an improvement offhand. It had a modest four post with a silk canopy. The ivy etchings of the wood had been painted green to give the illusion of a forest. The details in the wood matched the armoire in the corner, the dressing table and a settee. Furs hung over an accent chair. A small bistro table near the window that overlooked the gardens and distant forest held an intricate tea set. The fireplace was large enough for three people to stand in and chat. The walls had gold and green wallpaper, and woodland creatures were painted on the ceiling.

It was a room that Hera had once enjoyed decorating. Centuries ago. If she ever had children of her own, she envisioned that they would grow into this space when they were ready to leave the nursery. The settee was where she pictured conversations with her daughter regarding broken hearts and marriage proposals. The dressing table was where Hera would help her decide which earrings and hair ornaments worked best for the occasion. Where she would assist her with her first coronet. Hera would lecture from the doorway, as her daughter scoffed from the bed. She could have had a boy, of course, but she had always envisioned a daughter. A little girl who was her mirror by way of opposites. A daughter who would bring about a mother's headache that was persistent, yet affectionate.

Her placement of the discrepancy in this room was a last resort. Her ichor were here and in typical selfish fashion, they had assigned themselves entire wings and claimed their old apartments as if conquering lands. And this room was close to Hera's own. She needed to keep an eye on the girl.

"I get a room?" she asked as Hera went to the window to adjust the curtains. Hades leaned his shoulder on the doorframe. Hera could feel his gaze on them.

"Considering that you will be staying here, you will need some place to sleep."

"Really?" The girl turned with wide eyes. She was taking stock of the trinkets on the dressing table. The music box on the nightstand. The large pillows on the bed. As she brushed the teacup painted with lavender watercolor flowers, the girl retracted her hand as if it had come alive and bitten her. "Are you going to try to kill me again?"

Hades snickered and Hera snapped her chin at him. He pressed his lips together and cleared his throat.

"Behave," she said slowly, "and we will see."

"Yes ma'am. Um…"

"What?"

"What will I be doing?"

"What do you mean?"

"Is there a program? Or, am I to assume some occupation to earn my keep?"

Hera had already discussed her role with Hades and Poseidon. Although she wasn't in complete agreement, she would allow the girl to exercise Zeus' duties as if she were the Godking. Gradually. Until they figured out what to do with her or until they found answers. But now, examining her doe-eyed expression, Hera couldn't imagine the girl issuing command from the throne.

Hades entered fully and answered for her. "You will be serving Olympus in Zeus' stead."

"*I* will?" She blinked. "Zeus? As in, *the* Zeus? God of the skies? I am to be his replacement?"

"I didn't say that."

"Which part?"

"His replacement."

"Ah," she squished her features together. "An interim then. Do I have a choice in the matter?"

Hera turned to Hades, her feet firmly on the marble floors as she lifted her brows and awaited his answer with mock enthusiasm. It wasn't as though Hera couldn't rule Olympus alone. She knew the laws, the regulations and considered herself as much a conqueror as

Zeus. Hades cleared his throat, bringing attention to the hard work that must have gone into the birth of the area rug.

The girl sat on the edge of her bed and spoke freely to them. She squeezed her hands together and tugged at her fingers. "I told Adonis that I feel as though this is a dream. That none of you are real."

"We are very much real."

"Yes, well, it's as if my memories are...dream-like. You know? It's as if I cannot recall the details, only shadows. I know *of* you and I also feel as though I *know* you. As if certain things, mannerisms and behaviors are...easy to digest. Like I am comfortable, but I don't know why. Is that odd?"

"Yes—"

"No—" Hades exchanged glances with Hera, beckoning her sensitivity. "What Hera means is, 'yes, this entire situation is odd.' But you need not worry, little one. We will figure it out in due time."

She looked skeptical, and Hera felt the need to bring the conversation back to the facts at hand. She relayed to the girl that she was to join them for dinner, and that tomorrow they would begin her first day of work.

"Can we have ambrosia?" the girl asked, not hearing much past dinner.

"Haven't you had enough?"

"What else is there to eat then?"

She felt Hades' chuckle as she turned on her heels and left the girl to her own devices. Whatever they may be. In the hall, she massaged her temples, actively seeking any bottle of wine that might have been an arm's reach apart.

Hades said smoothly, "We have seen the ends of humanity. This is not it."

"Your juvenility is admired sometimes," she said without a smile.

"Is that all?"

"That, and your ability to always keep your hands under the table."

He examined his fingers as if he didn't understand her remark. Hades, ruler of the Underworld, could bury his intentions as deep as his realm. There was a time when the games he, Zeus and Poseidon used to play were ruthless and unwise. She would be foolish to think he wasn't capable of being multiple steps ahead. As if reading her mind, he took a step forward, shortening the distance between them.

"Ah, you think I am plotting something." His quick deduction validated her. "Hera," he lifted her chin with his fingertips. She was staring directly into his silver eyes. They were more lustrous than her husband's—when Zeus had a temper. She felt her body sway beneath him, but that could have been the wine. "I am not, and never would be, against you. We are on the same side."

"I feel as though this would be the first time."

He angled his chin and dramatized his shock. "Your *methods* need a bit of polishing, but you have always had the mind of a fair leader. Zeus and I rarely saw eye to eye, an issue that was only ever made worse by the fact of how often I agree with you."

She took a step back, allowing his fingers to fall. She didn't know what goal he was trying to achieve, but she wasn't going to allow herself to get lost in it. Hades wasn't selfish, but he wasn't generous either. Neither he nor Poseidon took much interest in Olympus. They stuck to their domains, and she stuck to her own. Currently, she wished he were in his realm. This open talk of partnership did funny things to her mind while his proximity did funny things to her body. But that could have been the wine.

The sound of arriving footsteps interrupted them. One of her butlers was approaching, along with a housekeeper. They relayed the rooms situation and expressed the staff's inability to keep up with Ares' demands. That, and when he wasn't scuffling with Poseidon, he was arguing with Athena—pushing her buttons no doubt. Hades placed his hand gently on Hera's shoulder and told her that he would handle them. She decided to retreat to her study where she and the housekeeper could go over the details of the evening. She needed the necessary distraction.

Their evening meal would consist of lime and cream soup, feta and zucchini flat cakes, pork soaked in orange sauce and artichoke hearts seasoned with wild lemon. She switched the beef to the stuffed chicken breasts with spinach and added savory carrots and fresh pita with cream spread. For dessert, there would be rice pudding and a chocolate and raspberry roulade. And wine. She requested extra bottles of wine.

When she was alone, she began on the place cards. Normally, those with the highest titles would enter first, making for an even number of pairs of lords and ladies to follow. She always entered with her husband, followed by Poseidon and Demeter, Hades and Hestia, Ares and Aphrodite (it was formerly he and Athena, but their constant bickering and competitiveness made her switch the order), Dionysus and Athena, Apollo and Persephone, and Hermes and Iris.

Hera tapped her pencil, glancing at the list. She couldn't enter with the girl, that would have been silly. This meant the discrepancy would be entering with Poseidon and she with Hades. Everyone would be shifted down, leaving Iris without a partner. This prompted a rare smile from Hera, as she now had a reason to invite Hephaestus. He was never a favorite of Zeus', but she always admired his silent wisdom and hard work. He would be paired with Persephone now, allowing Iris to be escorted by Adonis. One of those two would be secretly overjoyed.

She quickly penned a missive to be sent directly to Hephaestus and to the staff, to let them know the number for tonight. After, she performed a quick tour of the billiard room. Hermes, Ares, Athena and Dionysus were fond of cards. She might partake in a few games as well.

"Shall we prepare your dinner gown, my Queen?" Hera was asked as she returned to her wing. She nodded and proceeded to her dressing room which was behind a set of French doors at the end of the hall. A second, just off the entrance, revealed a staircase that led down to a private bathing pool while the remainder of the space was a giant wardrobe lined with gowns. The colors were arranged in the order of a rainbow, beginning in red and ending in violet. Her blacks, greys, creams and golds occupied a separate wall and were just as ample as those that were made of color. A servant was overlooking her wall of slippers, taking note of any that were in need of polishing. Her various riding habits and war attire had been shoved into a corner by her abundance of hat boxes.

Standing on her pedestal, one of her handmaidens had withdrawn a red and blue option for her consideration. She wasn't feeling any particular color today and gestured to something more neutral. When her servant held up a pearly grey gown, Hera's thoughts immediately went to Hades. How his eyes peered into her own, how his touch on her chin continued to linger.

Only Zeus had ever laid a finger to her skin. In the beginning it had been tender, but for more than half of their marriage it had been only to ensure that she was listening when he spoke. On those days, more often than not, she would retire to her room where a closet full of Zeus-stuffed-children's toys would be waiting for her. She would toss one into her pen of peacocks and smile as they ripped it to shreds.

"So pretty," a soft voice came from behind her. Followed by a pair of wide eyes. The girl was standing in the doorway, peeping inside. Hera, who was wearing nothing apart from her undies and silk chemise, instructed the handmaiden to find her something a bit darker in shade. If her husband was truly gone, she should be in mourning and wearing black. But she hated black. She hated her husband enough to excuse making the sacrifice. A deep silver would suffice.

"What are you doing?" Hera asked sharply.

"I was walking through the palace. I keep getting lost and it's truly exciting."

"It's *exciting* getting lost?"

She nodded and entered the room one step at a time. "My room is beautiful, this place is so beautiful, that getting lost means discovering something new over and over again. Although, I have yet to come across a library. Do grand houses like this one have a library?"

Hera wanted to moan. Naturally, they had a library. She was midway through her instructions when she realized it was pointless. Throwing on a robe, Hera would exert less energy if she just walked her there.

The library was a cylindrical and centralized structure, accessible by many doors and pathways that connected to the main house. In essence, it was built to resemble a birdcage with glass walls and golden leaf sheath scrolls that traveled to the apex, creating a dome with an open terrace. Zeus' eagle, Caelus, was flying outside. Always close to Zeus. Never too far from the discrepancy.

Books were organized along the circular tower shelves. The girl gasped and refrained from running ahead. When she turned to Hera for permission to roam, Hera lifted a shoulder. She needed to get back to dressing anyway.

"But do not stay too long, we will need to find a gown for you as well."

"Yes, ma'am." The girl smiled wide and was off.

***

The only one who appeared to have wept today was Athena, who had sheltered herself in a lonely corner. Hera didn't know how to feel, considering that no one wore black or seemed to be in the spirit of grief. Alright, she admitted, she was a bit tickled. As she leaned on the banister of the gallery, she observed her ichor and their lively mood. They all looked beautiful, including Athena, and were dressed in their best gowns, suits, and tails. Cocktails were held between their fingers as they discussed business and tidbits of their personal lives. They were under her thumb now, officially. She took a deep breath, the feeling of control settling over her with fluctuating anxiety regarding the unknown.

"Um, Mrs. Hera, my lady, um, my Queen…"

Hera turned to the sight of the girl in her dinner gown. She was wearing gold again and looked the picture with her pretty crown braids that gave way to long and wavy strands of hair. She wore ivory gloves and slippers that almost didn't make it in time for dinner. *She* almost didn't make it in time. The girl's apology for accidentally starting an electrical fire near the history and theology section of the library resulted in dozens of lost books, a burn to an irreplaceable tapestry and a blackened section of the window, was still on her face under a timid smile.

"Um…do we go down together or…?"

Hera and her *husband* would have made an appearance from the grand staircase. But what were they to do? Did Hera go first as Queen or the discrepancy, as the Godking? The order would set the tone for the rest of the evening and establish their roles socially. As much as she didn't find it fair, Hera would go first, allowing the discrepancy to be the latter and thereby, the more important.

"Why can we not go down together?" the girl asked.

"As a married couple?"

"As...friends..." the girl had the nerve to say.

Hera refrained from rolling her eyes. She signaled to the butler at the top of the stairs and took hold of her skirts as her name was announced. She began her descent in a polished fashion. She glanced over to the eyes of Hades who was smiling at her. As if she were coming to him, ready for his touch. She had to look away or else she would stumble. When she reached the landing, she cleared her throat and looked towards the top. She crossed her arms and waited for the girl to do as she was told.

When Hera could spot a glimpse of the girl's silver hair, she saw the butler's round livery come into view. He was speaking to the girl, low and with a plunge of his brow. The girl disappeared fully, and the butler's gaze went to the Queen in a convoluted expression.

"Is everything alright?" Hades had joined her side. As had Poseidon. Both were looking between Hera and the top of the stairs. It wasn't long before the delay had caused a ripple of murmurs throughout their party. A few of them had yet to see Zeus' replacement. News of her had reached each of the ichor by now, Oceanus and the Underworld included.

"Oh, for goodness sake..." Hera hitched up her skirts and stomped back up the stairs. When she reached the top, she grabbed the girl by the arm and pulled her aside. No one could see them from here. No one could see how disheartened the girl appeared. "What is the matter?"

"He...he..."

"What?" Hera stomped. The girl was embarrassing her at dinner. At a party, those of which Hera always hosted without flaw. "Out with it, now!"

"Have you tried not yelling at her?" Hades asked as he approached. Hera scoffed. She'd known it would only be a matter of time before he arrived. As if they were tuned to a timer, one by one her ichor would carry themselves up the grand staircase to gawk.

"Shut up, Hades."

He held up his hands and approached the girl carefully. In a leveled tone he leaned down and asked her what had upset her. It was at this moment that Hera realized the girl had the capability to cry her weight in tears. Very rarely did her ichor publicly display such a state.

"The butler...he asked..." she whimpered. Hades stood upright, took a breath and immediately understood.

"He asked for your name and you didn't know what to say, is that it?"

She nodded.

"Surely, we can't have him yell *discrepancy* at the top of his lungs, can we?" He slowly turned to Hera who averted her gaze out of pity. From the moment she emerged from Zeus' cloud, the girl had struggled to figure out who she was. She felt like she was in a dream, but even in dreams, one was the star of their own stage. No one matching her description had been reported in the papers and even now, Hera was forthright with the fact that they were figuring out what to do with her. As if she were some misplaced thing.

Had she parents? Friends? A lover?

"A name..." Hera forced herself to appear unconcerned. This was her attempt to lighten the mood. "Is that all?"

The girl nodded, drying her eyes.

"We need to call you something..." Hades gave Hera a gentle smile, as if acknowledging her change of tone. He also extended his handkerchief to the girl. "Any preferences?"

"Is everything alright?" As expected, Poseidon was next to emerge from the lower level. He looked dashing in his suit, but then immediately perturbed at the sight of the crying girl. As if someone had done their worse and he was prepared to summon the seas to defend her. Opposite of Ares who came shortly behind him, saw someone crying, spun on his heels and retreated back downstairs.

"What did you do?" Poseidon looked at Hera and Hades accusingly.

"We didn't do anything," Hades explained. "The discrepancy is in need of an identifier. Perhaps one that does not imply a mistake."

"What would you like to be called?" Hera tried.

The girl shrugged. "I wouldn't know."

"Well, we can't call you Zeus." Hades did that thing where he attempted to sound smart, albeit everyone knew he was. Hera felt they should hurry along and pick one, for if her calculations were correct, Dionysus would be the next to join them and he—too late.

"Is everything alright—"

"Yes," she said sharply. This time it was Poseidon's turn to relay their situation. Dionysus nodded intensively and looked at the girl with that same cloak of pity that somehow had infected the three male ichor before her. A foreign look for each of them. One only the discrepancy could extract. Dionysus, the god known for making Zeus' favorite wine, folded his arms and gave it some thought while she and Hades listed anything they thought would suit— Zeusette, Zeusaphina, Seuzena, Sarah, Zena, Anez, Zurithopia...*anything*.

Dionysus, who was studying the girl without pause, spoke affirmatively. "Zari."

She widened her eyes as he repeated the name—*Zah-Ree*. Her approval was palpable, as was her smile.

"Zari," she repeated. She looked as if a weight had been lifted from her shoulders. "My name is Zari."

"How did you just come up with that?" Hades asked.

Dionysus swirled his port as Poseidon and Hera both looked at Hades with lips that were pressed from the mistake he had made. When Dionysus spoke, his voice turned into a droll. The ichor was a slow mover, slow thinker. It was rumored that he would sit and watch the lifespan of a grape. Talking to it. Asking it about the nature of coffee beans.

"Well...as you have asked...I will tell you....I was in the process of making a new flavor of wine...named after Zeus. I am...not sure how it happened...but I gazed upon a wine bottle and...I thought..., 'my, how feminine a bottle looks.' Smooth...Nice...Slender. Zeus is too manly of a name...for such a delicate...drink. So, I thought..., 'if Zeus were a woman, his name would be...Zari.' Our Zeus...is a woman. Our Zeus' name...is Zari..."

By this time, the remainder of the ichor had come and gone up the stairs. By this time, Hera had found a drink. She inhaled it. Followed by another. And between her drinking she looked over at Hades who had the gallantry to smirk.

Chapter 6

Poseidon

I want this one.

When he came face to face with Zari in the amphitheater, the declaration had sunk into his mind and filled his body like the bottom half of an hourglass. There was no one to tip him over and relieve him from the absurdity of desire. A feeling she had awoken from deep within. A feeling that commanded his interest and summoned his need for possession. His nature to conquer. The implication that this woman was *Zeus* was far from the truth. The Godking had exacted loathing and contempt from Poseidon. Zari was everything but.

Poseidon didn't know what had happened to Zeus, but the world continued to function, he reminded his ichor. The skies were calm unless Zari was upset and Caelus, the Godking's companion, wasn't warning them off. He said just enough to liberate any question of whether or not he truly cared.

Ever since they were birthed, he, Hades and Zeus had always been close. Situationally speaking. The three had been sculpted in the same sitting, grew within the same decades, were equally powerful, and held established titles. Zeus was their *leader*, but only because he was the closest to Gaia. Zeus could turn into a human's equivalent of a nursing infant when it came to their Mother.

Zari's innocence was spiritual. Her cleanliness was concrete and pronounced. He could feel her call for adventure. He could see the unravelling of a beautiful world behind those golden eyes. Her curiosity was a playful and pleasant poke of a slender finger and ever since their initial meeting, he had watched Zari.

She admired the palace to distraction, interacted with the servants and assisted the elderly with their shopping. Happily, in fact.

When he decided to have some alone time near the natural lakes, he saw her and Adonis cheering on a fisherman as he reeled in a tough haul. Her feet were bare, and her lower body was knee deep in the green water. She laughed as she and the fishermen took hold of the behemoth and posed for a photograph. With playful inquisitiveness, she toyed with her abilities. He grinned, knowing there was a mischievous vein within her. With adorable fear she avoided peacocks as if they had the plague and, much to his jealousy, she always accepted flowers from Adonis, who acted as her guide and chaperone. Each time Adonis touched her, Poseidon wanted to do more than stone him.

While the discrepancy remained unknown, he knew that keeping his distance was for the best. Hera described Zeus as being gone within the blink of an eye—a showy array of sparkles and dust, of course. Poseidon had raised the question: Could Zari be gone just as easily? Would she be replaced with an old hag or a sticky toddler?

Looking at her now, as she examined the food on her plate, he hoped not.

"Are you enjoying the weather?" As soon as the words escaped his lips, both Hera and Hades, who occupied the seats across from them, created slopes with their brows. Poseidon was known for small talk. Rather, he was known for loathing it. If he ever spoke about the weather, it was a sure sign that he was *trying*. *Hard*. It was a miserable attempt that he would only admit to himself.

"I am," Zari replied happily. "Is there ever bad weather in Olympus?"

"Only when you cry." He should really go back to the sea. He had embarrassed her, and he felt his muscles constrict because of it.

Hades, whose help he did not need, inserted himself anyway. "Your emotions can interrupt the natural flow of things. Have you noticed? Why, even Poseidon here can disturb the waters when he is angry enough. His scowl means everything is alright."

Hades winked at her and she giggled. Although Poseidon had a reason to scowl *now*, Zari's laugh and light humor allowed Hades to cheer her at his expense. She turned to him, her gold eyes reflecting the light of the candelabras.

"Do you control all the seas? All the oceans, Mr. Poseidon?"

At Hera's grunt, Zari placed her hands under the table. "Did I say something wrong?"

"You called me 'Mr.'" Poseidon answered for himself this time, knowing Hera was a martyr for tradition. "'Mr. Poseidon.'"

"Are you not...male..." Her eyes followed the length of him and landed at his lap. He could not remember the last time he blushed, but in addition to his reddening, her comment made Hades choke on his drink and Hera inhale another glass of wine. The girl needed to be taught basic dinner etiquette, or everyone needed to lower their expectations with this one.

If he were his former self, he would have replied *I would be more than happy to show you later.* Instead, he cleared his throat and spoke flatly, "I am also a god."

"Right. I should have said 'Mr. God.'"

She was making a joke and it almost missed him. This dinner, this conversation, caused him to remember something—he was as equally bad at small talk as he was at courting. Not that he had any plans of courting Zari, but he assumed that the slow decline of his confidence, along with the buildup of his tension, would be the same if they were touring a museum. One would think it would be better considering they could talk about art. But he didn't really care for art. Or most things outside of his work. One of his builders had called him a dry businessman who needed to be taken in small doses. He agreed. Not always the brooding sort, he wondered when his humor had left him.

With the amount of energy that Zari appeared to have, he could easily imagine them being lovers for quite some time. Decades, maybe? They could sail across the seas and make love on his boat. Afterwards, he would grow bored of her, and this spontaneous desire of his could finally be put to rest. His feelings for Zari were as simple as lust. Nothing more.

He didn't blame himself. Not when the model of marriage was Zeus and Hera. The two made an eternity of matrimony look abominable. Zeus strayed and Hera became mean and surly. Their love, if it ever was, turned to dislike which turned to hatred and he couldn't imagine hating Zari, not for as long as he could remember how he felt the first time he laid eyes on her. Love, for all that it brightened, cast long shadows, and he had come close.

At this table, Poseidon concluded that love fell within one of two pits. The Ares, who had lost love and as a result was reckless, guarded and detached. Or the Hades, who wanted a love he could not have. The way he looked at Hera made Poseidon want to violate any code of their friendship that warranted support and his discretion to advise him to find his interest elsewhere. But there would be no point. After all, the reason that Zeus placed Hades in the Underworld was to keep Hades as far away from Hera as possible. Hera, he was sure, was still unaware.

Of course, he was forgetting Aphrodite and Hephaestus. An arranged union that was often overlooked and ignored by all parties. Additional support of his dislike for matrimony.

"Zari," Hades got her attention again. "You are the ruler of the skies. Everyone at this table is beneath you...literally speaking...I suppose. You need not address us so formally."

She made a face. "I'm not sure if I'm comfortable with that."

"Why not?"

"I don't know as much as you, or anyone else. I am not sure why a title outweighs experience." When the salad course was placed before them, she didn't reach for her fork like a proper dinner guest. She hovered her hand over it and used her powers to draw the utensil to her like a magnet. At her discovery, she beamed. She looked to Hera who shook her head disapprovingly. Poseidon's lips upturned, especially when Zari mumbled, "You should have people apply for the position, conduct interviews and select accordingly."

"And the ichor would form a committee?"

"Yes." Her eyes widened.

Hades chuckled, low and breathy. "We would never agree. Rarely do we reach the same conclusion."

She parted her lips and closed them again. She was pushing around the vegetables on her plate. Poseidon lifted his wine glass and sipped from the rim. He was going to ask her what was on her mind, but he needed to be civil by first allowing the alcohol some time to rest.

"Everything alright?"

Her gaze did not tear from her plate. "I've…I'm not sure if it's appropriate to say—"

"Then don't," Hera mumbled.

"But I've read stories…about Greek mythology…"

Poseidon would have come willingly to her rescue, had his ichor not been instructed to be more patient than usual. They were still trying to decipher the discrepancy. If they weren't, Zari would have received a variety of reprimand for calling them myths. Whether it was an exhibition between Ares and Athena, a lecture from Demeter or a curse from Aphrodite, to them it was as if she had called them invalids. To assume that a god wasn't real was to assume they weren't doing the very jobs they were made for. That humans were taking credit for all that they had built. "Apologies…" she said softly. She retreated behind her wine.

"Not to worry, Your Majesty!" Adonis sang from the other end of the table. "As a human myself, I will admit that the books we are given are a bit obscure when it comes to the history of the gods. Why, so much of it is so outlandish that it is difficult to believe what is real and what is not."

"Yes." Zari was relieved that someone had taken her corner. Poseidon wondered when he would have his chance to come to her rescue. Or, when it was appropriate to drown Adonis.

"Is that why you were at the library?" Hera angled her chin. "Before you set it on fire?"

"What was that?" Hades asked.

"Yes…" Zari said submissively. "It was an accident."

"Ah, a human's book is the equivalent of a god's tabloid, little one. Short. Brief. Often wrong, but never lacking in entertainment. A shorter explanation would be to tell the truth. Although, it is still a lengthy story. One you will learn in time."

"I suppose…" Zari quickly shook her head. "But if I am to rule, shouldn't I disregard past actions? Not unless I must. There is no precedent to my condition, so I think it's only right to give everyone the same opportunity. To begin again, I suppose."

"Are you saying that because you are too lazy to learn the history?" Hera smirked.

"Maybe…but even I know a few things that are not true."

"I would be abusing myself by asking. So, I won't—"

"Hades' abduction of Persephone, for one thing." Hades sighed behind his wine, as if to ask how on earth people always got that wrong. She then gestured to herself. "And that I...am a jackass."

Following an uncomfortable silence, Ares of course was the first to erupt into giggles. Followed by harsh chuckles. Iris followed suit, and then shortly Dionysus joined them. Hades turned to Hera, who was doing her best to hide her grin behind her spoon as the table shook with everyone—aside from Athena. Poseidon didn't know when he joined in or how it came to be in tune with Zari's as they locked eyes at one another. He wanted this one. And not just in small doses.

Chapter 7

Hades & Persephone

The bets had climbed to a hecatomb. It was how Hades knew it was time to remove himself from the tables. Cards were always just a warmup before the diamonds and clubs became sheep and ore. The gods would play a game of *Conquering the Table,* which often led to demands and bargains and, depending on who played, humiliating charades or sexual favors.

His drink was interlocked within his fingers. His wit was sitting on his shoulder. Poseidon was smitten, that much was clear. Hades had lived long enough, was deprived long enough, to read that look. And Hera, composed only on the exterior, was making her way through multiple bottles of wine. He wished he could understand what was going through her mind. Was she missing her husband? Was she truly missing him? He would assume she was nervous about ruling, but he would never find her incompetent. Hera was the strongest, most intelligent, most beau—

His thoughts were interrupted when Persephone stood before him. Simultaneously, Aphrodite stood before Poseidon, who was on the other side of the billiard room. The two were united, which wasn't good. Each with the goal of distraction. Neither were what they truly wanted. As if he and Poseidon were on the same wavelength, his ichor lifted a brow at him and finished off his drink. Hades sat his glass aside and stuffed his hands in his pockets. He turned to Persephone with a smile.

"Your Grace," she bowed her head.

"Lady Persephone, how are you fairing?"

"Very well, and yourself?"

When Poseidon and Aphrodite locked arms, it was to the distaste of multiple ichor in the room. Hephaestus could ignore it, but Ares, already excusing himself from the game, cursed and stomped after them. Hades felt Persephone brush the sleeve of his evening coat with her slender fingers.

"They are going for a walk. I was in need of one myself." She paused. "With you."

He could have said no, but there was no reason to deny her. A century ago, Hades wouldn't have minded Persephone on his arm. When he mentioned that he was considering marriage, Zeus had suggested Persephone. She was one of their younger gods. Time had not turned her habits into stone. And her habits were good ones. Mostly. She was the model of grace and her beauty was supple but ever present. He had imagined himself falling in love with her, as their exposed limbs moved without rest between the sheets of his bed. With Gaia's blessing and her artistry, they would give birth to children. A biological function that was not given to the ichor, but possible if their Mother took the time to cross their essence and plant the hybrid into her gardens.

But when he had asked Persephone to marry him, she hesitated. At the time, he credited her change of heart to Demeter. If there was a bond that closely resembled mother and daughter, it was between her and Persephone. Fortunately, Hades had taken Demeter's advice and brought Persephone to the Underworld first. He thought his kingdom was beautiful. He thought he had done his best. But she was born of spring, and instantly appeared withered by the lack of a sun. Her spirit, disheartened and uninspired. Very little grass was authentic. Fruit was difficult to grow. The Underworld was not a hideous place. But it was dark, and this did not suit her.

His decision to not marry her came as a surprise to Zeus, who did not accept it whole-heartedly. Hades knew why. Their gazes landed on Hera who, at the time, could be seen in the gardens tending to her peacocks.

"This has nothing to do with her," Hades had said. Which was mostly true. He was ready for marriage. He was ready to move on. And that was when he had a larger house and a larger piece of land and was competing with Zeus for how much wealth he could acquire. All to impress the wrong ichor.

Zeus' distaste had turned into pressure and belittlement. Hades wasn't going to force Persephone, or any bride, to accompany him down the aisle. His gallantry surprised even himself.

Under the moonlight and away from the dinner party, they walked as a lord and lady would. Each holding their own weight and each respectable of their setting. The wind was calm—Zari must be in a mild mood. The trees swayed gently, and the air smelled of flowers and coconut from the distant rain that she had cried earlier on the stairs. He could hear the faint sound of splashing water. Could have come from anywhere, really, considering the number of pools and water features that were stretched about the estate.

"It appears we are being followed, Your Grace."

He gave her a gentle pat on her hand. "I am aware."

"At least, one had the common sense to turn themselves into a tree."

He chuckled as he resisted the urge to glance over his shoulder. The giggling of their two invaders filtered through the otherwise peaceful evening. Hades wondered why Ares ever thought he could best Athena at war. Where she lacked in decompression, she made up for in her ability to master stealth. And Poseidon, the sly one, had left long ago. Perhaps using the excuse of taking Aphrodite on a walk to exit the dinner party completely.

"I apologize for using this time to call forth our previous discussion," Persephone said softly, ignoring their audience with finesse as he guided them slightly in the opposite direction. "But I do need an answer."

That's right, he thought. It was his turn again. They commenced with a dance of two steps—back and forth. Their feelings for one another never seemed to fall into harmony, and time in Olympus had not done her well. If Demeter thought a life in the Underworld would hinder Persephone, he wondered why his ichor did not tear her away from Aphrodite. But as much as she had changed, so had he.

"I am afraid my answer is the same. I cannot marry you."

"Can't, Your Grace, or won't?"

"Both."

Persephone waited before parting her lips. "I wonder who would do, if not me?"

"Conceit does not look well on you."

"Forgive me, but that is not what I meant. I assumed his lordship would want a wife of ichor. When I sort through the names, I often wonder who strikes your fancy. Unless there is a distant ichor I have yet to meet."

The sculpting and gardening of Gaia extended far beyond those at the dinner table. Their ichor stretched to the Underworld, Oceanus and even those who resided on Earth. There were ichor who sang to the waves, ichor who took the form of serpents. There were ichor with one eye—poor things. He couldn't confide in Persephone the areas he felt she lacked. He would feel crude and hypocritical. But he needed someone who could govern. He wanted someone with a bit of fire to them. Someone that made his heart leap whenever they were in the same room. His body longing for the end of normal separation.

"Is it the discrepancy?"

"Zari," Hades politely corrected her. "And no. I plan to match her to Poseidon. Do not look surprised. He is strong and would be good for her. And she would make him laugh."

"And where would they go? She would have to assume her husband's title. She would no longer be the Godking. Listen to me. *Godking.* I am so confused by it all."

"As are the rest of us. But we are taking matters one day at a time. Learning as we proceed."

"But you've already assumed much. That she is the Godking and that she will marry. That she will leave the throne and retreat to Oceanus—"

"Persephone," he patted her hand again. "That is for Zari to decide. And Hera."

"*If* it happens." Persephone lowered her lashes. "I thought he and Aphrodite were…interlaced."

A corner of Hades' lips upturned. This was the side of Persephone he did not like. The manipulative sort. Aphrodite was known to sunbathe on Poseidon's islands. Naked. Her blatant show of flesh interrupted the production of his builders, Poseidon had mentioned with a grunt. Maybe they had a brief stint. Maybe they did not. If he had to choose, he could picture it easily. Aphrodite was only rivaled by Zeus in number of conquests. So much so, he had to prevent the maidens from choosing Aphrodite by forcing her into marriage. That did nothing to deter her.

Hades stopped at the sight of Death. The deity stood before them with apprehension, as if he knew he was interrupting, but bowed when Hades gestured for him to remain.

"Are you on the clock?" Hades asked.

"Yes, Your Grace, as you know, Death does not take a break."

"No day off?" Persephone clarified.

Hades smirked and explained that it was one of the requirements of the position. The applicant must be willing to work without pause. It wasn't as though someone died, thought better of it, and came back.

"One of your servants has drowned in the pool." Death checked his clipboard.

"Those pools are only five feet deep."

"He was four foot eleven."

"Well…is that all?" When Death made a sound with his…bones, Hades asked Persephone to excuse them. She nodded and took a seat next to the tree Ares had disguised himself as. A tree that had been inching its way towards them. Aphrodite could be the grass underneath his boot for all he knew. Still, he walked a few paces from Persephone, not venturing far. He wanted to resume their walk and ensure her of his final answer.

"Is this regarding Zeus?" Hades asked.

Death shook his head. "You did, however, say you wanted to know if any important names were written by the quill."

"I did."

"Adonis."

"…Adonis." Hades grunted as he ran his fingers through his hair. "You and I may need to redefine the word *important*."

"Oh," Death said simply. "I just thought, since he was so close to the family and the ladies…" he gestured to Persephone, "I thought you might want to know, Your Grace."

Adonis' departure would break dozens of hearts. At the very least, every maiden he had ever passed a flower. And Zari seemed fond of him too. She would cry, and the thought of her tears felt like raindrops on his heart. Her tears would do that. They would turn the Soul King into a poet.

He was about to tell Death to have a special place reserved for Adonis—Hades was sure the man would receive visitors and sacrifices and a cult. But before he could, the grass shifted from underneath them. It twirled and spiraled into a heavy tornado. When the winds dispersed, they were looking into the fiery eyes of Aphrodite.

"Adonis!? Adonis!?" She stomped. At her reaction, Persephone had rejoined him. At her explanation, Persephone held a hand to her mouth and gasped.

"No…" Persephone said behind her gloved fingers.

"You will not have him! Never! If you so much as touch him—"

Death was about to explain that his *touching* was not something that brought about a person's demise. He was simply there to collect souls and escort them to the Underworld for processing. But he couldn't get a word in, not when Aphrodite was slapping his cheek. Death had to take physical therapy lessons to enact facial expressions without the benefit of skin and muscle. Currently, his skeleton face adequately managed to express complete shock. He stumbled back and held his hand to his cheek.

"Your Grace," Persephone replied behind glossy blue eyes. "Might you do something to prevent this?"

"It doesn't work like that. I am sorry."

"You will not be getting your hands on him!" Aphrodite gave Death another slap. Hades felt bad for Death. Briefly. He then remembered this was a part of the job. Death's job. Not necessarily his problem.

"For once, I agree with you," Persephone turned up her nose. She and Aphrodite wove their arms together, cursed Death and dared him to come for their precious Adonis. Hades was sure that Death knew that he could anticipate an additional slap from

Hecate when she learned she would have to chase down Adonis' soul from *two* gods.

"Damn," Ares was standing beside them now. No longer a tree. Good for him. "Everyone hates you, Death."

"I...I know..."

"Did you want to come inside for a drink and some cards?"

"Really?"

"No." Ares giggled and nudged him on the shoulder. "I was just trying to make you feel better. It worked for a second, did it not? For a second there, you thought someone liked you."

Chapter 8

Hera & Zari

Her husband was not always a sloth, hence Hera's decision to organize Zari's schedule with his former self in mind. First thing in the morning, Zari needed to have breakfast. Hera felt frivolous, having to add such a necessary requirement to their routine, but Zari liked to rise before the sun. Far too early for the likes of the ichor. Lounging until noon made the girl restless and bored. Each of which made her more likely to get into trouble.

Had the day been a normal one, Hera would have had a tray brought to her whilst in bed. Yet again, out of necessity to monitor the girl, she decided to join her at the table. Zari was dressed appropriately, thanks to Hera's appointment of a proper lady's maid. One who styled her in a pale-yellow skirt and cream-colored blouse where the collar intertwined through golden hoops and threaded into an elaborate bow at her neck. Her hair was pulled into a complicated braid that stopped at the nape and allowed the strands to hang loose over her shoulders. Zari wanted to complete her look with a crown, like Hera's. Her favorite was constructed of gold and petrified beech leaves fused with cypress and flowers. It weighed three pounds and had a diamond in the center. Hera had told her it was only when she achieved something great or got married that she could wear such a thing. Whichever came first. For now, golden leaves shaped into pins would suit.

Zari was full of additional questions as she helped herself to a second serving of the spread presented on the sideboard. Hera, sipping her coffee, paused to shoot Zari a look that said it was vulgar to eat so much. Luckily, most of her ichor were asleep at this hour. Poseidon had left for Oceanus to tend to his realm but would return shortly. As did Hades. She was alone with Zari and without any distractions to hinder Hera's strict regime.

Their meal consisted of creamed peaches drizzled in goat's milk and cream liquor, quail eggs with lamb and honeyed fried feta. Sumac bread, pressed to perfection, was soaked in olive oil. Steaming cups of coffee were promptly refilled by dutiful servants. Of course, Zari preferred a *Glykis* that was sweetened beyond its natural color.

"Where do babies come from?" Zari asked, making Hera fumble with her paper. No Zeus, no reprimand if she chose to read beyond the gossip sheets of *The Times, Titanfalls, Olympus Today, The Winged Messenger* and *Where Are They Now?* She could also glance at the estate books more thoroughly. Allowances to her ichor would need to be discussed.

"Pardon?" She bent down a corner of the crisp sheets. The butler nearly stumbled as he placed the silver hood over the eggs.

"I suppose I mean *god* babies. Do gods produce asexually? Demi-gods or…semi-gods…"

"So you know, this isn't appropriate talk for an ichor of your status…or the morning…or you." Hera tried to return to her reading but couldn't help lowering her paper fully and fixating on her meal. And *this* conversation. Hera was an advocate for education and would rather the girl know the truth from her than some lewd explanation from Ares. "Gaia crafted us from clay and planted us in her garden. You remember? That's hopeful. If a god were to want a child, Gaia would make it so. One must go to her and offer up their essence."

"So…yes and no…"

Hera sighed. "If you and another ichor wanted to have a child that was the combination of yourselves, Olympus help us, the two of you would offer up your essence to Gaia. She would create a form, infuse the essence into the sculpture, and plant it in her gardens. When the offspring comes of age, it would pluck itself from the ground and begin walking…"

Hera made a traveling motion with her two fingers across the table. Zari appeared stunned. At least she didn't ask about the birds and the bees. Hera couldn't begin to understand why humans would make something so pleasant sound so painful.

"So, you're not all sisters and brothers?" Zari smiled as Hera reminded her to chew slowly.

"First off, impossible. Secondly, that would make for crazy and psychopathic individuals who--" she stopped. She lifted a brow and shook her head. "No. No brothers or sisters."

"So, someone like Hercules is--"

"A myth," Hera said flatly. Gods and humans could not interbreed. The humans were a product of Gaia's stolen designs and their Mother had always been irritated because of it. Right down to their anatomy, the humans and gods looked very similar, albeit, they were two different species. Romances were possible but cross-bred children were not. "Hercules, the *half-breed*, is a myth. But Hercules, the *ichor*, is not. He is just one of hundreds of ichor."

"So, he couldn't have possibly bedded fifty women in one night who each gave birth to fifty of his sons?"

"Zari, not even Ares is capable of such an *accomplishment*."

"Still, I'm sure he wouldn't mind the *compliment*." Zari chuckled, causing Hera to grin behind her paper. She also reached for Hera's discard pile and flipped through the pages with her usual sense of wonder. "Someone is selling a beautiful little cottage," she pointed out to Hera. "A tiny house by the sea. It would be nice to live in a cottage by the sea, yes?"

"You live in a palace. Is that not enough?"

Not wanting to appear greedy, Zari nodded and lowered her brow to appear studious. Her gaze traveled between the news and missives among their stacks, which Hera took her time opening. She had suspected the Chinese and Egyptians had discovered that *something* had happened to *someone* here. The Orishas had already invited her to tea. Twice now. They usually only asked once.

"Odin?" Zari tilted her head to read the crest on the envelope Hera had tossed aside. "Odin, as in, father of Thor?"

"That's the one." Hera sipped her coffee.

"Wow!" Zari gasped. "Norse gods exist too?"

If the girl really wanted to be impressed, Hera thought, she should watch King Yan of China try to wrangle his Ten Kings of

Hell. Or Dionysus and Jesus debate over the best wines and vineyards. She moaned at the thought of him offering his judgement, which he felt was priceless only because he passed it freely. The arrogance of being an only child, a son, was what formed his *halo*. Not everyone could dress like paupers and live like peasants. And *the man*, what he called himself, drank ten cups of coffee a day and said things like *what's up* when he greeted people. Needless to say, any invitations to visit the homes of the gods that weren't their ichor, she disposed of immediately.

She did, however, feel the need to mention.

"You are never to interact with him."

"With Odin?"

"With Thor. Zeus and Thor had a habit of proving who could conjure the biggest lightning bolt. Many believe it was a meteor that wiped out all the dinosaurs."

"The dinosaurs?"

"Demeter's precious animals were torn apart so violently that they all became pink soup. There was very little of them left. A few toes, maybe. Burnt shadows that smelled of charred blood and withered intestines. Escaped feces." Zari swallowed as Hera casually took another sip of her coffee. Zari appeared to be finished with her meal, much to Hera's delight.

After breakfast, Zari was taken to Hephaestus. She needed to get fitted for armor in the case of a war or formal ceremony where she needed to display her militant attire. Currently, it would be devoid of patches, pins and emblems. Maybe that would change. Maybe, it would not. As of late, Zeus rarely joined a skirmish, but there was a time where he fought side-by-side with his ichor. Gallantly, Hera could remember. He and Caelus would claim the skies and face the Titans or any other deity head on. Inspiring those around them, herself included.

Hephaestus' workshop, a short walk from the main house, was supported by strong clay walls and sturdy wood. It was a small encampment, complete with a roof and a large wooden door that was left ajar by a heavy palm. The rest of the space was exposed to the elements. Workers chopped wood, bent metal and carried materials over their hefty shoulders. Hephaestus was near the anvil.

His hammer looked as if it was made of paper the way he swung it with ease. After Zeus, he was the largest of the ichor, visibly intimidating but intuitive and hardworking.

"Good morning," Zari happily bowed her head. Hera mentally added *greetings* to the list of *reminders* for Zari. "It's nice to see you again!"

Hephaestus grunted in her direction underneath a steady bow that Hera had to elicit with her gaze. The girl was without favor from most of the ichor. She was pleasant enough, but visibly unequipped and painfully misplaced.

"Zari is in need of armor."

"Are we at war?"

"No. But she does need it for, at the very least, her training. Fit her for the essentials. She has a tunic and a perizoma with her."

"Training…" Hephaestus examined Zari doubtfully. The girl looked as though she couldn't harm a fly. And yet, she killed her dear Robin and nearly disposed of the staff with lightning on her first day.

"She needs to learn to control her powers." Hera angled her chin. "We need a weapon for her."

"A Claymore." Zari nodded in a way that was meant to prompt the agreement of others. Hera and Hephaestus did nothing of the sort.

For the next few hours, Hera was very much involved in Zari's fitting. She had never been so hands-on before, dressing another ichor. Hephaestus had trained Hera in combat. It was how the two had become close. In a way it was as if they were coming around the bend and passing along the know-hows of master and apprentice to the next generation. A strange feeling.

Hera's weapon was a short sword and shield that made more for surprise mobilization than direct warfare. She was faster than she looked and used her thin frame to her advantage when it came to landing consistent attacks that could feel heavy when timed appropriately. Her grace wasn't compromised in comparison to the rigid style of the Spartans. Her combat methods, half Athenian and half Amazonian, made her equally as talented with launching arrows from the back of a horse.

"Are you a good fighter?" Zari asked Hera.

"I am decent enough." She undersold herself. Hephaestus grinned as he handed her a weapon. One that made Hephaestus lift a hand at Hera's reaction.

"We could dance around with sticks and spears and axes," he said. "But as I know you are not one to waste time, Your Majesty, we could skip to the end where I place in her fingers the weapon that is most suitable."

"I..."

"You recognize it?"

Hera nodded. It was her own training combination. The Cloud Sword and the Heaven Shield. The very first she practiced with until Hephaestus forged her permanent equipment. When he placed it in Zari's fingers, the girl handled it as if it were a part of her. Almost. She playfully swung the blade and waved her arm with the shield. Caelus took stock from upon the shack.

Hephaestus shoved training pads over Zari's shoulders. The girl allowed him to adjust her with little protest. A stiff leather belt cinched her tunic as he explained how to holster her weapons for quick withdrawal. When she was handed gauntlets for her arms and legs, she removed her boots to slip them on. When her toes touched the ground, she smiled at her bare feet on the earth.

"Do you make all of the armor, Mr. Hephaestus?"

"Yes."

"Like a blacksmith?"

"Yes."

"Do you only make armor, Mr. Hephaestus?"

"No."

Hera, seeing that Zari would have continued asking him questions about his work, hugged her waist as she pointed to where things appeared loose. That Hephaestus allowed her to meddle was a testament to their relationship. "He makes a few pieces of furniture," Hera answered. "Garden statues. Saddles for horses."

"Horses?" Zari smiled. "I've never ridden a horse before." She didn't know how she knew that, but she did.

"Neither has Zeus," Hera said flatly.

"Not even a pegasus?"

Hera withheld a sigh. "Pegasi are for the Valkyrie. We've bred a few but they're temperamental and not easy to ride or saddle, considering their wings get in the way. They do alright in the races. Zeus' horse usually won."

"I wish I could learn to ride one. Or a regular horse. Or even a dinosaur."

"Why, when you have Caelus?"

Zari turned her gaze to the eagle, her mouth hung open. Hera reached under her chin to close it. Caelus could expand in size to carry Zeus' weight. Zeus would soar overhead on the vast and spectacular wings of the creature. The skies would rain down on their enemies as the heavens parted to allow them passage. Lightning between his fingers. Energy charging them both.

"In time." Hera stopped her before she could ask. Zari pressed out her lips and whispered something to Hephaestus that made him pause in his work and chuckle. He never chuckled.

As Hephaestus gave Zari direction, the girl nodded and took his instruction to heart. Hera noticed that she was a quick learner— if not by books, then by action—and quickly became comfortable with handling the weapon. But when he told her to give it a specific combination of swings, she pulled her arm back with more strength than she realized she had, and the blade went hurling through the air, abandoning her fingertips. Hera saw a faint glimmer where the sword once was before it disappeared from view. There weren't many times in her life when she was at a loss for words, but Hera could only stare.

"I'll get it!" Zari said as she took off in the direction of the tossed sword. Caelus followed.

Hera massaged her temples and turned to Hephaestus, who had the boldness to grin. She approached him, slowly, and fiddled with the shield Zari left behind.

"What did she say? Earlier, that made you smile?"

But Hephaestus only motioned towards the measurements he had taken. That Hera allowed him to keep Zari's secret was a testament to their relationship.

Chapter 9

Aphrodite & Persephone

They had found Adonis in the meadow. As usual, he began his day picking flowers to hand out to the maidens of Olympus. He was truly radiant. His skin was the color of roses and milk, his tan lines were never crooked, and his curls were thick and fluffy. His lips carried a pursed smile and his narrow nose was blemish-free and relentlessly kissable. His hands were soft and plump. As were his feet. He was humming today. A song that most likely came from his heart. He was his own bard. All that was missing was his lyre.

Aphrodite remained hidden behind a hedge of flower bushes. She had a book in hand, although she wasn't reading it. She found herself distracted by her own reflection, admiring her perfectly shaped red curls and scrutinizing her ruby eyes, which looked as if she had lost a bit of sleep. She massaged the space just above her cheeks in tight, circular motions.

"What are you doing?" Persephone appeared. Aphrodite did not cease her movement.

"What are *you* doing *here*?"

"Making sure you were at your post."

"Of course, I am. Where else would I be?"

"Oh, I can think of a few names."

Aphrodite released a sympathetic chuckle as she lowered her fingers. She knew Persephone was speaking from jealousy. After all, she was desperate for more than a gloomy bedchamber in Demeter's cottage. She wanted a realm, a kingdom, a title and a family. Had *Aphrodite* been in pursuit of Hades, he would have no room to change his mind. But instead, Aphrodite was stuck with her own dull husband. To numb her sexual desires, and to rid himself of conquest competition, Zeus had arranged for Aphrodite to marry

Hephaestus. Her ichor was large and strong and industrious. He made a decent earning and built them a house that she could only describe as *quaint*. It had only six bedrooms. Two of which she had to convert into closets for her gowns. A third was her dressing chamber, and another she turned into a large bath. She tore down the walls between the bedchambers so that she could have a much larger space. When Hephaestus asked about where he was to sleep, she reminded him that he had a cot at his shop.

Without argument, he never returned home unless he needed to confront her about her spending. Like her, he knew the idiocy of such a match but complaining about it was futile. But with this new Zeus...

If one used her vanity as an insult, Aphrodite would have laughed as ruthless and as painful as Ares. At times, she was far past it. So much so, her pride had an assistant with an office built on pillars that towered Olympus. She was always wearing the latest fashions. Always dressed pristinely. She had a book club dedicated to herself. Among the humans, she was known as the most beautiful woman alive, and she liked the word *woman*. It sounded as if man was woe-ing for not having her.

After the dinner party and their cursing of Death, who was already cursed, she and Persephone had devised a plan to keep Adonis safe. They would watch over him, constantly, making sure the man would come to no harm. They had decided to take shifts, but considering they had a friendship that wavered more than Poseidon's seas, Persephone's presence was proof of their lack of confidence in one another when it came to such an important task.

"I am here. You may go."

"I am here too," Persephone, with her hair the shade of moonbeams and eyes that wavered from green to blue, settled in beside her. She was the perfect subject to a backdrop of pale flowers. "Might as well stay."

"Have it your way then," Aphrodite pronounced. It was one of the few times she would allow her ichor the privilege.

***

No one had ever given her flowers. She was around them all the time and yet, it wasn't the same as taking ownership from a caring smile to match. Adonis had wooed her with his warmth and softness. He was always a good listener and reliable keeper of secrets. He gave advice tenderly. He was a romantic. A pure soul.

When Hades was interested in courting her, he wasn't the lovestruck knight she had read about in her stories. There were no chocolates, no jewels and no desire to see more of one another. No offers to row her along the Styx or any river of that matter. No declaration of desire. However, she was willing to look past it. Undeniably, this time. She admitted that when she took her first trip to the Underworld, she was unpleasantly vexed. Now, she was ready to conform in order to rise above her station.

Persephone eyed Aphrodite, who she knew was only here to save her favorite. Her ichor was a collector of sorts. One who relished in the sport. Glancing at the book that had Aphrodite's name imprinted on the cover, Persephone sighed. Although her ichor was incredibly vein, she was also sure of herself. Never wavering. Never in the company of self-doubt.

Persephone looked to the meadow and watched as Adonis continued to pick his flowers. He hummed, cheery and innocent, as he thoroughly examined his selections before they took a ride in his basket. He picked another, gave it a sniff, whispered kind words to the flora and placed it on top of the others. She could get bored sitting there, watching him frolic. She was thankful that Aphrodite found something else to complain about to pass the time.

"What do you think of this Zari ichor?"

"She seems alright." Persephone knew better than to openly disown the new Zeus, if so, she was. She also needed to like the girl, considering Hades' apparent fondness of her. Then again, he also seemed fond of Hera.

"She's a pain, honestly. Did you know that Ares had the nerve to comment on her beauty? As if she were, in fact, beautiful?"

"She is."

"More so than I." Aphrodite eyed Persephone as if she were asking a question. Persephone took a moment to practice the slow upturn of her lips. She knew the implications of such a comparison would upset her rival. "I don't believe she is beautiful," Aphrodite scoffed. "I don't believe she is who she says she is."

"From my understanding, she didn't say she was anything. She seemed as confused as the rest of us."

"Zeus is never confused, that bastard."

"What do you suppose she is, then?"

"An imposter. An alien." Aphrodite clutched her book so tightly she damaged the spine. "It's obvious she's a trickster. I've considered that this is Hathor's revenge."

"Hathor? As in, the Egyptian god?" Persephone sighed. "What did you do this time?"

Aphrodite straightened her posture. She loosely folded her arms so that her fingertips could dance on her skin. Persephone blinked.

"You slept with her husband, of course."

"I slept with his brother, Set. You know me, I have a thing for the brash and the brazen."

"Opposite Adonis."

"Oh…" Aphrodite winked. "He can surprise you."

Persephone blushed. Aphrodite used any opportunity to remind Persephone of her purity and inexperience—a rare trait for any immortal being. Persephone was saving herself for her husband, and Aphrodite thought it was the most absurd thing. Especially considering that the notion of celibacy was used to scare humans into pleasing them, the gods.

Perhaps Persephone should take her leave. Aphrodite, although distracted by her reflection, was capable. She was about to dismiss herself when something shiny flickered overhead. Like a speck of fairy dust or a twinkling star in the daylight. A rapidly falling star. It made a sound like a flammulated owl as it pierced through the clouds. Aphrodite, whose gaze was also on the unidentified object, followed it with matching eyes. The star flickered again. The speck of gold was shiny and bright. The sun reflected the silver of metal that made their eyes widen.

It was a sword.

A sword was flying towards them.

A sword that was heading straight for Adonis.

Chapter 10

Zari

She could run. *Fast.* The lightning trailed behind her like a tail of ribbon tied to the mast of a ship in a heavy storm. She giggled at the feeling. At the sight of the earth blurring behind her. She wondered if she had ever liked running. If she had not, it was because she had never come unhinged. She had never felt the vibrations of space and the living things around her working so uniformly in a perfect dance.

Moving so fast, she was able to tour Olympus in a way she would have never experienced. From the pulse of hummingbird feathers, to the rapid beat of a scared rabbit's heart. She looked into the eyes of a panther, bathing on a rock and ever so splendid. She eyed the drops of moisture that erupted from the fountains. She took note of each lingering scent. There was a sense of momentousness in the air. The earth was alive beneath her toes and she could feel it breathing. She spun around and around and around in circles. Feeling what it was like to breathe with no air.

Oh, right.

She hurried along in the path the sword had been thrown. It was strange, feeling comfort from a place she had never been before. Like a cartographer making quick work of mapping a new discovery. Caelus was keeping up with her. His eagle cries were overhead and leading the way. She knew what he was saying. She could feel him, the clever creature. At times he would arch his wings so that the primary feathers curved behind him, allowing him a burst of acceleration. As if he were diving towards his prey. She would push herself harder to match him. Laughing. Giggling. The two of them in sync.

When Caelus circled overhead, she came to an abrupt halt. The start of a scream tickled her ears. When she arrived at the point in question, she realized that she was in a meadow. A slow-moving meadow. Time progressed gradually as she surveyed the area, blades of grass swayed as if lulled by the delay in wind. To her right, Aphrodite and Persephone were mid sprint—the skirts of their day dresses suspended behind them, revealing legs through intended splits and ankles without stockings. On her left, Adonis, sweet Adonis, was standing with a flower to his nose, oblivious to the two ichor running towards him.

Overhead…

She furrowed her brow and held her hand to her chest. Her sword was hurling towards Adonis, aimed perfectly to stab and kill. Adonis was human, she remembered quickly, but she could not recall the rules regarding murder among the two species. Nonetheless, her vigor had arrived with her. Rescuing him made her determined beyond words. She extended her hand. She reached for the hovering sword like the fork at the dinner table. She did not know what would happen. She did not know her limitations. But in her heart, she knew that she had to do something. In her heart, she knew that she could.

The lightning moved with hesitation. Slow stems of electricity reached for the sword like a careful drawing of branches from a tree. She willed her body to push itself. To command more. The sky illuminated like an explosion. Her chest trembled with force. She pulled with all of her strength. The stubborn blade was coming towards her now and the pressure bore into her heavily. Her knees began to buckle, and her body surprised her with its exhaustion. Her nostrils were beginning to burn as Caelus' cries swung overhead, warning her from her mission.

My husband killed himself by playing with lightning, Hera's words echoed through Zari's mind. Was it possible? Could this be the end of her? As she returned to her questionable reality, she braced herself for impact. Time was no longer hers and the sword was being pulled to her with an aggressive build of animosity. Any part of it would rip her to pieces, that she knew, for it was flying, twirling, spinning with such force—fueled by power that was only in possession of a

Godking. Her only hope was for the end to be as painless as possible.

Or...*wet?*

She assumed it was her own blood being splattered across her face. She felt something warm and hard pressed into her. Something tight and consoling was wrapped around her body. The scent of almonds and coconut replaced the burn that had made its way through her skin earlier. She slowly opened her eyes, unaware of when she had closed them, and found the source of the sharp winds and heavy waters that were spiraling around her and creating a vortex of protection against the impact.

"P-Poseidon."

When the funnel subsided and the air around them began to calm, she was able to take a deep breath. His strong hands were steady around her. She couldn't stumble if she tried.

"Are you alright?" he asked low and breathy. His eyes met hers in an instant and she felt the electricity within her on the verge of a frantic emission.

She took a few steps back, suddenly insecure. She appeared far from the woman who would stand by the side of the Ocean King. Her armor was worn and mismatched, her feet bare and her hair disheveled. Attempting to right herself, and remember her current mission, she spotted Adonis nearby, who was being coddled by the ample bosom of Aphrodite and the nurturing fingers of Persephone. His spirit was gallant and amusing as he swung their hands in his own and happily dug into his basket for their appropriate flowers.

"The sword?" She looked around quickly, wondering if she had blown it to smithereens. When she had the courage to lock eyes with Poseidon, he pointed to his left. The sword had done its best to split the wind and water shield he had created around them. But it failed. It ricocheted into the earth, as if to await the day when it would be able to try again. "You saved my life," she refrained from panting. "I...I can't thank you enough."

"You don't have to thank me."

Oh, but she did. For he also saved her from humiliation and perhaps a painful injury. Her smile spread, as did his own. Her body was warmed by him as if she were sitting next to a cozy fire, ready to snuggle into a bouquet of coconut leaves. His smile extraordinary and from what Hades had implied, rare. Her heart hummed with the distant sounds of waves and resting droplets of moisture that were still hovering among the winds he had created. The dew reflected the rays of the sun and made his eyes appear every shade of blue. Some woman, somewhere in the world, was lucky to wake up to such a pair on every blessed morning.

"You are strong." She folded her lips together. "Much stronger than I."

He looked away, and she didn't blame him. Poseidon was not the type to learn how to admit to one's own superiority without sounding insensitive. Bluntness was a dose she swallowed with the shame of a scorned puppy. Slowly, he told her "In time."

"I hope so."

"Until then, you must be more careful—"

Without time to blink, she felt herself being thrown to the ground. His body on top of her own. His hand cupped firmly on the back of her head, keeping her pressed into the soft and damp earth. She didn't see what prompted him to take defense. She heard it. It sounded as if a giant was pursuing them in search of a promised serving of ambrosia. Heavy stomping. The ground was trembling. She felt the air being sucked from within her body into a void of nothingness. She became nauseous. Dizzy.

Wind. Lightning. Trees. Branches. A…panther.

She lifted her chin to see that everything was hurling in their direction, on the tails of her draft. The aftermath of her power felt like an apocalypse. The impeccable meadow with charming flowers was a disaster zone of catastrophic chaos. Grass torn. Flower beds uprooted. Trees snapped in half as if they were chicken bones. Leaves flung past them like throwing darts.

She leapt to her feet as soon as she was able and hurried over to Adonis and her ichor. Aphrodite and Persephone were nearly naked under their torn gowns. Hair was intertwined like the mess she made when she attempted to knit. Adonis was between them still, looking pudgy and soft and slightly distressed. It wasn't until the two ichor pulled themselves away from him that she noticed he had a large lump on his head that was horrifically discolored. His grin was crooked. His voice unsteady.

"I am fine…" he mumbled.

"No! You are not fine!" Aphrodite stood so fast that what remained of her clothing had fallen from her in shreds. Her breasts twerked as she poked at Zari and shoved her on the shoulders. "You hit him in the head with a fucking panther! What is wrong with you!?"

"It was an accident…" Zari tried to refrain from tears. The scene was unsettling, as were her emotions. Poseidon stood between the two of them, far from sympathetic regarding Adonis' injuries, nor was he phased by his naked ichor. He didn't look away, as if he had seen her bare skin dozens of times. In fact, when he removed his coat, he handed it to Persephone who accepted the garment with as much politeness as she could muster under her rosy cheeks.

"She said she was sorry," Poseidon said so low Zari thought he was growling at her. Even Caelus grunted as he took root on whatever debris he could find. Zari apologized to Adonis over and over again. Speaking between mouthfuls of blood, he assured everyone he was alright. Persephone used the scraps from their dresses to nurse him as Aphrodite continued to battle Poseidon.

Between Zari's sobs and the unwanted smell of a heavy rain that curtained them instantly, she had missed the arrival of Death. At the glare of Aphrodite and Persephone he did not hesitate to declare, "I came for the panther." He backed away slowly. "Just here for the panther."

Chapter 11

Ares & Poseidon

His club was located in the land among the humans. Down at the base of Olympus where the water met the beaches. After, one needed only to hop into a hansom and be driven into town. Where the stone, clay and stucco structures were stacked and as crowded as the Underworld. Homes fluctuated sporadically between shades of salt-eroded creams and vibrant blues, yellows and pinks. Windows above sinks were flung open to welcome the breeze.

Olive gardens grew in wooden troughs as rows of melons, figs and peaches lined fences. Lemon trees provided shade. Resting dogs lay in the darker corners of the narrow alleys. Following a winding road that opened to a steep incline lined with shops and restaurants, Club Ares' red door painted with the symbol of a boar's head marked the entrance to a guilty evening.

The floors were made of polished stone and the wood ceiling formed a pattern of diamonds within diamonds. Walls were compiled of clay or brick. Sometimes the texture changed in no particular fashion. What was once a parlor, was still a parlor. It was simply for gentlemen to lounge in comfortable chairs before the oversized fireplace. Drinks were poured so frequently that one wouldn't dare to place their fingers over their cups for fear they would soak their rings. The dining hall was replaced with tables for cards and checkers and dominos. Lunch trays and spirit exited the kitchens with rehearsed speed. The cellars underneath were stocked with wine, whiskey and Dionysus experiments.

The rooms upstairs had been converted for billiards and lodging. Each with a window to the ocean or the neighboring bustling activity on the paths below. The paths were being cleansed of last night's secretions and evidence of romps between a woman and her client. The third story parapets, as with most of the homes on the side of the mountain, were accessible for sea gazing, private drinks and rowdy gatherings.

Poseidon wasn't someone who liked to gamble, but he also couldn't remain at the palace. Not tonight. Hades had undersold the feeling that overcame him at the sight of Zari in tears. His heart was tearing in two. As if someone had reached their hands into his chest, tore apart his muscle and stitched it back together, leaving him in an agonizing phase of recovery. It was like watching a baby chick struggling to take a sip of water. The shouting between he and Aphrodite didn't help. All of this was over Adonis.

The human was taking residence in the palace and nursed by almost every woman in the village of Olympus. Flowers decorated his room and tear-stained handkerchiefs were strung to the ceilings like Colosseum flags.

"Sai!" Ares signaled to him when he entered. Not that he needed to, Ares was rarely without a crowd.

His ichor was sitting at a card table with a woman on his lap. His arm was wrapped around her waist while his other hand shuffled a pair of dice. Before tossing the bone onto the velvet table, Ares placed a kiss on the woman's dress—the area that protruded from the shape of her teased nipple. His fate was anticipated among the silence of observers until suddenly, the guests erupted into cheers. No one knew that luck was *literally* on his side. Ares had within his pockets, a token from Tyche, the bringer of fortune. What his ichor had done to receive such a thing was perhaps acting out one of Tyche's scripts. She was an aspiring playwright and desperately lacking in talent. Her fortune unable to look upon itself, she relied on the false praises that were given by those in need of her blessing.

Ares nudged the woman from his lap, granting her a sloppy parting kiss. With his chin, he gestured for Poseidon to precede him upstairs. The uppermost rooftop was theirs now. Servants made quick work of arranging a long table with white wine, chilled flutes and frozen watermelon cubes. Marinated chicken souvlaki rested on skewers next to a bowl of heavy tzatziki sauce with minced cucumber. Fresh pita was warmed in a cloth lined bowl over a light flame. Lamb and rice were stuffed in grape leaves and soaked in lemon juices. Orange and olive oil sponge cakes topped with dove orchids were cut into finger-sized squares and displayed on a porcelain pedestal. Poseidon took a glass of wine and overlooked the scenery. From this side of the terrace, more private than the others, he had a clear sightline of the cascading houses, the groves of grapes and the blue waters. The air smelled of salt and spring and the night's rain from Zari's tears on Mount Olympus.

"You never told me you were coming." Ares took a bite of chicken and winked as a servant poured him a glass of wine.

"I needed to get away from the palace."

"Ah. That business with Adonis." Ares chortled in a way that threatened to evolve into one of his booming eruptions of glee. "Our Zari hit him with a mountain lion?"

"A panther."

"Why didn't I think to simply throw animals at the man?"

"It was an accident."

"I heard she destroyed everything."

"The gardens mostly--"

"And that Aphrodite tried to ring her neck."

"Where are you getting your information?"

"Perhaps I will throw one of those ghastly Pomeranians. They're cute and all, but they're so vicious you won't actually miss them when they're gone."

Poseidon drank for his own pity. He was walking in the gardens that day, hoping to not see Zari. He had talked himself out of the puerile affections he felt for her. It was obvious, as each ichor was grown with a certain trait that made them unique, Zari was born to evoke affinity. It was her nature, her way, to make him want to come to her aid when he should have allowed the sword to do its duty. Upon her fatality, perhaps the real Zeus would reappear, or they would rid themselves of a Godking outright. But he couldn't. His body reacted long before his mind had the chance to think clearly. He wouldn't have allowed anything bad to happen to her. Just thinking of the opposite outcome made his drink disappear quickly down his throat.

As much as he wanted her was as much as he knew how detrimental it would be for them both. She was the Godking and ruler of Olympus. He ruled the oceans. They were built to outlast this world and he couldn't imagine himself with a single ichor for the rest of his life. Nor could he imagine the day in which he would tire of her. When he returned to Oceanus the first night, he took two women to his bedchamber, grew bored instantly, and nearly destroyed his trident in a sparring match with his oldest friend. His aggression was building. His former restlessness warned him of an eruption. One he wanted to release into her.

Luckily, he could dive into his work with the ships. He had become so hands-on that he was sure he was hindering the builders. But he could lose himself, briefly, over the columns of numbers, schedules and progress. Like this endeavor, he realized, the pursuit of Zari would be a long game.

"What are your opinions of the little lightning cub?" Ares gestured for them to sit at a table and eat. He gazed at Poseidon behind dark lashes. In the sun, his earthy brown features were littered with hues of red.

"I have no opinion."

Ares turned up the corner of his lips, knowing that Poseidon had taught him the art of lying much better than that. The two had grown close over the decades—tolerating one another was the true test of friendship. Ares asked for coffee and stirred it slowly as Poseidon sat in silence. Their allegiance was about to be pressed.

"I like her," Ares said as he sipped his drink. "She's funny and so happy it makes me sick to my stomach. Like too much candy. Sweet and decadent. I wonder if she tastes sweet." Poseidon slowly turned to Ares, proving that he hadn't been listening to a word Ares had spoken after the mention of Pomeranians. Shame, Ares thought, as he went into full detail on the specific cut, color and breed of the dog he would sick on Adonis. "All of that energy, squirming beneath me as I took her, we could probably go for days in my bed. I'd fuck her so hard—"

Poseidon knew he was taking the bait. But he didn't care. His fingers gripped the table between them and tossed it aside as if it were a children's toy. It snapped in half when it hit the wall of the club and splintered into jagged edges. The staff had the sense to abandon their post without permission. Glass and wine sprayed the floor. Distant laundry lines strung with towels and sheets and linens thrashed in the violent beginnings of a storm. Poseidon had taken hold of Ares' designer lapel and raised his fist to his chuckling ichor.

As he was now, Poseidon knew a match between them would end in his loss. He was too infuriated to think clearly and Ares had trained with him enough to know every move that Poseidon would make. Ares could disarm and counter with ease. Poseidon needed to get a hold of himself.

"Calm yourself." Ares grinned from halfway in his seat. Poseidon towered over him, his chest expanding with steam. "I am only searching for answers the only way I know how."

"By being an ass."

"By being intuitive to habits."

"I don't have a habit with women or ichor, unlike yourself."

"Sai, you have a need for conquest. It is in your nature. You can deny it this century with your I'm-too-good-for-the-pettiness-of-you mentality, but deep down, you are like the rest of us. Pure champions bred from chaos. Grown for beauty, duty, war and nothing else really." He blinked. "Zari is someone you want. I won't get in the way. But as for you not having a habit—"

"You wouldn't be in the way, I assure you."

Ares chuckled as he removed Poseidon's fingers from him. "Arrogance runs deep in us all. And greed." He sighed as he examined the mess of the terrace. "And destruction."

"Zari is none of those things." Perhaps, a little destructive.

Ares shook his head knowingly. "Which makes her appealing to you."

As the staff shuffled about the stone laid floors, Poseidon took a breath. Vases were broken, spilling soil in mounds between the grout. Linens were torn and food was everywhere. Poseidon sat firmly in his chair, eyeing his ichor, who adjusted his clothing without breaking their gaze. He smirked, which made Poseidon wish he had punched him. As if they were actors on a reset, a replacement table was wedged between them. A cloth was laid on top with saucers and wine glasses. The mess had been cleared in under three minutes. Food was replaced and it looked as if Poseidon's loss of control had never happened.

"Be careful," Ares said as he took hold of his wine glass.

Poseidon knew he shouldn't ask but it wasn't like Ares to offer sound advice. "Why?"

"Take myself for example. I like the Godking as a lively member of our troupe. But her incompetence makes her an easy target for manipulation. Had your emotions not gotten the best of you already, I would say that we could use this to our advantage— loans, repayments, the assumption of the islands to Oceanus. You know? But since your emotions *have* gotten the best of you, it makes this so much harder."

"Makes what harder?"

"Her being a ruler. She likes you. I can tell." He lifted a shoulder. "Then again, she likes everyone. A few years in the game of odds and allies will change someone. When friendships are lost and relationships severed upon disagreements."

"What are you saying? Really?"

"I am saying that I don't want you, my friend, to lose sight of what's important because of the Godking."

"Zari is—"

"Different, as I've already stated. But you seem to be overlooking one obvious thing."

"What is that?"

"*She* likes everyone. That includes Hera, who is incapable of change."

***

Ares knew that Poseidon was out to prove himself. Like a man ready to take the hand of a woman he loved, he was ready to take back his coherence when it came to being a king. Poseidon asserted that he had what it took to separate the hold Zari had on him from his duty. Ares responded with a lift of his brow as they went in search of the Godking. They found her in the study.

Zari sat behind Zeus' desk, which was built to accommodate his large frame. She was hunched over a stack of books and papers with a quill between her fingers. Caelus was in the corner near an open window. His eyes must have been closed as his feathers rustled from his interrupted nap and his wings expanded at the sight of the two ichor entering. When Zari looked up, they could see that she was wearing spectacles. Goofy looking things that did not help her appeal. That did not help his ichor, whose heart appeared to have stopped as they approached her. Poseidon was helpless at this point, and it would be infeasible to pry what they needed from Zari by force. Ares would have to be a friend to her as well, which would bring his total count of confidants to three. He was alright with three.

"Hiya!" Ares said so loudly it startled her. Her hair was pulled into two high tails and flowed over the shoulders of her blue dress. "I didn't know you wore the glass, Your Majesty."

"Oh," she adjusted them. "I found them in a drawer. As with anything here, I thought they were magic."

"Magic?"

"I thought I would see things differently."

"Do you?"

She shrugged. "Just a bit blurry."

"So, mission accomplished. I say, if it makes you feel better, you wear those spectacles." Ares smiled as wide as he could. Zari did as well.

"I want to be a good ichor, like the rest of you. Hopefully, as good as Zeus."

"Well, I mean…" Ares' voice caught at the sight of Poseidon's expression. Ares knew to choose his words carefully. Right, he would begin with a compliment. "You are reaching some aspects of his potential in strides."

"Am I?" She beamed.

"Why of course. Right now, you are hated almost as much as Death. And Zeus was hated almost as much as Death. You are following in his footsteps well. Almost there, I would say."

She removed the glasses from her face and her smile faded as she looked away from them. Caelus began to fidget and crow. Ares could tell that Zari was once again on the verge of tears.

Poseidon, cursing his name, joined her side as Ares stood on the other. Each of them reached out to touch her and then recoiled, wondering if it was the right thing to do. Their lips moved over her head, mouthing words to one another as they tried to think of *something* to say that was comforting and apologetic—with the exception of an apology, for neither of them were experienced enough to make it sound sincere. But Ares was only capable of the truth while Poseidon feared his passion would either repulse or break her.

Ares placed a bold hand on her shoulder and did his best to move it in circles.

"The truth hurts, lightning cub. But if you stretched it as much as you stretched yourself, you would hurt too."

What? Poseidon mouthed with a slow blink and a glare at Ares' hand on Zari. To further humor himself at his friend's expense, Ares tapped her flesh with his fingers as if he were playing a piano. Slowly, very slowly, he took a lock of Zari's hair and smiled into the silky fibers of silver. If the goal was to agitate Poseidon and Caelus, it worked. The three of them, forgetting the objective was to cease the Godking from crying, were teetering the edge of a battle with no one able to offer a sound explanation.

"You're going to kill me now." She sniffled and turned to them. Their movements came to an abrupt halt. Her golden eyes were as glossy as tempered chocolate. She was truly expecting them to be rid of her.

"No, my darling, you are more than capable of doing that yourself."

"Shut the fuck up, Ares! You're making it worse!"

Ares meant it as a compliment but was met with the trembling of the Godking's lip.

"No, no, no," Ares said, patting her over and over as if he were beating a rug. If he ever beat rugs. "You're not crying. You're not upset. You're simply...allergic...to this life."

Ares knew it was only a matter of seconds before the tears would come. Out of all the wars, battles and scuffles with Athena, he wasn't prepared for this. He released his hold on Zari to seek the string for the servant's bell. When the servant arrived, his eyes lowered, displaying the pity of a resting Zebra at the tear-stung ichor. Her ability worked on humans, Ares realized. His voice shook the servant from his trance.

"Hold it together, man! Ambrosia, I need it now!"

"W-we are out of it, my lord."

"What!? How the Hades do you run out of *fruit*?"

"We are doing our best to make more. But Her Majesty eats so much of it…and the gardens were destroyed by…Her Majesty…"

"What do we do?" He mouthed to Poseidon who was also holding on to the possibility of the dessert bringing an end to this. For it was no secret, the Godking inhaled it with record-breaking speed. Before the two could enter a match of silent arguments and wailing limbs, Poseidon gritted his teeth, brought Zari to her feet and pressed his lips to her own.

***

He was only going to leave it for a second. Or two. But when he kissed her, the brief distraction turned into a moment of sharp attraction. His lips latched onto her own as if they were coming home. Yes, he was greedy. Greedy as he waited for her body to relax into his hold and the shock of the kiss to become a reality to her. When she slackened into him, her hands hovering lightly over his morning coat, he removed his lips away slightly, within an inch of her own, only to allow her a moment to breathe. He then pressed into them again, hoping she did not feel the shudder of his desire.

His body was on the verge of doing wicked things to her. Of performing acts of arrogance that would leave her sensitive at the peaks of her breasts and sore between her thighs. His chest fell, heavily, as his mouth lingered over hers. As her body became stiff again.

"Zari, no more crying…" he whispered on her cheek. "Alright?"

"Y-yes."

"If you do, I will have to kiss you again. Understood?"

Her throat muscles shifted as she took a swallow of air. She gave a quick nod as he looked into her eyes. Eyes that were a bit terrified at his abrupt liberties. She was only recently hatched and already, he had done something ruinous. This ichor had *too* much power. Not only did she command the skies, she commanded him and the need for fostering that was foreign to most of their ichor. He put a short distance between them, followed by an abrupt turn

94

of his expression. Ares and the servant were watching with interest. All that was missing for them, were two comfortable chairs.

"Zari," Poseidon said simply, calming himself. "I am here to bring forth a former request."

"Y-yes." She blinked.

"I once informed Zeus that I wanted to annex the islands of Oceanus. Milos, Icaria, Rhodes and Cythera. Ares and I have a business venture that we would like to pursue, but unfortunately a war that your predecessor involved me in placed my lands in a financial bind and depleted our timber. I would like to absorb the islands as a part of Oceanus, but also, I need Demeter to grant us harvest."

"I...um..."

"In exchange for a thousand ships. It's only fair."

"I..." She was shaken by his turn of formality. He placed his hands in his pockets, waiting for a response. She searched vigorously for a pen and parchment. She was trying to recall all he said and make sense of it. He could tell she was confused. And frazzled. Ares took the moment to relay his own demands regarding land and money and how Athena should not be granted her own jurisdiction and how she should allow Aphrodite to leave Hephaestus and that she should make her marry him. That they would get a kick out of being husband and wife. And then when they wanted, perhaps in a fortnight, they would divorce one another. And that Adonis should—

"I...I would need to speak...to Hera..."

"No, you wouldn't," Poseidon's response was so brisk, it shook her. "You are the Godking. Say it is so and you can make it happen."

"I..."

Poseidon withdrew a copy of the agreement from his pocket. He placed it before her to sign. She didn't know what she was looking at or if she should be in the presence of such sensitive materials. She was still flustered by the kiss and his coldness. He refrained from showing the same discombobulation by being the devil himself. Her feebleness was worth the rescue, but he wanted to hold his ground. This was a test for him more than it was for her. This was proof to Ares that he could set aside his emotions to take hold of what he truly wanted. But as she raised her brow, an inch of sadness at the corners of her mouth, she reached for a quill and pressed it to the parchment. Poseidon placed his hand over her own and stopped her.

It was as it was with the sword in the garden. His body reacted before his mind could explain what he was doing.

Staring at yet another change in his mood, he realized she was not deserving of his firmness. If not for his compassion, he would have easily gotten anything he wanted. As much as he wanted to be done with this and return to Oceanus, he didn't have it in him to exploit her for his own benefit. Ares' point was made. And it was accompanied by a heavy smirk from his ichor.

"If any of the ichor, if anyone, comes to you directly asking for things, you must deny them." Zari blinked as Poseidon took a breath. "If I had a tenant who needed funding for a new fence, I would never hand him the funds directly. Nor would I sign something I am incapable of deciphering. No one wants to be swindled and unfortunately, you've been inserted into a race that does just that."

"Swindling?" She seemed shocked. "Your family?"

"Your family too…"

She lowered her chin and appeared unsure. "I make a mess of things wherever I go. Hera told me to stay here for the rest of my life. She said I was the worst thing... all the time."

"Ah." Ares gave a spry nod. Poseidon silenced him with a sharp turn of his chin.

"I will never be good at this." She sat heavily in her chair and stared at the array of everything before her. Her textbooks, her documents. Their history. Hera had barraged her with studies although Zari admitted she wasn't an avid student. It didn't matter to the Queen who couldn't wait to begin her mathematics tutoring.

He lifted the cover of one of the books entitled the *Titanomachy: The Battle of Thessaly*.

"That was a big one…" he said softly.

"Are not all wars big?"

She wasn't wrong and he acknowledged her with a smile. "This one was a war of independence. And perhaps, the one time the Titans were all united."

He flipped through the pages of the book. He pointed to various places on the map and drew invisible circles with his fingertips. He chronicled the beginning of time, as he knew it. From what Gaia herself had told them when they were children to present day. She asked many questions that he answered with more patience than he thought possible. He decompressed, blissfully, as he had found their *something to talk about*. Until Ares made sure to insert himself as the more flamboyant narrator—calling upon the servant to perform the role of dying soldiers and villainy as he acted out important scenes from the war. He seemed to be rushing through the early parts of history so that they would arrive quicker to that point at which he ascended to become the God of War. And the servant, he twirled and fell to the floor pretending to be covered in blood. Zari watched intensively, and happily in her seat. She beamed.

Not a tear in sight.

Chapter 12

Hera & Hades

Hades had his hand on her shoulder as they stood in the doorway. She noticed it only after she had relaxed. She was ready to pounce on Ares and Poseidon. Her prized peacocks had the scent of each of them and she would not hesitate to castrate her ichor. Poseidon, although handling their predicament with minimal involvement, was not unselfish. There was no such thing as nobility when it came to her ichor. They had been alive for far too long and she was waiting for the moment when one of them would try to take advantage of Zari. Although Hera was the Queen, the universe had acknowledged Zari as the Godking. Decisions were in fact hers if she made them so.

"See," Hades whispered over her. He had been preventing Hera's pursuit. After feeling the coming of an unnatural rain, they went to the study and saw the debacle that was Ares and Poseidon's attempt at consolation. Hades convinced Hera to wait. He wanted to see how they handled the situation, perhaps for the simple sake of amusement. "She is enjoying herself."

"I don't like her alone with them."

"You need not worry yourself," Hades said in a low voice.

"You need worry more--" She stopped as they turned at the sound of heavy shuffling. Something tall and covered in a wad of fabric was being guided down the hall with two of their ichor surrounding it. A pair of feet peeked from underneath. They belonged to Adonis. Hera had seen enough of the man frolicking through her meadows to be sure. Aphrodite, along with Persephone, scowled at Hera.

"He should stay here," Aphrodite demanded. At the very least, her ichor was presentable in their appearance. When they arrived wearing nothing but rags, Hera was still overseeing the mending of Hephaestus' shop, which had been in disarray due to Zari's sudden burst of speed.

"No," Hera said flatly.

"He's too weak to be moved." Aphrodite lowered her eyes and whispered aggressively. "It's not safe out there for him."

"I do not care. Your lover is not staying in my house."

Aphrodite growled and stomped her foot. Rejection was as much of a stranger to Aphrodite as mercy was to Hera. She would have had it tiled at the bottom of her pools. She would have painted the word on the door of the palace in the blood of a pig had her point not been made. She wanted Adonis gone. He wasn't her problem and she had enough to handle at the moment.

"You have no heart, Hera."

"I do. I felt really bad for the panther."

Aphrodite huffed as she beckoned the wrapped Adonis along. Persephone lingered for a moment before extending what appeared to be a coat to Hades.

"This belongs to Poseidon, but I have not been able to locate him."

"I will ensure he gets it."

"Seems as though the two of you have a knack for providing shelter for the distressed. Her Majesty," she turned to Hera, "the King, would be well cared for, if he's half the gentleman you are."

Hades released an earthy chuckle as Hera lifted a brow in his direction. This was news to her, if said news was an implication of Hades attempting to match Zari with Poseidon. It was almost overshadowed by Persephone's flirtatious behavior toward Hades. Hera scoffed, knowing the ichor would teeter her affection when Hades tottered his own.

Even so, the annoying tulip pink cheeks of Persephone were showing up more and more within Hera's presence which meant that she was in the company of Hades for far too long. Her list of inconveniences was expanding by the minute.

When Persephone took her leave, Hera folded her arms and turned to him. Hades looked to be at a loss for words as he ran his fingers through his hair and smiled sheepishly.

"Lady Persephone, always polite."

"And blunt without effort." Hera lowered her brow. "Poseidon?"

Hades' eyes widened for a moment, as if he were expecting her to mention something else. Persephone's advances, perhaps? But she did not care for the private life of her ichor. The only one she concerned herself over was Zari, the ichor whose future Hades was attempting to plan.

"It's not as though she's *your* husband."

"Of course not, that would imply that I am the Queen."

Regardless of their genders, their occupations were the same. She wasn't going to displace herself when she had worked hard to build her home and her kingdom. Beginning again, finding a purpose, was not a journey she intended to take.

"You are the Queen," Hades agreed. "And she is the Godking. She is also eligible and there is no harm in agreeing to a match that appears to be settling naturally." At her expression, Hades took a pause as a few servants approached the room. Ares had asked them to join the stage for an extended and complicated scene. They came equipped with brooms and mops to act as their props. Hades took the opportunity to pass along Poseidon's coat. He also seemed appreciative of the moment to start again. "Roles aside," he spoke softly to her, "Poseidon is fond of Zari and the girl is certainly drawn to him. I don't see the harm."

"Sexual pursuits are the last thing she needs to worry about right now."

"*Romances* are necessary."

"Why?"

He tilted his chin at Hera's defiance. "Imagine, for a moment, that you are Zari. You have no idea of who you are or what you're doing here. Every day is a mystery. You have the power of a god. Let us add, you are a ruler. A king among kings. The responsibility has been handed to you, whether you like it or not, and to make matters worse, you are aware that you are unworthy of the title that has been thrust upon you. She has been a jewel that none of us would have been. Gentle, forgiving and, well, a good sport. But it is only because she has us to rely on."

"Not romances—"

"I believe that romances are extensions of family. When you hand yourself over to those that can uplift you, that take the time to learn about you, and accept you, when you feel wanted and supported, beautiful things can happen. And Poseidon, although he is not half the gentleman that I am—" he made a show of playfully adjusting his collar, "—he has a good heart. We should be thankful that she doesn't have an eye for Ares."

"I disagree, but I won't argue with you further." Mostly because she was as ill-equipped to understand love affairs as Zari was to be the Godking. After her husband's betrayal, her insecurities had nibbled away at her heart. Rotting her from the insides.

His silver eyes smiled at her as he took hold of her hand. With his thumb he brushed over the curve of her knuckles and studied her fingers, as if longing for the removal of her gloves that separated them. He placed her hand in the crook of his elbow and guided her away from the door.

"And to answer your question, I do worry. Constantly." She looked up at him as he gave a tender nod. "Zari has the ability to ruin us all, but as does any infant that is born into the world. Her nurture will help overcome the natural quench of conflict we gods gravitate toward. She will be better than us. That is my hope."

"You are so sure of her...you place so much faith in her—"

"What else am I to do? We as gods have been tossed into the matchbox and shaken violently before. We adapt and we overcome. We've been cursed, swallowed, eaten, drowned, stabbed, betrayed, squashed, squished and tossed aside. Some of us, forgotten. Most of us, overlooked. But we do what we can with what we have."

"And if she is not long for this life?"

"Then she is not. But I have not ended the search for Gaia and Zeus. We will get answers."

"And if we don't?"

"Then it will be one more thing we cannot understand. Even as gods, we don't know *everything*. We cannot control everything." He smirked, mostly to himself. "We would turn out like our mother. Where is the fun in that?"

She didn't like his use of the word *fun*. But she did agree, there was nothing they could do at the moment aside from carry on with their plan of having Zari act in Zeus' absence.

Hera said nothing as they continued their walk, nor did she question why he was escorting her through the gardens. It was a pretty day. The clouds from Zari's repressed cry had parted beautifully and the sun warmed them gently. The palace gardens were beautiful with the babbling sound of the fountains accompanying the fresh scent of new blooms. Demeter was hard at work in the nearby meadow, rebuilding all that Zari had broken. Hera wished she had worn a Greek day dress instead of her English one. But as an aristocrat and the Queen, she would wear the lesser, and more ornate fabrics when spring was officially welcomed, in conjunction with the Garden Party and Floral Ball.

"I was wondering if I should send out a redaction for the ball. Canceling it altogether."

"I don't think that's necessary," he said. "The normality and the high-spirited event send a good message to the realm, and I always enjoyed your water lilies."

Hera often arranged them in the ponds, pools and fountains as clusters of soft petals among candles and spring fireflies. The Garden Party was an event in which she would open up her palace gates for a week so that anyone from her kingdom of Olympus could walk the gardens, bathe in the waters, have their photograph taken, tour the portrait galleries and watch the chariot races. The Floral Ball would be held at the end of the week on a raised floor under the moonlight. Her peacocks would be on display, happy to be fed and admired.

"Are you bringing Cerberus?"

He beamed. The tenants loved getting their photo taken with the three-headed beast. Although nobody enjoyed it more than Cerberus herself, who always knew when a camera was aimed at her. This event was so popular that they had to create a schedule of each god and their animal companion to appear during set times to control the masses. Hera and her peacocks, Hades and his hound, Athena and her pegasi. Hera wondered if Zari would be interested in introducing Caelus. Zeus liked the fact that his domineering eagle was a menacing mystery to the people and never allowed him to be approached during social events.

"Cerberus has already chosen her outfit. It's adorable, really."

"Is that so? I'm not sure anything can beat her performance of *Struwwelpeter*. What was it, each head was Peter, Fred and then Alice."

"On fire," they said in unison. Hera chuckled at the memory.

"Was that your favorite?" he asked.

"*Little Women*. Cerberus looks lovely in a bonnet. As do you..."

Hades laughed, which made a surprising amount of pressure build within her chest. She liked his laugh. She hadn't seen or heard it enough. It took a brave ichor to accept his own silliness. It took a special person to go the lengths of wearing a gown and a hat to complete their quadrant. All to make Cerberus happy and please their visitors. She imagined him with a child. A little girl who wanted to play teatime or a boy who wanted to play pirates. Hades would shed the dinner coat and fasten his neckcloth across his forehead to make for a one-eyed bandage. She imagined him rolling on the grass as they attempted to bind him.

Building her nursery, she had pictured Zeus with children. She then pictured him without them, as he never gave her the suggestion that he would have liked to be involved in parenting until his sons came of age. He was a king who only rolled around with concubines.

"Cerberus wants to do *The Wonderful Wizard of Oz*," he said, pulling her from memories of what should have been. "So I am afraid there will be no bonnets. Although," he lowered his voice as if confessing a secret. "I might be wearing a pair of beautiful silver slippers. You wouldn't have some that I could borrow, by any chance?"

She laughed so hard she couldn't help but to lean into him. He squeezed her hand against the top of his arm as she took hold of it. The scent of his soap and aftershave reminded her of another time that the two of them were close.

Many centuries ago, prior to her marriage, Hera had gravitated towards Hades. She wouldn't have called it love, for she was still unsure of what the word meant. But he was the one who prompted a smile from her when he entered a room and always knew how to shift her mood with his playfulness. Or tease her to tears, followed by a bashful apology. Growing up with him was always an adventure. Hades was the lively and prankster sort, Zeus, courageous and a bully and Poseidon, protective and pragmatic. Over time, Zeus' entitlement turned him into a bossy tyrant, and Poseidon began the act of distancing himself from the rest of their ichor. Only Hades remained the same. Always a relief and overall, happy.

He accompanied her on walks and listened if she ever complained. He had a way of making her feel as though he was understanding which, in turn, made her feel understood. But then, with Gaia's blessing, Zeus made an offer for Hera after the war. He was a strong, gallant leader who had just assumed Olympus and was declared the God of the Heavens and God of the Skies. His power was something a companion wanted in their mate. It didn't matter if he did not know how to make her laugh, he was adamant that her beauty and strength, in his eyes, were unmatched.

Then, there was a delay with having children. Gaia would look at them and shake her head, citing that she was having a case of *artist's block* when it came to sculpting their offspring. And Gaia was a perfectionist, therefore, there was no solution or hope for a child in the near future. *Funny*, Hera thought, as Gaia seemed to have a burst of inspiration when it came to the models that followed. Hence, the additional hecatoncheires, cyclops, gigantes, erinyes, furies and nymphs. All the nymphs. And then Persephone and Aphrodite. Each ichor was the beauty and innocence she felt was fading within her.

The world around them, each with their depictions of exotic refinement, were absent in her features. Her hair was dark and boring. Her eyes, equally so. She was intelligent, but not a genius like Apollo. She was strong, but not as virile as Athena. Not even her temper could match Ares at his worst. All she had was an empty bed, an empty nursery, and an empty heart.

She understood now, without Hades needing to say more. Zari must have been feeling similar—not enough and never enough. And Hera had assumed Zeus' character of being imperious and overbearing. In a way, their roles had switched, and it wasn't fair for the either of them. It was their nurture that would guide Zari into believing she was worthy. Like no one did for Hera when she needed it.

She felt their paces slow. She turned to Hades, overcome with her thoughts.

"Zari wants to do well. She is...depending on us to show her how."

Hades' smile was gentle. "She feels bad when she disappoints, especially you."

"Not sure why..." Hera looked away, unable to find one reason why the girl would admire her to any extent. She quickly added, "She needs to get her powers under control. And learn some basic manners."

"She will make mistakes."

"I'd be surprised if she didn't."

"We will be there to clean it up."

We. He was making a habit of including himself and she could not understand why. He gave her another one of those smiles. One that made her look away from him and continue her walk, with or without him. Hades was acting as if what they had was a partnership. Was he using her? Was he using Zari? He was the King of the Underworld and a master of manipulation when it came to chess and his ichor. He was always calculating, always several steps ahead. But what if he wasn't? What if he was truly here to help Zari? To help them both?

She didn't know what she feared the most. Hades with a plan, or Hades being tender for reasons her heart couldn't bear to begin to consider.

Chapter 13

Death

"No animal is safe with this one." Death held up his pocket watch when he entered the office. Another soul was inside, and not a human one.

"What is it this time?" Hecate asked with her boots on the desk. Animals passed everyday—food and clothing and sport. But the ones that had a place in Death's pocket watch were souls that were once loved. It was what caused a soul to maintain its form in the afterlife and prevented it from becoming a conduit for the Underworld in the River Styx.

Someone had loved the peacock, the panther, the flock of chickens, a barnyard owl and now, a sperm whale. Death was carrying the soul of a whale in his pocket.

"Apparently," Death removed his cloak and hung it on a hat stand in the corner, "the Godking doesn't know how to swim. So, when she and Hephaestus were training near the docks, she fell into the water and was swept away by a current. Poseidon was there and jumped in to save her. However, the girl panicked and sent shockwaves that stretched about twenty feet. An old sperm whale was nearby."

"Who adopts a whale as a pet?" Hecate asked.

"I believed it was Jonah's."

"The whale that ate him?"

"Some people gain affection for their captors. Besides, the whale practically saved his life."

"Damn." She threw a wad of paper in the air. She caught it and tossed it again. "No animal is safe with that one."

"That's what I said." Death took a seat at his desk, which he noticed had been pushed further into the corner near the bathing chamber. He wished he could have had the extra workspace on the opposite side of the room, but Hecate and Janus claimed they needed the extra surface for their things. Hecate had her pistols and her hats and spurs. Janus had her files and a collection of porcelain sphinxes. She had been to Egypt over a decade ago and could recall her trip as if it were yesterday. He knew better than to touch anything of Janus'. Her second face would turn to chastise him faster than Hecate could withdraw her pistols if he so much as moved her hat. Even if they were on his desk.

"I'm glad you're here," Hecate said, catching the wad of paper again. "We need to talk."

Death swallowed, although there was no air within his lungs to push down. It was a pointless habit, but he hoped the mannerisms of animated expressions would help him seem more affable. Not that it was working very much. He understood how much he was disliked. He also understood why Hecate was looking at him as if she were ready to use him for target practice. "Adonis."

He made a gesture of running his fingers through his hair, then proceeded to examine his pocket watch and schedule. Perhaps, the Godking was murdering some little girl's dormouse.

"Not that she's not apologetic." He tried to change the subject. "She cried so hard at the demise of the poor whale. She likes animals. They simply don't last long when she's near."

"Adonis."

"I believe Demeter is hiding her deer in a shed. They're allowed out in shifts to use the bathroom and eat. It's like a prison."

He stopped at the wad of paper getting lodged into his empty eye socket. Janus released a monosyllabic laugh before returning to her work.

He felt his face for the paper Hecate had thrown. Using his bony fingers, he pulled at one of the folds of parchment. He had to be careful. Once, Hecate had thrown a pencil at him and it fell into his body. He learned, disturbingly enough, that his sockets did not look into the form of a skeleton. The eyes of his body opened to the darkness of the abyss. Deep within were constellations—his eyes were one of many doors to the universe. Searching the universe for a lost pencil, it was a nightmare.

When he was successful in removing the wedged piece of paper, he turned to Janus. "Do I have any other appointments?"

"No," she said sharply, also awaiting his explanation. Adonis' delay in retrieval meant more paperwork for her. Her golden quill continued to scribble but paused to shake its feather at him.

"Hades asked me to tell him if any important names came up."

Hecate folded her arms. "We need to work on your definition of important."

"He's so well liked in Olympus. I thought—"

"What's he going to do, frolic among the graveyard picking corpses for his tiny basket?"

Obviously, no. But Death kept his thoughts to himself. He examined his desk. It held his clipboard and a notebook that he rarely used. He was so busy retrieving souls that he rarely had time to sit there and stare at the walls. Plus, he didn't like being around Hecate and Janus when they were upset with him. It was difficult being the new guy.

Hecate sighed. "Aphrodite and Persephone are trying to shield him. It won't work. Tell them that."

"Um, where do I put the whale?" He turned to the two of them. Janus chose to ignore him, and Hecate chose to not answer. He stood to his feet and reached for his cloak. Shame, Mrs. Federer served delicious tea and biscuits at this time and always greeted him with a smile. One of the few people who did. "Well, before I go, any news on Zari and or Zeus?"

Nothing.

"What of Gaia? Has Iris located her?"

Again, they said nothing.

He tugged on his hat and proceeded downstairs. He saw the tray Mrs. Federer was in the process of preparing with beautiful lemon biscuits, freshly baked scones and petit fours. And tea. He could go for a cup. Perhaps, some would be waiting for him when he returned. Mrs. Federer often said she would save him a serving, but only to her surprise would his stash be depleted. He dared not ask her to reserve a portion for him. The old woman was exhausted over finding creative hiding places that were always discovered.

When he left the office, he examined his pocket watch. It was gold and intricate, with a ruby eye in the center. Inside was the soul of the whale. It still amazed him that at the end of the day, all bodies were merely shells for what was important. Life that never extinguished.

Formerly a deity himself—one of the lesser known ichor of the lesser known—being in the land of souls was far more interesting than the land of the living. It was also a place and time for rest. Souls who were brought here that did not want to repeat the formula of working until their bones ached remained dormant. They might join the unloved in the Styx or the Hypnos deities for an endless slumber, taking the shape of stars.

There were also those who were forced into centuries of hibernation for law breaking in the Underworld. The Penitentiary for Souls was similar to the layout of a department store he once visited in America. Aisles of souls were resting in glass jars—or if they couldn't find an equivalent, anything that could hold them such as bottles and terracotta pots. They were arranged by their violation into departments and paired with a unique barcode for easy sorting.

Those that wandered had jobs or some form of vocation that earned them coins to pay for their homes and shopping. It was similar to life on Earth, but everything moved at a pace that could not be described as slower or faster. It was its own. Women still shopped for their evening meals, men visited clubs and children attended school.

School.

He grunted, forgetting it was time for the schoolhouse to release its antsy students. The one he was passing taught boys up to the age of twelve. Before he could quicken his pace, he had the attention of a familiar group of children who were heading towards him on their bicycles. There were five of them, ranging in size but not in insolence.

"Look who it is," one said to another. Of course, they rode in circles to block his path.

"He can't look if he has no eyes."

"Hello...young men..." Death said softly as he tried to find an opening. His mother had always taught him that if he couldn't say anything nice, to say it anyway because kindness was simply *good*. And to never strike a child, although right now he found her morals more difficult to uphold. "And I have eyes."

"Death, we have a question for you. How did you become Death?"

Oh. His sockets widened. Not many people asked, and he was proud that he was selected by Hades personally. The Soul King had told him that his decision had been a difficult one. That bit of encouragement often helped him through his day. He held up a finger to explain but was rudely interrupted by the rehearsed punch line.

"He became Death because he got fired from Life." The children laughed as he slowly lowered his finger. He had to admit, the joke was one of their better ones. Still cruel, but an improvement if they ever wanted to perform comedy in the *proper* setting.

"Death, you would be the only one at your funeral. But do not worry, we would all approve and not question it."

"Why would he have a funeral? He would only get his own receipt from the parlor."

"Because he's dead?"

"No, because no one would pay for a casket."

"Don't worry, we would all chip in to make sure you got the biggest casket there is. Something big enough to hold you and your loneliness."

The children sang. Death hung his head. He knew they would get bored of him eventually. Although, there was that one time they teased him until the lampposts came on. Until their mothers bellowed for them to come inside for supper. If he tried to walk through them, they would run him down with their bicycles. He would have waited this out, had he not had a prior appointment.

The children tightened their circle. He asked them politely to let him pass. When they refused, he released a heavy sigh. He was going to ask them one last time with the hopes of—

ZAAAAAPPP!!!

A flash of lightning and the sound of heavy thunder made him cover his head with his arms. It sounded like an explosion. Like the detonation of a thousand fireworks. When he opened his eyes, he noticed the children had toppled from their bicycles. Their eyes and mouths were agape at the figure before him. A girl with white hair stood between them. She was wearing a bathing suit made of a deep blue rayon, consisting of slim-fitting trousers that stopped just above her ankles. Her turquoise top looked like a dressing robe, complete with short, bell-shaped sleeves and buttons that insinuated her cinched waist. The gathered fabrics flared naturally behind her, as did her hair, which was pulled in a long tale on top of her head and secured with multiple ribbons. She had no shoes on her feet and her face was twisted in fury.

"Y-Your Majesty?" He swallowed. Her gaze never left the children.

"Bullies!" She stomped her foot and lightning branched from the impact of her skin meeting the pavement. Electricity fizzled around her ankle like a bloom of sharp wires, emphasizing her emotions. He could feel her energy. He could feel it in his bones.

"W-w-who are you?" The children, although scared, did their best to appear brave.

"I am Zari. The Interim of Olympus." She grinned and displayed a handful of energy that wove between her fingers. Her gaze was menacing, and her smile gave him chills. With a flick of her finger, she sent a pea-sized current to their feet. The children leapt in place and proceeded to take hold of their bicycles, which she wound so full of electricity the static prevented them from doing so. "Apologize to Mr. Death."

One child tried to make a run for it, but she stomped her foot again, sending another wave that traveled through the ground and staggered him. And if that didn't stop him, Caelus' massive wingspan and boisterous screech made the children huddle together like cowards.

"I said, apologize."

In a chorus, the children bowed their heads and asked for his forgiveness. Death had to fight the overwhelming for more. He brushed his coat and accepted their apology. When he turned to the Godking, pretending to be satisfied, she nodded and communicated with Caelus to let them pass. The children, in their damp trousers, took hold of their bicycles and hurried away. Death looked around them to see that a crowd had gathered at the sight of his rescuer.

"Are you alright, Mr. Death?" She smiled at him. He was in love.

"I…I think so…"

"Those children were awful. What horrible things to say to another being. And their pedaling, how many circles could one possibly travel without getting dizzy?"

"I…I've wondered the same…" Realizing he was not being formal when it came to the Godking, he cleared his throat and knelt before her. Causing her to giggle. "You didn't have to do that, Your Majesty. They would have gone home eventually."

"You may rise," she teased, as if this were a game. "And you can call me Zari. I couldn't stand by and do nothing. Unlike the rest of them." She slowly turned her head to those who were on the street. Those who ignored Death's assaults and sometimes participated in them. They either hurried away or acknowledged him with a quick bow of their head. A new respect would be given to Death, beginning today. He could feel it.

"What brings you to the Underworld, Your Majesty, I mean, Zari? Is there anything I may assist you with? Anything at all is the least that I could do."

Her smile vanished and he wished he had not asked. With her bright hair, her russet skin, golden eyes and selflessness, she was an affection that breathed life into his bones and seeing her upset did something strange within his chest. Where his heart would have been.

"I am hiding."

"Hiding?" He tilted his chin. "From whom?"

"From everyone and everything that has a pulse." She held one of her arms. "I don't need to tell you that I am a hazard. I haven't been here long, and I've already killed a peacock, a panther, a whale, destroyed the gardens, set fire to the library, eaten all the ambrosia and almost stabbed Adonis in the heart. And I've cried enough times to cause severe flooding. And…I cannot swim." She looked ashamed. "I figured that I couldn't make a mess of things here. Not really."

He understood her logic but did not know what to say. After watching Caelus circle around her and landing on a nearby fence so that she could pet him, he offered, "Would you like to take a walk? I can show you around. Or maybe you have, with Lord Hades and I—"

"I would love to." She smiled as she wove her arm through his own.

Physical contact. He breathed. He couldn't remember the last time an ichor or woman had allowed him to escort her. Even when he was among the living, full-time, he wasn't popular in the ballroom and rarely did he receive an invitation to shows or the theater. He was what they called *a wallflower.* Dull and forgettable.

"So, tell me what you do, exactly, Mr. Death." Her politeness hit him like a splash of cold water. "I am curious about your work."

"R-Really?"

"Yes," she giggled. As he began to explain, she gazed at him as if he were the most interesting being in the universe. She even had pity for him when he explained that he was the most hated. "That's horrible. You are simply doing your job, if no one else will. However, I suppose I can understand the need to cast blame…I think…" They were crossing a bridge over the river that would lead them into a nearby park. She stopped and turned to him. "And a god has never died before, Mr. Death?"

"Not to my knowledge."

"Not even the Titans, from what I've been told."

"They are locked away. Imprisoned. Captured when weakened and never released."

"How sad…but, that was why I was called *the discrepancy.* I understand now."

"Do you remember anything from your past, Zari? Anything at all?"

"No…" she sighed. "Just a feeling of comfort and familiarity with the others. And darkness."

"Darkness…" The bones of his brow strained as they lowered. "That is something."

"Is it?"

"It means you were alive. Otherwise, how else would you remember?"

"I never thought of it like that before. You are so smart, Mr. Death."

If he had veins pumping with blood and skin to hold it all in place, his blush would have been so strained, one would think he was ill. "Do you remember smells and sounds?"

"Maybe. Maybe not. Everything is so faint. Like a distant dream."

"We've been trying to figure it out as well." He looked away, feeling as though he said too much. Hades was very clear that her peculiar situation was to remain between the office staff. To avoid panic. To his surprise, however, she nodded.

"If there is anything I can do to help…as long as it doesn't involve animals or managing a senior group of gods who know I am absolutely senseless, please let me know."

He didn't believe her to be so hopeless. If anything, he admired her courage and ability to smile even though she felt that life was against her. She was facing her own bullies and a family who were lying in wait—for her failure, for Zeus' return, for *something*. He was Death and she was Zeus. They were perhaps the most powerful beings in the world and yet they were both feeling mighty small.

He eyed his pocket watch and held it out to her. "The sperm whale you…the spirit of the deceased is inside. I was looking for a place to release him. He might like it here." She looked over the railing of the bridge to the river. Her long hair shifted in the wind. She then looked at the watch, smiled and awaited instructions.

"Simply press the latch and set it free."

She cautiously took hold of the instrument, as he had done on his first day of work. "What if I mess up? What if he doesn't like it here?"

"Then he will roam until he finds a place to settle. If it is a true inconvenience, Hecate, my co-worker, will capture him again and give him to an agency that would release him where they see fit."

When she opened the face of his trinket, she was engulfed by the sudden burst of light as the sperm whale emerged, a makeup of celestial luminosity and fuzzy things. From its pocket-sized starting point, it expanded into the sky until it reached its full potential. Larger than any animal she had ever seen. It released a lyrical whisper as it hovered over the river. It stopped and tilted the upper half of its body towards Caelus, who was flying among the Hypnos. The body of the whale contorted until it lifted itself into the air and used its tail to push off into the vibrant sky of blues and violets. Its fins created strings of light that trailed around him as he spun in a circle and performed tricks for all who stopped to see. It paused before them, as if to give thanks. The whale had spent its life under the sea. It was now ready to continue its journey among the stars.

Chapter 14

Hera & Hades

"Thank you for calling me," Hera said as she materialized through the rotary. Iris had to ask her multiple times to verify her identity, and if she was truly wanting transport to the Underworld. It had been decades since she had been in Hades' mansion. She rarely ventured downstairs in her own palace.

She materialized in his parlor. It was a spacious room with a perfect blend of Louis XVI and Victorian furnishings—opposite the Greco-Roman style of the palace. He had sofas with decorative scrolls trimmed in rich woods. The oak floors were herringbone and restored professionally. He had plants underneath small heated lamps and rugs to frame the sitting area near the fire. A heavy sideboard was littered with crystal decanters and glasses. It was filled with whiskey, rum, nectar and wine. It was also messy with literature.

Hades was an avid reader who loved purchasing books as much as he enjoyed getting a new suit. Hera picked up one of the few reading materials she could easily gain access to. As much as he loved his books, he did not treat them very well. They were propped under vases, piled in corners and wedged between the cushions on his seat. She ran her fingers along the stitching of *Pinocchio, The Story of a Puppet*.

"I haven't heard of this one."

"It's new. From Italy. Perhaps, one of the humans' better works." He had his hands in his pockets as he watched her flip open the pages.

"The illustrations are a bit creepy."

He chuckled as she sat it down and scanned his other titles. His home, although significantly smaller than the palace—even smaller with the clutter—felt like a warm embrace. Each area appeared to be lived-in and loved. No traces of a feminine touch were within sight. She noticed that. Following the trail of books, across the foyer and to the dining hall, she also noticed a sunroom that contained a piano. She brushed her fingers along the keys, releasing a soft musical sequence.

"I used to play," she said, remembering a time when she enjoyed music. She used to gift herself new compositions for the holidays. When she was younger, and in Gaia's care, she used to sneak to the land of the living and purchase tickets for their operas and concerts. Like Zari, she was accustomed to running barefoot through the grass at music festivals. She was once happy, if a bit naive.

"I know." He stood beside her. She could feel his warmth and the smell of new fabrics on his body. He reached above her, to a shelf she hadn't noticed among the clutter. He pulled down a book stuffed with old parchment. When he opened it, it had a variety of sheet music. His fingers rummaged through the stacks until he found one that made her chuckle instantly. "You remember this one."

"I remembered what was happening when I played it."

She was staring at the notes for *Watch My Cow*. It was centuries ago when she performed it for her ichor. Before she was married to Zeus and had been attempting to impress him. Athena, also musically inclined, tried to justify the modern piano over the traditional clavichord. Hera was skilled with both instruments, but always felt the clavichord was the proper choice for a lady who would uphold traditions when she became Queen. The two of them, somehow, initiated a duel of keys. Since it was at a formal dinner, their ichor were available to do what they did best: judge.

Hera was victorious, but when the dinner was over and she retired to the music room, she sat at the piano and played *Watch My Cow* without fault. More beautiful than Athena could ever hope to accomplish. Hades had been watching her from the doorframe. Encouraging her to continue playing when she was startled by his audience. As he was doing now.

"You don't seriously want to hear this."

"I do." He took a seat on the bench and patted the vacant space next to him. She smirked as she adjusted her skirt and removed her gloves. She liked the feeling of the carved, Japanese spruce trees and smooth acrylic when her fingers ran across the keys. She noticed him watching her, with each inch of skin she revealed. As she looked in her immediate vicinity for a place to lay them, Hades took them from her, brushing her fingers with his own. Once again, she had a similar feeling of springs under her skin. She avoided his gaze as she looked to the piano and began to play.

The song wasn't impressive, but she could feel him smiling as her fingers massaged the keys. She could even smile back at him, showing off that she could recall the composition in her sleep. He chuckled as he tried to mimic her from his end. He was horrible. So much so, she found herself flinching each time.

"Play this sequence," she offered.

He tried. Again, he failed. His frustration at being inadequate was enough to make her laugh. She would have thought he was performing poorly on purpose, but he admitted to simply being that bad. She was about to offer additional instruction when she heard a familiar sound on the other side of the window. The piano was blocking most of the view, as was the clutter of books on top of the body of the instrument. As she leaned over the keys to look out the window, she gasped.

She hadn't realized that she had forgotten her gloves. Or that she had welcomed herself into his gardens without permission. But her heart leapt at the sight of *him*. Her precious Robin. Full and happy. He hurried to greet her, as well as three other peacocks she had lost over the years.

She counted them. She petted them. They were all there.

When she felt Hades standing beside her, she did not look at him, out of fear that he would see the tear in the corner of her eye.

"I am not sure if you are aware, but peacocks are dangerously aggressive," he said simply.

"I am," she smirked. She was proud of their protectiveness, their strength and their beauty. She brushed her fingers along their feathers. She could feel their contentment. The closest she had ever come to children. "Why do you have them, if they are so much trouble?"

"No trouble for me." He shrugged. "The shelters don't particularly have a place for them or the wildlife habitats. They form a gang and terrorize the other birds."

She looked out the corner of her eye to see that he was handing her gloves to her and outstretching a hand to help her to her feet. He had been keeping a watch over her birds. He didn't have to, but he did. She knew he didn't do it for selfish reasons considering he never told her or suggested that she should visit them. She had always imagined that her birds were resting eternally. Among the stars in the sky. Not living beyond their years. They were at home within their group, familiar in their family.

"You can lay them to rest, if you like." She didn't want to be a burden on him, nor did she want him to use her children as leverage against her. But as the words escaped her lips, she couldn't bear the thought. Not after seeing them now.

"Is that what you want?" After a short pause, she shook her head. It would have been easier to do had he simply done it. "Then they stay here. Guarding my home."

She glanced at him, watching his eyes flicker with the stars that hung overhead. Standing there, he looked the part of a tempting villain. As sleek as his suit. As smooth as his smile. He did have a reputation for being contriving but he was a gentleman. No matter if she couldn't explain his kindness towards her, she questioned his eligibility.

"Why have you not taken a wife?" She was maneuvering her gloves past her elbows, ignoring the expression on his face. She took her time, if only to keep her hands occupied. "From what I can observe, Persephone is ready for marriage." And fair and lovely. Opposite Hera in every way.

"Perhaps, I am not."

"I find that difficult to believe. Tell me, is it the peacocks?"

"More or less."

She meant to tease, but his tone spoke otherwise. She felt him before she met his gaze. She inhaled his scent, dwelling in the sense of comfort that washed over her. He was close. Too close. He was tall, but she was only a head shorter. She could see the stubble under his neck. She could see the movement of his throat as his lips slowly parted. His fingertips were to her chin, guiding her to meet him directly. Her heart caught as she leaned in.

***

He was so close. So ready. His name on her lips made his chest swell. However, when she called his name again, it was not one of pleasure or anticipation. She jerked her head back and kept her fingers on his chest to separate them. Her gaze went over his shoulder and to the sky.

"Hades, I understand that I have not ventured to the Underworld in some time, but what is that?"

He furrowed his brow and turned towards the sky. Appearing slowly over the tree line was a whale. A large one. The biggest whale he had ever seen. He had never cursed Zari or found her to be a complete inconvenience, but somehow, he knew that Zari was to blame for this—interrupting what he had been longing to do for as long as he could remember.

For centuries, he had imagined kissing Hera. Of holding her. Of listening to her play the piano just for him. He rarely had regrets, but if he could repeat the past, he would have made her his before she could ever question her place among their ichor. He would not have settled for pleasant friendliness. He certainly would not have held his tongue at the match of her and her husband. Zeus would have done worse than cast him to the Underworld, but he wouldn't have cared.

He had suppressed these urges when he had told Gaia that he was in love with her. Their Mother shook her head over her workstation and said that only Hera was a match for Zeus. It crushed him to feel as though he wasn't worthy of her. However, with all that had transpired, he often wondered if Gaia had been speaking in a literal sense. If Hera was the only ichor who could grow strong enough to not crumble under the weight of Zeus' thumb.

Be that as it may, he felt that it wasn't fair to Hera to go without love just to grapple the ego of her husband. She deserved to be worshipped and cared for and kissed and loved. He wanted her, he wanted her at any hour of the day. If she had convinced herself that her marriage to Zeus and time as Queen had changed her, she was mistaken. He could see the intelligent and free-spirited fire that burned within her. It was hidden, smothered by centuries of neglect, but it was there. Waiting for him to provide oxygen to the flame that would burn brighter than the sun.

"That girl..." Hera massaged her brow. She assumed her position as Queen again, putting the necessary distance between them and straightening her back. Remembering herself. The self that everyone expected her to be. "Do you know where she is?"

"I have an idea."

Only this morning, Hades had been informed of a call waiting for him in the parlor. He took the phone and was greeted with an assault of tears. He couldn't hear a word between the sobs, but he could hear Iris in the background, in her office, cursing the rain that was leaking through her window. She must have taken the headset from Zari, as she told Hades—not asked—that he was about to receive a transfer.

Suddenly, a flash of thunder had erupted from the earpiece, so loud that he feared he would be forever numb in his left ear. It took many cups of tea to calm Zari. The Underworld was safe from the heavens, so he did not fear rain or floods. Although, she was vibrating with electricity. So rapidly in fact, she couldn't hold her hands to her face without shaking her entire body like a pack of crazy jumping beans he once had when he was a child. He gave her some laudanum. The dose was meant to sedate a tiger, but for Zari it only leveled her. Slightly. She was able to form full sentences and become her regularly distractible self as she took note of his home.

She had asked for a tour, which he gave. She had asked for more tea, which his cookmaid served with a questionable glance. Looking out the window, she mentioned that she always wanted to come to the Underworld. She wanted to explore.

Offering his permission, he was in the middle of asking her to wait for him to grab his coat, but she was off in a quick burst of speed, making him spill his tea on his shirt, coat and settee. Then, the rotary rang again, and he was suddenly met with a blast of wind that scattered open books and loose papers all over the room. Hades nearly lost an eye at the emergence of Caelus flying through his parlor. He yelled for the cookmaid to open the door. Any door or window.

Alone again—and wondering how a bird could use a rotary— he had taken some time to put himself together. His hair needed to be combed, he needed a new shirt, and trousers, that were not drenched in tea. He also wanted to reorganize his mess to the piles of which he preferred. Afterwards, he called Hera, who did not sound surprised that Zari would retreat to the Underworld. A bridge of trust had been easily built between them.

Walking with Hera, Hades tried to interlock their arms, but she unwove them and cleared her throat. She attempted to make small talk, which he did not want to do with her. They were past that, if not for the intimacy they almost shared, then for their essential friendship. Taking his time, figuring they would begin their search at his offices and enlist the help of Hecate, he studied the carve of her features. Her smooth skin, her small nose and perfectly arched lips. Her dark hair and dark eyes reflected the evening colors of the sky above.

He could have taken inventory of her countless of times before a gossip of a woman stopped him. She informed him of a parent who complained of their child's complaint that a deity that had assaulted a group of children with lightning and fire—Death accompanying—the woman pointed in the direction of the park.

"We can add that to the list," Hera moaned. "And that she seems to have made a friend…the most unlikely pair…"

"Now, now." He massaged his jaw, watching as Zari and Death walked arm in arm under the moonlit trees. "Remember: friendships, families…along with everything else I previously said."

Hera shook her head as she accompanied Hades across the bridge. He expected her to summon Zari immediately, but she took her time, admiring her surroundings. The parks were clean, the sky was beautiful, the waters calm. The Underworld was far from decrepit, a contrary to what was illustrated in books. In fact, there were places on Earth that were much more befitting of the name *Hell*. His home was welcoming by comparison. And the constant night, he wondered if Hera would have minded it. Seeing her, quietly marveling at everything within reach and beyond, she was the picture of a thousand stars. She was appreciative of how well his realm was maintained and how he allowed his residents to speak to him directly and not wait in line for admittance to the throne room.

Hades called to Death who was watching Zari jump up and down. Her feet were creating pulses of electricity that rippled like a pebble in a pond. Ripples that danced with vibrant colors each time her feet met the floor. A new trick that he knew would drive Hera mad. He chuckled at the thought.

The eyeless servant turned at the sight of them, appeared to have frowned at the interruption —Hades knew the feeling— and tugged at Zari's arm. When Zari spotted them, however, she trotted towards them.

"Did you see the whale?" It was the first thing she asked.

"Yes," Hades said. "And we heard about your run-in with children."

"Oh…"

Before she could explain, Death had offered them the truth. That Zari had rescued him from the bullies.

"Are you usually tormented by children?" Hera asked flatly. Death hung his head.

"Death was showing me around," Zari spoke next. When she did, Hades noticed Death come around again. "He's so smart. Very efficient with his job."

"Not sure about that…" Hades eyed his imaginary wristwatch. "Tell me, how long have you been away from your desk?"

Death stumbled, acknowledging that he had lost track of time. He bid farewell to his friend, wishing her luck before he parted. Zari turned to Hades with half a pout.

"Why is Death an around-the-clock employee?"

"Because he works, around-the-clock."

"Why not a working man's hours? So that he can have a life?"

Hades chuckled and Hera nudged him. Although, she was wanting to laugh as well. He knew her well enough to spot her hidden expressions. "Death's job is never done. And only he can do what he does."

"Are you sure? Is it not possible to have *two* Deaths? Or two and a part-timer?"

"Well I…" He never thought of offering help for Death. Especially considering no one really wanted the position. But as Hera mumbled his own words, something about comradery, he sighed. "I suppose I will give it some thought."

"I could do it," she said confidently enough. "I can retrieve souls." Both Hades and Hera looked at one another. She held up her hands to explain. "Death informed me of his duties. If we could agree on reasonable working hours, I could do this."

"And who would rule Olympus?"

"Hera, of course." Hades could feel Hera's bewilderment, although she did not show it. "You practically run it anyway. Not sure why you need me. Or, I could rule the Underworld. You see, I can't kill anyone down here. Mr. Hades and I could swap. Or Hera could take my place. I will come down here and—"

"Zari." Hera held up a hand exhaustedly. "Just. Stop."

"But I—"

"Listen to me," she said sternly, but also with a bit of warmth. She approached the girl and took her arm. The two of them walked in the direction of his home and Hera looked over her shoulder to make sure he was following. "What you did for Death, although a wasted effort, was kind. But you will not become him. You are Zari. You are currently taking the place of Zeus and whether it is for our benefit or our demise, you—"

Hades cleared his throat. He gave his chin a brief shake, trying to communicate to Hera that this wasn't the time to be this *and* that. She needed to convince Zari that she could be *one* of those things. Preferably the one with pleasantries.

"You need to have confidence in yourself," Hera began again. "Believe that you can do it and you will."

"I don't know Hera…"

"Tell me this, how is it that lightning is not something that frightens you?"

"Hm…" Zari looked to the skies as if they had the answer. Caelus flew overhead. "I don't know. Instincts, I guess."

"Describe that to me. Describe that *feeling* to someone who will never know what it's like to command the skies."

Zari's smile lit up like the sun as she struggled with her words. How to describe what took root in someone's heart? In their soul? Hera imagined it sounded a bit like trying to describe love. Only this was a love she could physically reach out and hold. A love that guided her, protected her and was made just for her.

"It is a power that is difficult to ignore, yes? It is there, speaking to you loud and clear. Confidence is within you, Zari. Once you listen to yourself, fully trust yourself, you can shine brighter than the bolt that murdered all the dinosaurs, you will see."

Minus the dinosaurs, Hades approved of that message. He tapped his fingertips together when Hera looked back at him, applauding her efforts. And then, Hera stumbled. Zari leaned her head into Hera's arm and made a motion as if she were snuggling her. Her cheek to her fabrics and her hair just below Hera's shoulder.

He grinned as he walked past their display of affection. He did however peek back to see that Hera was slowly smiling. She ran her fingers through Zari's hair and gave her a kiss to her crown.

Chapter 15

Zari

He had ambrosia.

A combination of hops, skips and begging was a different sight indeed. She could tell by Hera's expression that she was not going to grow accustomed to it, but Zari was prepared to use any means to convince Hera that she really, *really* wanted to stay for dinner.

"I have ambrosia," Hades said again.

"He has *ambrosia*," Zari begged. Again.

When they returned to his home, Hades had asked them to dine with him. Hera was quick to decline the invitation and Zari, normally, would have complied with Hera's wishes. But then, Hades mentioned ambrosia. Zari noticed that Hera and Hades exchanged a look between them that meant trouble for Hades later. But the sort of trouble that would be accompanied with a laugh and some innocent teasing. Hades displayed wide, puppy dog eyes to Hera on Zari's behalf. Zari mimicked him and excelled far beyond his reach. Hera's chagrin was accompanied by a slight upturn of her light pink lips as she finally buckled, picked up the rotary and sent for a dress to replace Zari's swimwear.

While Zari bathed and changed, Hades had his cookmaid prepare them a meal of bread, stuffed vegetables, mouthwatering chicken with potatoes in simmering stock and a side of spaghetti squash salad. It was an assortment of vibrant colors and delicious flavors as Hades admitted his cookmaid was thrilled to have more than him to feed. Cooking was her priority as Hades' organized chaos prevented her from tidying properly.

As the three of them sat at the table, Zari kept tapping her foot at how slowly Hera and Hades ate their meal. They were torturing her in the form of discipline. She had agreed to have her ambrosia after dinner and was already regretting that decision.

"Manners, Zari," Hera said with a soft raise of her brow.

Zari was conflicted. They were having dinner, yes, but they were in Hades' home. A place where Zari felt free of criticism. Where she felt comfortable. She even noticed the two of them glancing at one another from across the table. Hades was bringing about a more relaxed side of Hera. Well, when she wasn't sighing at Zari to take smaller bites.

"But...ambrosia—"

Hades couldn't help but chuckle. He then took a breath and looked at Zari directly. "Listen to Hera. The ambrosia is not going anywhere, alright? I will make sure of it."

Zari pushed her lips to the side and took a moment to reset herself. She adjusted her back in her seat, refolded her napkin on her lap and held her fork properly. She did want to please Hera. She wanted to be like her. Zari had always admired Hera's strength and poise. Even the way Hera walked—gliding across the floor as if she were skating on ice—made Zari practice in her mirror when she was alone in her bedchamber.

She wanted to make the Queen accepting of her, proud, if possible. It was the least she could do, considering Hera had chosen to acknowledge Zari. She raised her glass of wine and sipped, keeping her fingers tucked. But as the bitter liquid coated her tongue, she coughed. There were some things not even she could tolerate.

"Wow," Zari puckered her lips. "That is...horrible."

Instead of scolding her, Hera gestured to a servant and told him to bring her nectar. Zari noticed how Hera commanded Hades' servants as if she were the wife of the house. And, most importantly, how Hades allowed her to do so. Nonetheless, she was grateful for the wine substitute. It was fruity and tangy and pure. Almost as tempting as ambrosia.

"Now," Hades said to them after he swallowed a bite of chicken. "Would someone like to tell me what I have done to have two beautiful creatures at my table this evening?"

Hera shook her head and grinned as Zari took her time explaining what had happened. She was training with Hephaestus near a cliff's edge. Their scheduled sessions were nothing out of the ordinary and from what Hera had observed, Hephaestus was without complaint to have Zari as a student. She was punctual. Polite. Receptive. Poseidon and Ares, having spotted the pair on their way to the cliffs, invited themselves to come along. Ares wasted no time claiming that he was an even better fighter than Hephaestus and Athena combined.

Hephaestus' inclusion of them was not warm. Nor welcome. Zari didn't mind the company, although, she was nervous to see Poseidon again. She paused in her story to tell them what they had already witnessed, that Poseidon had kissed her in the study. Hera and Hades exchanged a smirk behind the rims of their wine glasses as she continued.

"And then, I slipped."

"Slipped?" Hades asked. Her self-pity was obvious.

"They distracted me. Ares was yelling at me and Poseidon was yelling at him and Hephaestus was yelling at both of them." She had been discombobulated as she accidently maneuvered too close to the edge. And then, as she said, she slipped.

She had learned that her body was durable, so she didn't fear the impact of her flesh to the waters. But what she didn't account for was the cold and hungry waves that pulled her further out to sea. That, and she couldn't swim. She remembered swallowing water and being surrounded by nothing more than the curvatures of liquid tunnels and the tail fins of fish caught in the spiral that twisted her. At one point, she didn't know which way was up. She was kicking and kicking and felt she was going nowhere.

"Caelus did not catch you?" Hades' voice brought her back again. She shivered from the memory.

"Caelus gets a bit anxious whenever I am stressed. I thought it best to keep him in the palace and under the care of the royal groomers. That, and I don't believe he likes many ichor. But he must have sensed my panic, for he flew through the palace, through the closest window he could find. The one in the grand hall, I think. He made a mess of the groomer's station, ruined a few portraits and of course, there's glass everywhere. I saw him briefly just before I plunged into the water. He did not reach me in time."

128

"Poseidon was there. He didn't save you?" Hades disregarded Hera's moaning of the state of the palace. Zari pinched her lips together and nodded.

She remembered the feeling of electricity emitting from her body as she kicked and screamed under the vast blue void. She remembered closing her eyes, preparing for the end, and then opening them again at his familiar scent. He was carrying her. Holding her. Waves shaped his body as if they were friends, and his face, although handsome, was twisted in pain. She reached out to touch him and recoiled when her fingertips began to spark. She wasn't trying to shock him, unaware that she had done so already.

Still halfway in the water, she felt something brush against her cheek. A sea of muddy color surrounded her. She thought it had been her vision, blurred from trauma. Only it wasn't. It was fish. Hundreds, thousands of dead fish that had perished in her horror. It was as if Poseidon was carrying her through a seaside graveyard. The smell should have been horrific. But it was if the energy she radiated into the water had sucked the life from the salt and charred flesh of grouper, salmon and gutter critters. The air smelled of nothing.

Now, her ambrosia didn't taste the same. She completed her dish but with half the enthusiasm. As they took tea, cheese and fruit in the parlor, Hera whispered something to Hades that caused him to nod and excuse himself to another part of the house. Hera sat next to Zari on the settee near the fire. Zari, in her melancholy state, relied on her training to substitute for words. Her fingers positioned the handles and cups appropriately.

"Do you want to talk about it?" Hera asked as Zari settled in with her own cup.

"About what?"

"About what happened between you and Poseidon."

"Nothing happened." Zari sipped. She was so depressed she *sipped*. "I mean, a whale died but he seems happy now. I mean…" Zari allowed her shoulders to wither. "Poseidon tried to save me."

"As you said."

"I think I…I think I hurt him. If not him then my pride…or what little of it I had…oh gods…" She shook as Hera removed the cup from her hand. She placed her fingers on Zari's back and shoulder as Zari heaved with tears. "I completely made a fool of myself in front of him."

"Darling, I am sure he didn't find any humor in your drowning."

"Ares was there," Zari gasped. "He laughed so hard I could hear him between swallows of water. At one point, I almost thought the situation was *meant* to be funny. That everything was a joke I had missed."

Hera cursed Ares. But then, she slowly turned the conversation back to the Ocean King. "You like him."

Zari bit the inside of her mouth. She did like him. She liked him a lot. Behind that rare and wonderful smile was a patient individual and practical genius. When he was comfortable, relaxed within his element, he had a confidence about him that was expressed through his wide and pressing strides. He had enough endurance to put up with Ares and her combined. He encouraged her to speak her mind, without judgement from him. And twice now, he had saved her life without a second thought.

She couldn't die by drowning—as Ares and Hephaestus reminded them both—but that didn't stop him from securing her safety.

"Do you...do you not approve of him?" Zari asked, visibly curious of what Hera might say. Poseidon had been alive for a very long time. She was sure he had a storied and complicated past. She and the Ocean King were still learning of one another and she noticed that he rarely spoke of himself outside of his work. If she ever tried, he would shine the light on her once more. His answers were nothing shy of facts. With so much time spent on this world, it had crossed her mind that she might never come to know him, fully. If Hera did not approve, with a heavy heart she would keep their relationship a professional one.

As if seeing her wish reflected in her eyes, Hera gave Zari a pat on her hand.

"He is a good king."

Zari's chest lowered with relief. "I should be checking on him, making sure he's okay but...whenever I get close to him, I get..."

She showed her fingertips to Hera. There were tiny fractures of electricity erupting from them. It was her nervous condition. As if her emotions were searching for a release. She was doing her best to contain herself, but she had so much energy she could not fathom how it was possible. It was no wonder Zeus had been in a constant state of debauchery. "I like him a lot. I don't think he likes me. Especially after... He'd be insane."

Hera squeezed her hand and instantly, the electricity vanished. "We will see, won't we? Perhaps he will ask you to dance with him at the ball. When it comes to such things, he's rarely made the effort."

"Ball?"

Hera gave her a blank stare. One that made Zari bite her lip. Hera *might* have mentioned that there was an event that welcomed the spring season. A ball of sorts. A garden party. But Zari *might* have been too busy thinking about other things. Like her existence. Like her powers. Like an Ocean King.

"Of course, I know of the ball. That one..." Zari tugged at a thread on her dress. "...I don't know how to dance."

"Dancing?" Hades said upon his return. Even with the absence of his dinner coat he still looked handsome and distinguished and ever so charming. With Hera's hand on top of her own, Zari could feel it constrict slightly. As if his amiability would destabilize her. The Godking was *new*, but she wasn't blind.

"Zari here was telling me that she doesn't believe she can dance."

"I can barely handle my footing on the ground."

"Ah." Hades approached, slow and appealing. He gave her a dramatic bow and extended his hand. She chuckled and accepted him. As she did, Hera stood to her feet and headed for the sunroom with the piano. It was hidden behind clutter. Clutter that the cookmaid had only shifted to make more space for the guests to roam. Space they were using as their floor. Hades positioned them and nodded to Hera.

"I will lead. You need only follow."

"That means nothing to me," she said looking to the wood, trying to anticipate where his feet were going. As he turned her around Zari's struggle was instant. She had already convinced herself she was not good at dancing. That she wasn't good at much of anything. But no matter how much she stumbled and struggled, Hades would stop them, calm her with a smile and begin again. Until she finally found her rhythm. Hera's music was easy to sway to.

"This isn't so bad…" she said with a giggle.

"You are doing an easy waltz," Hera said from her piano. She then added quickly, "But you are doing so beautifully."

Zari lifted her chin as Hades increased the difficulty. Until the song came to a close and he playfully took her hand and spun her in a few circles. The feeling of accomplishment was the equivalent to a breathlessness of running. That, and dancing, which she discovered she loved very much, made her feel as though she were floating. The hem of her gown hovered about her legs. Her hair fell into place. He took her hand and danced with her again, their pace in sync and their movements faster.

And at the end, he spun her again. She giggled uncontrollably as Hera's music became a seamless sound of happy riffing. Until even Hades was moving to the upbeat tune. Until Zari spun again and again.

Spinning. Spinning. Spinning.

Until she laughed so hard it hurt her stomach. It was then that she realized that she was the only one laughing. Pieces were falling from the sky. Pieces of *something*. Zari had spun so vigorously she created a tornado of gray and silver wind. It had begun at her toes and circulated through her entire body with comfort and fun. The same funnel pierced a hole through the ceiling of Hades' dining hall, through the bedchamber, into the attic and out of the roof. Everything and everyone was a mess. Especially the room which was—well, it was messy before—but now it had a draft.

She stood there and eyed the two ichor. Each of them expressionless.

Hera leaned over to Hades and whispered, "What was that you were saying about allowing her to make mistakes?"

Hades, who neither smiled nor frowned, indicated his exasperation through silence. Zari hung her head, knowing that this was simply another place she could no longer show her face.

Chapter 16

Aphrodite & Ares

"Aphrodite? Sweetheart? I would like to come out now."

A knock came from the other side of the door. Aphrodite was on the floor of her corridor, in front of the entrance to her dressing chamber, which she had barricaded with locks and overgrown foliage from a nearby palm. In between her legs was a carton of ice cream. Normally, she would ask for a serving in a petite crystal egg bowl to monitor her portions. And to look more appealing when she ate. This time, she sighed and dug her spoon into the milky substance. Eating and eating until she would grow sick of eating.

"No," she said with her mouth full. She gazed at the clock, seeing that either the staff forgot to wind it properly or—

Another knock.

This time, from downstairs.

She sighed as she heard the servant open it. She got to her feet, chucked the carton and spoon into a vase, smoothed her skirts and ran her fingers through her pinned ruby hair as she planted her feet before a decorative mirror—her home wasn't shy of them. She took a breath, and repeated her words of self-admiration.

You are beautiful.
You are beautiful.
You are beautiful.

When she was ready, she walked to the foyer to greet Persephone.

"You're late," she told her ichor, who only lowered her brow. Persephone was wearing a pale blue gown with lace and a modest, yet impactful cascade of soft flowers. Graceful as ever, and the complete opposite of how Aphrodite felt.

"Must have been a difficult morning." Persephone scanned her ichor. "Considering you are complaining about having more time with him."

"And you don't appear to be in a rush to retrieve him." Aphrodite narrowed her eyes at Persephone, who matched her stare until her ichor scoffed and made a gesture as if to summon him. When her servant was given permission to release—um, *call upon*—Adonis, Aphrodite went to the receiving room where she had a large muslin sack she began to stuff. "His blanket. His book. His lyre."

"Has he eaten?" Persephone sighed at Aphrodite's pause. "Must I always be the one who feeds him?"

"It's barely dinner time."

"He should be fed *by* then. By the time we return to my home it will be past it and I have to prepare him a—never mind." Aphrodite saw Persephone's gaze and knew that Adonis was behind her. They tried not to argue in front of him. They didn't want him to believe anything was wrong. "Hello, lovely."

Adonis' smile was careful and timid. Routinely, he approached Aphrodite who extended his sack. He gazed into its contents, noticing his basket was missing but did not comment. It meant he wasn't going to be picking flowers tomorrow. He withheld his disappointment.

Aphrodite gave him a kiss on his cheek as she ushered him into Persephone's arm. Once the two had disappeared, she gazed out her window to see their coach moving away. She slumped down onto her settee.

She took a moment to gaze at her surroundings. Her iridescent wallpaper had flying doves embellished in gold fabric. Her floors were made of marble and roses filled her oversized urns—including the one with the ice cream. She was about to retrieve it, not to throw away but to continue eating, when a knock came at her door and she cursed Persephone who she assumed must have forgotten something. Much to her surprise however, it was Ares. When he came into the room, looking at her as if he arrived at the wrong seminar—*How to Coddle and Enjoy It*—he appeared to want to turn away. But she approached him with familiar vigor as their mouths claimed one another with immediate passion. Her fingers threaded through his hair and wrestled over the buttons of his clothing. His own attacked her stays.

For the past few weeks, she and Persephone had been keeping a close eye on Adonis. It wasn't out of the ordinary, considering Zeus had commanded they share the human to avoid future strife. Only this time, it wasn't out of want, it was out of need. She felt the only way she could protect him from Death was if he were kept under their supervision. Under no circumstances was he to be left to his own devices.

No frolicking.

No flower picking.

No swimming.

No vices.

Knowing her own habits, she had to refrain from their lovemaking. She knew she could be rough with him. She knew she had a reputation for leaving trails of love bruises on his soft and doughy skin. Her needs were difficult to suppress and she was running out of ice cream. So, when Ares appeared in her home, looking dashing as usual, she wasted no time ravishing him.

Their sex was often housed between a triangle of passion, hate and punishment. Always lively. Always frantic. His fingertips undid her bodice in record time. How she longed for the warm season, when there would be very little clothing for him to remove. He unpinned her hair and pressed her firmly against the wall between her receiving room and her foyer. His shaft between her thighs, he lifted her skirts, and then lifted her onto the hall table.

"Dottie, have you gained weight?"

She wanted to slap him. But how fortunate he chose that precise moment to plunge into her. His hips thrusted without interruption as she wrapped her legs around his waist and matched his pace. Her nails dug into his back and shoulders. He returned the favor with a bite to her breasts and deep, hot, life giving kisses.

Tiny trinkets fell to the floor as her eruption came. Her quivering continued as he hoisted her over his shoulder. If the ice cream had made her heavier, he carried her with ease. He took to the stairs, two at a time, as her hair dangled past his rear. They passed the vase with the ice cream. She wouldn't forget about it. When they entered her chamber, Ares flung her on the bed, rolling her to her belly and removing whatever clothing they had left. He bestowed kisses on her lower back and rear. He kissed her where he wanted to go and she took a breath as he entered, hard and fast.

She released a cry of pleasure, clutching the sheets. Her body rocked with his power. With a force that made the floor tremble beneath them. She was unhinged. She was lost in ecstasy. She vaguely remembered his feral growl between her shoulders as he gripped her thighs and bucked, collapsing onto her and then onto the floor. She used her last bit of energy to kick the covers that had gathered around her body. Her heart felt as though it was going to burst through her ribs. Her lungs were pleading for air as her body struggled to reform.

And, she was hungry.

"Ares, do you want dinner?"

He grunted. Normally, they had signals when they were exasperated. Taps of fingers on one another's skin, nibbles on whatever part of the body one's lips were closest to. Flexes of an arse cheek. However, she was too exhausted to drag herself to the edge of the bed to see him.

After what felt like another hour of them going in and out of sleep, he finally joined her. Waking her in the process. It was the first time their eyes had truly met since he'd been there. The sun was beginning to rise, and he did not ask her permission to enter her once more. They tousled. They giggled. She knew he was trying to encourage her to ride him. He always liked the sight of her body on top of his. Especially in the sunrise. Her hair looked as if it was on fire and the curls between her thighs were visible to him from this position. But she was so tired. She collapsed onto his hard chest and held on as he pumped inside of her. Her thighs gripped him like an experienced horsewoman as she moaned with another wave of heavy release. She was usually a match for him but today, she was lazy.

And, she was hungry.

"Breakfast. In town." He lifted her head and smiled at her. Handsome and wicked all the same, he rolled her off of him as he strutted about her house in naked glory. He helped himself to the bathing chamber which was underneath the house and filled with the natural waters of Olympus. He commanded the servants, who were used to him, to ready the coals. When the coals were burning, a lattice grill was placed on top. Ares used a ladle to pour water onto them, filling the room with the sound of simmering steam. When she joined him, her nostrils opened at the smell of warm water and eucalyptus.

He had his head over the heat, directly ingesting it. Aphrodite lowered herself in the water and released a heavy sigh. They said very little as she angled her chin on the bath's edge. Their strenuous activity had worn them both and the heat of the bath would soothe the pleasant aches they would feel later.

When they were both dressed and in the foyer, he escorted her to his coach. She pressed her fingers to her chest where he bit her. He smirked and she smirked back.

"Did you want to talk about it?" he asked.

They couldn't help themselves. They both joined in the laughter of his starting the day with a joke. A funny one, she thought. Those who *communicated* their problems for the sake of good relationships were those who had little time in the world. It was one of the benefits of being immortal. Since their time in the world was unlimited, they did not see the need. This was what made them friends. Friends who did not need to explain themselves to the world or each other.

"Where are we going?" she asked when the laughter subsided.

"A new place opened on the same street as my club. It's very tasty."

She nodded.

They arrived at a restaurant with clay walls, coffered ceilings and large windows that overlooked the cascade of homes glowing in the morning sun. Breakfast wasn't a popular meal on the coast. Only servants were about at this hour, purchasing food for the day's meals and picking up supplies for the maid closets. She would still be in bed, or lounging bare near her private pool, sipping on tea and nibbling on toast.

But she was hungry. She was also in need of some air.

They were shown to a table on the terrace. The morning was fresh and crisp. Birds chirped as they bathed in puddles and tugged at trees bearing fruit. Breakfast consisted of smoked salmon on muffins, honey and almond ricotta with fresh peaches, apples and grapes. Ares consumed an entire stack of yogurt pancakes with feta. And for dessert, fresh coffee. Ares was flipping through his newspaper while she cycled through magazines the establishment was more than happy to provide for the elegant couple. The two of them together were truly a picture. It opened many doors when they were out, increasing their notoriety.

"It's not ironed," she told him as she observed the black smudge on his fingers. He grunted at the state of his hands, discarded the paper and took hold of one of her magazines. When he opened it, he scanned a page before turning it to her.

"A coat just for smoking?"

"You could use that."

"Not sure if it's for my benefit or the benefit of my staff."

To anyone less than them, Ares might have come off as pompous. But that was what she liked about him. He was so sure of himself that it left no room for doubt or unanswered questions. He was strong. And strong willed. He was also jealous. Unlike her husband, who was so quiet, brooding and passive it drove her mad. She would never be the source of Hephaestus' envy. Nor would she ever be the center of his concern.

Zeus had arranged the marriage in order to refrain her from seducing the young maidens that he felt belonged to him, and without her concerns being taken into consideration. She had her eyes set on everyone and no one. Until she met Ares. With his persistence, he assured her that she wouldn't regret having him in her bed. He introduced her to pleasure beyond her wildest dreams. Unknowingly, unlocking her inner ravisher and creating a haven for wild experimentation. It was no secret that she was beyond ruined on her wedding night. With Hephaestus being such a large ichor, she had high hopes for his performance. But he asked her if she wanted to and, since given the choice, she said no. He left her bed without a fuss and thereby labeling their marriage: pointless.

138

Then on, she and Ares had an unspoken agreement. One of physical pleasures when the other commanded it. The conversations that followed, conversations befitting of two narcissistic individuals, was an added benefit.

"I am surprised to see you without your better half." When she spoke, he did not look up from the advertisement.

"Sai is in bedrest."

"Do I want to know?"

"Yes."

She chuckled into her coffee. "Go on then."

"Zari—"

When he mentioned her name, jealousy slithered into her veins. She was tired of hearing about Zari. Everyone was fond of her in some way. Even Adonis claimed to miss his friend. Her beauty was new and exciting, her personality was fresh and enthusiastic. She was innocent only by her introduction to this world and was easily impressed. A weak ichor if there ever was one.

When she looked up from her coffee, she saw that Ares had his elbow on the table, uncharacteristically, and allowed his chin to rest on his raised knuckles as he gazed upon her with a quipping grin.

"What?" she asked, undoubtedly annoyed.

"I don't understand why you don't like her. When she's not being adorable, she is quite terrifying and fun. Not a dull day with that one."

"Bedded her, have you?"

"I would never do that to my *better half*."

"Has he offered for her?" Aphrodite scoffed. "She's a barbarian."

"My dear, you are the barbarian." He gestured to his shoulder. The one she branded with her nails. "That, and you're keeping poor Adonis on a tighter leash than usual."

"Do not speak as if you care for him."

"I care more for the stones I throw at him. Even so, I miss throwing stones."

She gritted her teeth. She hated when he hurt Adonis. All to spite her. But he would soon get his wish. Adonis was marked for Death. Sooner or later he would see his end. She was worried she might miss the opportunity to stop it. Especially considering Persephone seemed to be preoccupied with her *feelings* as of late.

Something was shifting in the air and she couldn't make it out. Something was changing among her ichor after Zeus' disappearance. Hera and Hades had amiability that wasn't there before. The two had been united from the moment they introduced Zari to their ichor in the amphitheater. Poseidon hadn't given Aphrodite a second glance, even when she implied. He was above harmless flirting and looked past her if the Godking were ever in the room. Persephone's indifference for Hades was quickly turning into jealousy. Her rival was so laughable Aphrodite nearly pitied her. And her husband...

Her husband... Aphrodite bit her lip. Once, she spotted him around the palace smiling at Zari with unprecedented kindness. His tall, husky body looked surprisingly gentle. He even bestowed a tiny kiss on the top of her head as she skipped past him with Caelus at her heels. Swinging her sword and shield as he instructed. Without flaw.

Affection. Feeling. Laughter. It was a disease.

Iris. Adonis. Death. Even Ares.

Only Athena made a show of being defiant—blaming Zari for Zeus' disappearance and her ichor for being dismissive. But she would be affected too. Sooner or later. If Zari were the Godking and Athena was adamant on serving, she would eventually bend the knee.

Aphrodite blinked as she felt Ares' fingers on her own. He looked her in the eye and leaned over the table for what she thought would be a kiss. But he parted his lips and whispered.

"I will ask you this, only once. And when I do, I will mean it." He paused, making sure she did not look away. "Do you want to talk about it?"

He was looking at her in a way he never had. A way that was uncomfortable for them both. One that meant he must have felt she was in need of conversation. A confidant that she considered a friend. That would imply that she was feeling uneasy, and in short order, weak. Everyone saw Aphrodite as the unbreakable. Her beauty was as thick as Athena's armor. She would not dare to lower her shields and show that she, too, was vulnerable. She withdrew her hand and sipped her coffee. He leaned back in his chair, accepting her answer.

At least she knew he wouldn't ask her again, he returned to the pages of his magazine. She ignored the small part in her heart that wished he had.

"Dottie." His pet name for her always made her smile, even if she did not show it. "Do you mind coming aboard my ship?" She furrowed her brow. If this was his attempt at seducing her, he had used worse analogies. As if reading her mind, he chuckled and waived her assumption away. "The project Sai and I have been working on."

"Your pleasure yacht.

"My *luxury ship*."

"I am not a fan of boats."

"I know," he beamed. "That is why you are the perfect test. For months Sai and I have debated whether or not we want to appeal to women and the likes of you. I was against it, but Sai assured me that men do not like being surrounded by other men while drifting helplessly through the waters. Nor do they want tired whores. So, we have to make the voyage appeal to women."

"That is not how I want to spend my time."

"Very well... We will go the day after tomorrow. First thing."

Had he not heard her? Yes, he had. And the fact that he wasn't going to take no for an answer was enough to make her want to slap him, as well as be touched by him, and risk another violent romp on this very terrace. Ares, the ichor who cursed when he remembered the paper wasn't ironed, was one of the few to openly deny her. It was nice to know that if there was one soul in the world who would prevent her from plummeting off a cliff to her death, no matter how much she wanted to, she would be caught on the descent.

Chapter 17

Persephone

"Eat your dinner."

"I'm not very hungry."

"Darling, if you don't eat you will wither away. You've already lost some weight. You're not as plump as you used to be."

Obediently, Adonis took a bite. His mouth moved slowly as he chewed. She understood his mood. Surely by this point he was beginning to feel like a prisoner being policed by two wardens in alternating shifts. But this was to keep him safe. They both wanted him alive to the very end. Until his hair turned grey and time did what it did to humans. They thought it best to not explain their reasoning.

Tilting her chin, however, she took a long look at him. Something was changing within her to where she wasn't as obsessed with Adonis as she had once been. She remembered being the ichor who fought over him with Aphrodite, tooth and nail, until Zeus intervened and she had to make nice with the renowned blackguard with breasts, the collector of flesh. Adonis served the purpose of drawing her attention away from marriage. Away from being left in the Underworld. A place she had feared since she was younger.

Now, everything was different.

After the presentation of Zari at the formal dinner, the night Hades denied her offer of marriage, she assumed they would resume their circle of being asynchronous. That he would ask her next and it would be her turn to decline. But he did not. Hades was smiling more these days, his appeal growing in her heart. She even heard him laugh when she was walking the gardens of the palace. Unfortunately, none of that was for her.

He was often with Hera and Zari. Something about the three of them, an uncomfortable sting, burned in the forefront of her mind as they meandered through the topiaries. She wondered what it would be like to have his arm as his wife. To have him looking down on her with a gentleness she knew he had but had rarely seen outside of their brief interactions with one another. Hades was, she dare say, a bit childish. Those years of him playing dress up with Cerberus, she now knew, was not to embarrass or mock her ichor as Demeter had convinced her. It was to please his companion and bring smiles to the children who marveled at the sight. She found herself smiling at the memory of him in a cloth, as naked as Mowgli, and each of the three heads dressed as a different animal from the jungle.

She wanted a husband. Hades had the characteristics that she wanted in whomever she would choose. If she could find it, if she knew of it elsewhere, she would not intrude on the strange romance between him and Hera. Contrary to everyone's presumption of her, she did not like competition. It was exhausting and petty.

"I am finished." Adonis was subdued. She gave him a brush on his arm and sent him off to bed. She tucked the covers around him and nodded at a servant, gifted from Aphrodite for this purpose, to stand guard. Adonis was not to leave his room. The windows were barred, and the door was to remain locked.

Her home, Demeter's home, was built like a cottage. With more garden than house to accommodate the grazing deer and farm animals. The ceilings were low, and each window had a view of green hills and fresh flowers. The staff was kept to a minimum, but they made up for their short handedness with excellence. She had a handmaiden who could mend anything, a butler who doubled as a reliable chauffeur and a single maid who helped in the kitchens. What their home lacked was a proper cook. After her childhood cook had passed, the duties of preparing meals fell to Persephone who enjoyed the art. More so than watercolors or playing an instrument. She and the maid had used all of their informal lessons to prepare delicious meals for the house and Demeter.

Not quite ready for bed, she decided to get started on a dessert. She picked fruits and vegetables from the gardens. She had fresh lemons from her trees and honey she brought with her from the palace pantry. Her phyllo pastry dough, which she had started on earlier in the day, was already chilled and layered with perfect cubes of butter. Tonight, she would begin on her filling. She was going to make a glazed, golden brown custard pie.

"Baking again?" Persephone gave a dry nod at Demeter who was returning from her evening in the woods. She often visited Artemis, another daughter-like ichor that was with her before Persephone was planted. Artemis carried herself like the elder sister no one wanted. She was too independent for her own good and openly disagreeing. She enjoyed separation. She lived among the trees and animals and felt that the woods were the better of Gaia's creations.

Artemis wasn't alone, however. Far less than Persephone, in fact. She had a camp of women--experienced artists, spinsters, orphaned daughters and nonconformists—who worked the land, protected the woods, monitored Gaia's invalids who lived there and trained by way of archery. If Persephone were ever desperate enough to escape this life of rules and structure, she might have joined them.

"Careful now, you don't want to put on weight."

Persephone said nothing. For the past few weeks, ever since she and Aphrodite had split the shifts of watching over Adonis, Demeter had chastised her. She was an unmarried ichor, living with a man of ill repute. No matter how many flowers Adonis had brought to Demeter, she never liked him. To make matters worse, Demeter did not approve of Hades either. She didn't like the thought of Persephone moving so far away if the two of them were ever married. Demeter's splendor struggled to remain hidden whenever Hades denied her. Now, Persephone was brewing with a loathing for Demeter. For filling her head with such nonsense in his regard.

The time she had wasted.

The opportunities she had missed.

Her feuding with Aphrodite, her blind trust with Demeter and her lusting over Adonis had been a distraction. Glancing at her mixing bowl, she chunked the contents into the bin and decided to begin again. She wanted this one to be perfect.

***

As she sat in the boat, she lifted the blanket of her basket and eyed her custard pie with concern. One would think she was transporting a swaddled infant. The smell had filled the nose of Charon who mentioned more than once that he would have welcomed a bite. Luckily, she had almond cookies that she didn't mind sharing. Her baking was rumored to be exquisite. She learned to make extra for anyone who asked. She hoped her food would earn her friends here. Although, she was reminded that fresh ingredients would be difficult to come by.

When Charon dropped her off, she took her time admiring the Underworld with a fresh set of eyes. It wasn't as cryptic as Demeter had once led her to believe. Her ichor made such a fuss, that when Persephone eventually visited on the arm of Hades, she couldn't see through the mental picture that Demeter had already painted for her. She warned Persephone of slums, dirt and uneducated sorts. Like most places, the Underworld had its seedy side, but it also had its beauty.

The homes were well maintained. The streets were being swept free of trash. There were small gardens with heat lamps and baby peppers. Neighbors knew one another by name. Children ran past her, chasing a hoop. A puppy nipped at their heels, completely oblivious to the rules of the game. She inhaled the scent of something she could not identify but could get used to. The Underworld fragrance. The sky looked like a collection of dreams and the river was enchanting.

Hades' home was more modest than she remembered. When she blinked, she realized it wasn't the same place he had brought her during her first visit. The estate he had intended for her to run was the size of a miniature Olympian palace. This Victorian, however, was happily hugged by wrap-around porches. Tall windows with dramatic ledges were free of curtains. The shingles were made of wood and ivy molested the sporadic angles in some places. There was a lot of land. Perhaps acres that went unused, granting him the space he needed. There was an attic and a tarp that clutched the roof.

145

Visibly out of place. She wondered what happened. Perhaps, he was going through a renovation.

As she reached for the gate that would welcome her to the garden she stopped at the sudden appearance of vicious wads of blues and greens. Peacocks. A pack of them. They were prodding their beaks through the iron and making a noise that caused her to place a hand to her heart. Sounds of footsteps and heavy demands that the birds return to their side of the garden bellowed from Hades. He began shooing them along with his hands. One turned to him, barked with a teenage rebellion, and led his siblings around the side of the house.

"Persephone." He smiled at her, opening the gate and welcoming her along the path that led to the front door. She suddenly felt nervous in his presence. She had worn her green dress today, hoping it would push her eyes to the color she preferred. Many thought they were blue, but she always noticed the glimmer of jade in her irises. Her hair was braided and pinned, and she adorned a new pair of pearly silk gloves. Around her neck was a cameo pendant outlined in silver filigree and tiny stones that mimicked stardust. The marble portrait was made in her image. He had gifted it to her after he first expressed intentions on marrying her.

His smile vanished when he saw it. Quickly, his eyes found something else to gain his attention. Her basket, which she lifted with two hands.

"I made a custard pie and cookies, although Charon had a handful."

"Did we have an appointment that I missed?"

She shook her head. She was being impolite for arriving without notice. And, it was before teatime. Improper for a call. But as a gentleman and her ichor he invited her inside anyway. Shielding her from the irritating birds that were peeking their heads around the corner and watching them disapprovingly.

He held onto her basket while he rang for his cookmaid. She nodded with the instruction to serve the contents with tea. He immediately turned to help her remove her cloak and hang it on a hat rack. One that was absent of any signs of another ichor or woman's garments. No trace at all, thus far.

What she also noticed was the state of the dining hall and the chill that permeated from the hole that went further than she could see from where she was standing. When he met her gaze, her cloak still between his fingers, he cleared his throat.

"On second thought, you might want to keep this on."

"I'll be...fine..."

"Then please, sit by the fire. The hearth is massive and raised. The stone is mostly smooth."

"What happened?"

"Zari..." he said with a strained grin. "It wasn't her fault. Well, it was. She gets over excited and accidents happen." When she took a seat, the flame warming her back and arms, he sat on the chair adjacent to her. "Had I known you wanted to visit, I would have dissuaded you."

"Have you begun repairs?"

He lifted a shoulder as he stretched his legs in his chair. "I'm sifting through estimates, but the situation is growing more and more complex."

"How so?"

"Since I will be having builders in my home, I figured now would be the time to make modern updates. Such as electricity in every room, plumbing throughout, expanding the bedchambers, building a proper library to house all of my collection and refurbishing the servant's hall. All of which I would have delayed had not Zari forced my hand. I suppose it is a blessing in disguise. One I intend to drag my feet on."

"It will be beautiful, I'm sure." She wondered if he would accept decorating tips. Lighter wall colors. Plusher furniture. Cotton drapes. She could see herself making this place a home for them if he allowed her.

The cookmaid arrived with tea and a serving dish of her delicious custard and cookies. She watched him as he took a bite, pleased with his expression and relishing in his endless compliments.

"Forgive me, I am so infatuated with your baking I forgot to ask what troubles you."

"Why would I be troubled, Your Grace?" He looked at her, as if her question needed deciphering. She took a delicate bite of her custard. It was perfect. The vanilla, cinnamon and lemon balanced well—a harmonious trinity of sweetness, spice and tart. "It is no secret that I am now in pursuit of you."

"Am I not in pursuit of you yet? Only then would our dance continue." He was polite in his tone and admitting to their history of back-and-forth. But as she took another bite, she allowed her lips to curl.

"A dance I want us both to say yes to. Your Grace, I do not plan on descending from the other side of the hill this time."

"We do not plan a lot of things. But they happen."

"Hades." She looked at him directly, studying the shade of his eyes and dropping their formalities. They were quite stunning and reflected the fire beautifully. "I want to marry you. I want to move to the Underworld and be your wife."

He was silent for a long time. Both of them set their custard aside in favor of the strongly brewed tea. He relaxed in his chair, his arm on the rest and his expression one of contemplation. He looked mostly to the fire, as if the answer was there and bright within the embers. He lifted his leg onto his knee and tapped his foot slowly.

"Why?" he finally asked. "And please, do not answer with whatever it is you have rehearsed. To prevent me from assuming the worst, from assuming you are doing this to best Aphrodite or escape Demeter or claim a status, I need the truth."

It was her turn to delay her answer. She was afraid that if she told him, he would laugh at her. Call her a dreamer and a fool. But seeing him lately, watching his true demeanor, she couldn't imagine it. She would grant him his request.

"The sun shines differently on you now. Or perhaps, it has finally shone on me and I am able to notice what I have failed to see before. I truly believe that we would be happy as husband and wife. I believe our children will be happy and loved and adored." They would sit by the fire as they were now. Enjoying her baking as he moaned to his eldest to keep their pets off the sofa. "You make me forget about Aphrodite and whatever pointless feud we may have. Demeter will come around, once she sees how well we are together.

Being your Queen would be an honor, but if it were you without the title, I would not change my mind." She could see in his eyes he did not fully believe her. He doubted her so much, she almost questioned herself. "Your Grace, please tell me what reservations you have. Tell me what has changed. Perhaps, we can put your mind to rest."

After an even longer pause, he spoke so softly she had to lean forward slightly to hear him. "It is as you say, the sun shines differently on me. But...it is not because of—"

He was interrupted by the sound of his rotary. From what Demeter had told her, only the primary three had access to *that* assortment of lines. When the cookmaid went to lift the receiver, he kindly waived her away, taking the call himself. As he placed the headpiece to his ear, he smiled and adjusted his cuffs.

He spoke a few words she could not hear, but he did glance at her direction. His face sunk, slightly enough, as he hesitated to lay the phone on the pedestal. Just then, Hera materialized before him. Mid-sentence. Smiling. Happy. Whatever had her in chipper spirits was forgotten when she spotted Persephone. She rose from the fire and bowed before the Queen.

"Persephone." Hera's tone was leveled but questioning.

Hades cleared his throat. "Persephone brought some of her delicious custard to share."

"Is that so?" Hera leered.

"We were discussing marriage." Persephone, wanting to prove her intentions, stepped forward with a courage that shocked the room. "My past behaviors, unfortunately, make him understandably reluctant. But my intentions are pure."

"Marriage between ichor," Hera said slowly, not waiting for Hades' reply, "must be approved by the Godking."

Approved by *you*, Persephone wanted to say. Instead, she smiled and nodded with patience. "Zeus has approved. It was his idea, if you recall."

"I do recall. And Zeus is not here."

"Past agreements do not end with his disappearance. So much would be undone, if that were the case. Your Majesty."

"The agreement was marriage. At *that* moment. You two declined one another. Over and over, as *you* have implied." Hera lifted a shoulder. "Marriage requests need to be presented before the new Godking."

"Zari." Persephone blinked. "You must be—" Persephone caught herself, remembering how much Hades was fond of the girl. "I am wondering if this is truly a matter she should be burdened with, considering that she seems to have *other* things to worry about…" Persephone gestured to the dining hall. Hera did not alter her gaze.

Hades cleared his throat. "Look at the time. We will be late." Persephone knew that he wasn't speaking to her, for they had no program scheduled for the day. Hera, who refrained from showing anything other than her power, did not blink. Hades once again took the floor. "We were going to visit Poseidon and Ares' boat of pleasure—I mean, *luxury tour.*" He cleared his throat again as Persephone flashed an innocent smile at him. One that she knew he would not resist, simply because she knew how kind he was. "Would you like to accompany us?"

"I don't want to intrude. Although…I have been curious to see it." She turned to Hera whose lashes lowered a centimeter. Enough to let her know she would be. Intruding, that is. "Is Zari going?"

"She will be there," Hades said carefully.

"Taking the opportunity to mention a union?" Hera said dryly. Persephone grinned politely.

"Yes. But I will also take the chance to know her. I feel as though the two of you have been hogging her, I have yet to exchange cards." Hades mentioned they could all return through the rotary as he excused himself to retrieve her cloak. When he presented her fabric, she turned her back and prompted him to help her into its warmth.

Contrary to everyone's presumption of her, she did not like competition. It was exhausting and petty. She would avoid it if she could. She then locked eyes with Hera and silently entered the ring for one more fight. Having competed with the most beautiful ichor for centuries, Persephone felt she had been trained well.

Chapter 18

Poseidon

He had walked the length of the ship twice now. He was sure his staff were cursing him under their breath. He wasn't the type to hover, but he needed his work to shine. To be perfect. His ichor were coming to see his efforts. Among them would be Zari. She had been avoiding him lately, if not, brief with their interactions. At times, he'd notice her scuttling away if she ever saw him approaching from the opposite end of a corridor or the gardens. His spontaneous, hyperactive, carefree crutch to his heart no longer wanted to come near him. His mind churned with the rhythm of a chef's knife, slicing and dicing every vegetable known to man into tiny organized little squares, as he tried to deduce the reasons for her behavior.

Was it something he said?

Something he did?

Without a chance to confront her on his own, his anger began to build as Ares' warning came crashing into him.

Hera.

Poseidon felt that he had made himself clear. He wanted Zari. He'd be surprised to find someone who was oblivious to his intentions when it came to her—although not even he himself could explain precisely what those intentions were. Her smile, laughter and joy were fresh air. Within her, the budding rays of a new sun. She was more than he deserved. His nature made him want more than he deserved.

He did not approach Hera in the traditional sense. There was no need for it. Civil as the gesture might have been, Hera was not Zari's mother or official guardian. Zari could do as she pleased and that would be the end of it. He did not need anyone's permission to pursue her.

Hera could have felt otherwise, thereby proving herself hypocritical. She was taking advantage of the Godking's admirations, layering her own influences and ideals that her husband had once discarded. Hera liked to be in control. It was why she and Zeus were constantly at odds. It caused her to insert herself into matters regarding the three kings. She would attempt to fill Zeus' head with condescending remarks to ensure that he was doing what needed to be done for Olympus. To manipulate him using the greed and anger that influenced his decisions daily. Her defiance and bluntness when it came to her king, and husband, always put Zeus in a foul mood. Neither were the sort to be bossed about. Neither were the type to bend.

Regardless, Poseidon was the voice of reason. Speaking the facts, which were as they were. Hera didn't have a vote, thereby her opinions only caused unnecessary strife. And no matter how hard he worked and proved himself to be a fair ruler, she would never feel more for him than passive respect. The feeling was mutual, and both adopted a rule-and-let-rule policy towards one another

Now, there was Zari. An object of attention that each wanted for themselves. And in the closest of ways. If Hera were shielding Zari as a mother would, he was prepared to extract her from her clutches. As a lover would. Sharing was not something he did. He often laughed at the concept.

Now, he had to make Zari see for herself that he could do right by her. He had not touched a woman or another ichor since he laid eyes on her, under the flickering chandeliers of the amphitheater. She looked at him, and in that moment, he felt…special. From that day, she forever ruined his standards when it came to tender company. Only she would do.

"Everything will be fine." Ares patted him on the shoulder. When he arrived, late as usual, he had Aphrodite with him. He knew she hated ships. Time spent on his beaches weren't for the sake of going near the water, but not even he could argue with Ares' reasoning. Aphrodite was a perfect exemplar of their feminine demographic—prestigious, picky and wealthy. Her overcritical nature needed to be swallowed like spoonfuls of sugar. Sugar that would taste like salt.

"Sai," she said behind a yawn. She glanced at the ship and looked instantly bothered. She then fixed her eyes on him. "I never liked it when you combed your hair. You can never do it right, so it looks as if you truly tried…and failed. Which is unfortunate for the Ocean King."

He grunted, pretending that her comment did not faze him and found the nearest water closet to retreat to. He held his fingers under the waterspout and ran them through his hair. Until it relaxed into its naturally shabby shape that fell where it pleased. He had shaved, but his stubble was already casting a dark shadow over his face. He was beginning to look like he hadn't tried at all. As if he was preparing for a day of heavy lifting.

At the sight of Aphrodite entering the closet behind him, he studied her eyes and relaxed. There was no twinkle of sexual pursuit. Fortunately. The space was too small; he would have to destroy it to put the necessary distance between them. She had her arms folded and was arching her brows.

"Lose the cravat," she said. "This isn't a dinner. And open the top button of your shirt and switch to your leisure coat. In fact, if you can go without, you don't need one. A coat I mean. And roll up your sleeves. You have arms that deserve to be on display."

He obeyed her every command. Stripping himself of the last signs of polishing. She took her fingertips and ran them through his hair one final time. When he turned, he lowered his hands on the pedestal sink.

"I look like myself."

"Anything else, and you look ridiculous."

His appreciation was within his smirk. Aphrodite wasn't one for *helping* others, but if he asked, he knew she would admit to offering her advice for the sake of her own beauty. That she was so alluring she did not think it fair she be in the presence of homeliness. She nodded and allowed him to sink back into himself. He was comfortable now. If he floundered in front of Zari, he would do so without starch. Allowing Aphrodite to leave first, they returned to the docks where a coach was emerging from the distance. Caelus' outstretched wings, pushing the air behind him, signified Zari's arrival.

When the coach came to a halt, Hades, who emerged first, appeared to have had a journey that was not worth repeating. Persephone was with them and clinging to Zari's arm. They were chatting about baking and pointing to the vessel before them. Hera and her signature scowl acknowledged him briefly. Anytime a group of his ichor gathered, the atmosphere was odd and mixed in favor.

It didn't matter. The only one he wanted to concern himself with was Zari, who had yet to make eye contact with him. She was stunning in a dress the shade of an amethyst's eye. Her long white hair was braided behind her and her wide eyes were fixated on the ship. She did not smile. She did not gawk. Nor did she prance about the docks as he expected. Her energy was refined. Her movements, careful. When she wasn't leaning on Persephone, she kept her arms pressed firmly against her body.

It made him doubt every decision he ever made regarding his endeavor.

"Welcome, you down and forgotten-looking bunch!" Ares extended his arms. Before anyone could speak, he took a moment to hold up a hand. "Sai and I have worked very hard on this, and the last thing we need is for all of you to bring your problems on board. This is a pleasure—I mean, *luxury ship*. Problems stay at home with your nursemaids to keep watch. Fun, *fun* beings only. Alright? Now I ask you, first impressions, what do you think?"

"I think it's lovely," Persephone said with kindness. "Is it not, Your Grace?" She turned to Hades. "Such splendor and craftsmanship—"

"Where is Adonis?" Aphrodite interrupted her without apologies. Clearly, she wasn't expecting Persephone to tag along. Neither did Poseidon. They would need an extra setting at the tasting he had prepared.

"I hired a nanny for the day."

"A nanny!? What qualifies this nanny to keep an eye on him—"

"He will be fine--"

"No, no he won't!"

As the two bickered, Poseidon and Ares exchanged glances. This day was going to be more tiring than they thought. Zari was still avoiding him and hovering near Hera, whose scowl could be felt on the tips of his hair. When Poseidon turned to Hades for an explanation, his ichor's mouth moved rapidly, practically begging them to begin the tour.

***

Their luxury ship was painted in a shade called *cloud white*. It was Ares' choice. He said white was more elegant. Poseidon wanted to paint it black or a deep shade of navy. Understanding the conditions boats encountered in the waters, he wanted a darker color to disguise the dirt, grime and rust that the vessel would eventually subject to. Poseidon allowed Ares this win, given that he himself usually had the first say in terms of function and practicality. Together, the two of them had built something truly magnificent. She was called *Olympia*.

Her body was trimmed in gold with the ornament of a mermaid resting at the helm and guiding their way. The statue was meant to be the final piece that was placed on the vessel to signify the end of its construction. However, present company considered, Poseidon allowed Olympia to assume her position early. She looked at peace up there, high above them.

The ship had six floors of rooms, two additional floors for communal spaces and three levels of exposed decks and terraces. Like railroads, they were utilizing steel and reinforced glass and polymer. It was another disagreement among a sea of disagreements. Ares, naturally, wanted her to be built entirely of glass so that when other ships passed in the night, Olympia looked like a beacon for a good time. The envy of all private parties.

The incline to board the ship was the first object of Aphrodite's scrutiny. Ares sighed at her, but then mumbled to Poseidon that they should consider adding hydraulic lifts to decrease the amount of walking time for women and ichor in their slippers. The assistance would benefit the porters and the portly. If not, perhaps they could use pull carts to carry people on board.

Poseidon gave a half nod, glancing over his shoulder to Zari who was speaking closely with Hera. Persephone walked alongside Hades. Poseidon lifted a brow to his ichor, who shrugged it off with a bend of his lips. When their feet touched the ship, Poseidon heard Zari gasp. Her eyes widened as she approached the vast open space. The welcome area needed to be grand. It was their parlor away from parlors. It would be where everyone gathered before moving to their designated areas.

"Once you step on board, you will immediately be handed a drink." Ares snapped his fingers. On cue, servers with golden trays carrying glasses of red and blue froth appeared. Everyone took their serving, except for Aphrodite.

"That will turn my mouth an odd color." She turned up her nose at the offering. "I will not drink it."

Their theme of *tropical gardens* needed to include coconut. And pineapple, perhaps. Ares relayed the request to the server to notify the kitchens. Although rude, Aphrodite's advice was sound.

Zari slowly chose a drink, unsure of which to try, she looked to Hera who took hold of a red one. As did she. She sipped and smiled as she examined the frozen treat. Her eyes scanned the ship's interior, widening upon examining the walls.

Their ichor enjoyed the romantic curves of exposed flesh. Their portraits and statues went far beyond the religious renderings of virgins and fruit baskets. Each subject was nude and surrounded by garlands and grapevines and waves and clouds. Pegasi with women warriors rode on the cathedral ceilings. They were carved into the vases, into the wood of the counters and sewn into the fabrics of the cushions. Gold and cream and velvet and glass were everywhere. Their ichor had been invited into the clutches of luxury, and the Godking could only nod.

Was she...underwhelmed?

"We will have a live band here." Ares gestured to a suspended area with a stage, which was wedged between a total of four grand staircases that continued the path of the marble tile. The steps were lined with palms and windows that oversaw the ocean. Ares guided them to the second floor where Aphrodite offered her opinions. Heavily.

"Are these the only shops?"

Thus far, they had only planned for food and wine and cigars.

"What did you expect, a haberdashery?" Ares furrowed his brow. Her sideways glance prompted him to signal to a servant to begin writing things down.

"And a dressing room," she said matter-of-factly. "Fabrics from around the world. Gloves. Shawls. Swimwear. If a lady had forgotten anything, she will need to purchase it here. If she is to be trapped on this monstrosity, that is. Slippers for the ballroom. A tearoom. A place for sweets. Trinkets to purchase. Bathing items. Jewelry. Souvenirs. Goodness, must I go on?"

"Yes…" Ares grunted, making sure his servant was keeping up with her.

Speaking of servants, she asked, "How would we ring for them? Do the bells in each room connect?"

Poseidon and Ares looked to one another. When they were crafting the ship for gentlemen, they knew that most could do without. Most could dress themselves and tie their shoes if need be. And if one brought a servant, they would simply pay for an additional room. But the idea of servants being *paid* to occupy the quarters on the same floor as the guests made Aphrodite gasp.

"Why can't they share the same hall?" Zari whispered to Hera. Poseidon slightly turned his chin to eavesdrop. "Or sleep in the room with their employers?"

"Zari, I've explained how to run a house." Hera tapped her hand.

"I know, but it's not the end of the world. I would assume the servants will be wanting to have a good time as well."

"Most likely the servants will not have itineraries. They are here to work."

"So…they're going to be on a boat, gliding across the ocean and expected to stay indoors? All day?"

"They do that now, sweeting."

Luckily, they weren't too far into the design where they couldn't make changes. Poseidon understood Zari's concerns. He made his own mental notes on how they could divide the rooms. They could turn the upper floors, the accommodations with balconies, into suites. Charge more for them. It would help manage the capacity anyway at no fewer cost. The rooms underneath the suites could be designated for servants and have a direct line, a bell that ran through the floor. The servant's rooms, mirroring the size of the suites, could easily fit multiple beds. Each man would require a valet. Each woman would want a lady's maid. Perhaps it could be a service they provided. Temporary servants to further comfort their guests who stayed.

If it were him, Poseidon would gladly take on the role of undressing his wife. He looked to Zari and looked away quickly. If he allowed his mind to wander, if he pictured himself freeing her from her gowns and spread on top of her—he grunted and took refuge in the front of the tour group as he led them into the ballroom.

His ichor were pleased, as dancing was a popular sport among them. A large, crystal chandelier swayed gently with the sea. The lacquered floors were shined to perfection and his workers were peeling protective covers from the furniture. A mahogany grand piano sat in the corner. Mirrors covered the walls more so than wallpaper. Aphrodite and Persephone practiced a twirl. Hera ignored Hades' glance and Zari, once again, was tucked in a corner.

Poseidon wanted to go to her. He wanted to bring her close to him and ask what was bothering her. But Ares was pressing the tour along. They had to visit the gambling halls, the smoking rooms, a library and the lounge. There were two music clubs and a theater for performers. They had time to spend on the upper decks before retreating to the restaurant for luncheon.

One of many pools was glistening before them. More for fashion than function. It was thin and carried the length of the ship. There was a hidden, glass retaining wall that caught the spilled water and redirected it back into the pool. Lounge chairs and other furniture were in the process of being bolted to the floors. Olympus was a sight from up here. Beautiful. Like a precious oil painting. While everyone pointed to the various zones of the mountain, Zari was looking out to sea.

"Join her." Poseidon turned to see Hades approaching him. His ichor was sipping on another drink. Poseidon believed he was on his fourth. "A lovely should not be alone and in need of company."

"She's been avoiding me."

"Yes, well, she's trying to be on her best behavior." Hades paused to close one eye and use the other to ensure his serving was empty. Poseidon made a gesture to the server that meant to up the dosage of water in lieu of alcohol if Hades asked for another. "Something about a whale. And that was before she blew a hole through my house."

"What was that?"

"And you've invited her to a cocoon on the sea. She's doing her best to not kill us all." Hades was smirking. Still himself, but a bit depressed. "All two floors...plus the attic...and I am making repairs. Only, I'm not sure what color to paint the walls. Do you ever find that difficult? As a builder yourself? As a carpenter? That you're torn between two paint colors? Should you pick the safer option? Or...the one that makes you happy? Said color might be an...acquired taste? Funny thing...paint..."

As Poseidon helped Hades to a chair, something told him that his ichor was not speaking of paint. "Water." Poseidon gestured to a servant. "And toast."

"Yes, Your Grace."

Knowing there was no time like the present, Poseidon left Hades under the market umbrella and approached Zari with his hands in his pockets. He leaned his back on the railing and smiled. She did as well, expecting to see someone else at first.

"Hi," she said, shifting her gaze back to the sea. She didn't flee from him, which gave him time to examine her profile. Round were her features. Not traditionally sharp or chiseled. Her nose was perfectly curved, and her cheeks were full. Her chin was petite, and the thickness of her dark brow accentuated the vibrancy of her eyes. Loose strands of hair blew in the wind and she tried to catch them. Those that she missed, he took hold for her, keeping the silkiness to himself for a while. Keeping her to himself for a while.

"Do you like the ship?"

She nodded. "It is a lovely vessel."

"Which part was your favorite?"

"Everything was delightful."

He made a sound between a groan and a chuckle, seeing Hera's training in her. But she wasn't Hera. She was Zari. And Zari wasn't the sort to curb her enthusiasm. Tapping his fingers on the railing, he gave her hair a gentle tug to get her attention. She turned to him, surprised to see he had it wrapped around his fingers.

"Did you want to see a secret?" he whispered.

"A secret?" Her expression nearly undid him. How beautiful she was, at that moment. Leaning into him, his oceans behind her, the breeze splitting her mane but bringing them closer together.

"It's a place I haven't shown anyone. My favorite place. Come with me."

He extended his hand. She did not take it. When he reached for her, almost immediately, he felt a subtle buzz entering his fingertips.

"I'm sorry," she said, pulling away. "I don't mean to do that."

He examined his hand, not a stranger to the sensation. It wasn't a painful one. Not like the flash fry she had given him when he carried her from the waves. This was a tender buzz. An intimate poke. He took her hand again and smiled.

"Come, sweetheart."

"But what about—"

"You don't need to worry about anything, Zari." He squeezed her hand. "You're safe with me."

"I... I know."

He could see her shoulders relaxing as he led her away from the group. They walked the path of the deck until they arrived at a pair of glass doors that placed them on the most direct path to the other side of the ship. Underneath the captain's quarters, yet above his own private rooms, he stopped at a winding staircase, ensuring she watched her step. She clung to his arm as they maneuvered through the darkened space. Her electric pulses were dancing on his sleeve, flashing beneath her fingertips. Revealing her blush.

When they reached the landing, two oversized doors were before them. Brown wood trimmed in gold with glass panes that were covered in tarp. They were at the back of the ship. Pressed far into its edge. He opened the door and allowed the light from the curve of windows to illuminate what was before them.

"It's…it's…beautiful!" she gasped.

Poseidon shut the doors behind them, keeping them there and uninterrupted. Presenting her with his gift. Although it was incomplete, the carousel was remarkable. There were places where its skeleton was exposed for updates and wiring, but the artistry had not been compromised. The platform held over twenty, hand-painted horses with frosted glass eyes and clear hooves. They varied in shades of white, bay, honey, grey and midnight. Their leads were made of garlands. Their tails were decorated with grapes and berries.

The murals around them were of the sky. Heavy with clouds and under a revolving sun. Zari's skirts brushed the tassels that covered the base of the platform. She made a complete circle, admiring each and every piece.

"I've never been on one of these before. I don't think."

He stepped onto the platform and extended his hand. That tingling sensation was in his fingers again as she looked nervously around them. As much as he appreciated her determination to refrain from damaging anything, he guided her around the structure anyway. Pointing out the details she might have missed. Encouraging her to stroke the horses as if they could respond. To run her fingers along the scrolls of the trimmings. To tap the hanging tassels from the tiny chandeliers.

"Which one do you like?"

"All of them."

"No preference?"

She pointed. He guided her to the precious bay horse that was wrapped in a wreath of gold ivy and grapes. He lifted her onto the horse so that her feet dangled on one side and she was now at eye level with him. The air had fled the room as he studied the color of her eyes. He pushed a strand of hair behind her ear. His fingertips brushed the side of her cheek. Although the windows welcomed sufficient sunlight, they were on the side of the carousel where the shadows embraced them. In the darkness, he could see tiny flickers of electricity emitting from her skin.

She was pulsing. Heated by his touch. He laid his palm flat against her cheek, at the groove where her chin and neck met and left it there. Waiting. Waiting for her to attune to him.

"I…" she tried to say but couldn't. She also tried to pull away.

"It's alright, Zari."

"I can't control it."

"You will, in time." She shook her head, calling upon his humility. "Do you know how it will work? The carousel? It uses a generator. A motor underneath our feet. The generator will store electricity and fill the carousel. There's no electricity now. But if there was…Zari."

She quickly dismissed the idea. "I will have us spinning out the windows."

He chuckled. "No, you won't. He lowered his hand to her own and guided her to grip the support beams that punctured the horses to keep them in place. "Try."

"I will hurt you again. I don't want to hurt you again."

"Why does everyone believe I was on my deathbed?" His laugh was low and breathy. Sure, he had needed rest while his limbs remembered how to function again, but it was no more than a sting. And he recovered quickly. "When I began my training, my powers were also unstable."

"They were?"

"It was how I came about my trident. It was a channel, something to help me along the way. Until I learned myself. Sometimes…" his other hand took hold of her own, "Sometimes, I am still learning myself. But that's what happens when one is immortal, you have plenty of time to make mistakes." He smiled. "Tell your power what you want it to do. Imagine it. Command it. Or in your case, try asking it nicely."

"To not hurt you."

"And?" he chuckled.

"To move the carousel." As soon as she said it, they felt the ground shift. A noise hummed beneath them and a brief melody played and stopped. Poseidon held on to her waist with his free hand, keeping her steady on the horse. With a smile, he encouraged her to try again. And again. Until they got further each time. Until they kept going.

The tune of *Nani Nani* signified the awakening of the ride. The ceiling did as he designed and slowly began a transition from day to night. The clouds were replaced with stars that twinkled from tiny glass bulbs. The sun made way for the moon.

The idea of a carousel came from a distant memory. When he was not quite small and on the verge of losing what little cheerfulness that remained. He had watched Hera sneaking away from the mountain one evening. Back when her rebelliousness prompted her to embark on adventures that carried her away from a house full of ichor. She used to whisper to Hades about the humans and their music and their dancing. It wasn't long before a small group of them shifted from their beds and scurried down the mountain with her at the helm. All except for Zeus, who was Gaia's favorite. He was a snitch who would expose them if given the chance, landing them all in bird cages.

Poseidon hadn't been one for large crowds and rowdy celebrations. But after persuasion from Hades to join them, he did. He was pleasantly surprised by the race Gaia had often cursed. The humans were a humorous bunch, falling over themselves and making up words. And because they looked like them, they were visibly appealing. And creative. And smart. And obnoxious. Interacting with them was the moment that induced change. Or *poisoned* them, as Gaia had put it. His ichor might have been gods, but it was seeing their likeness in an entirely different species that prompted them to ask worldly questions and ponder their purpose.

Her name was unimportant.

He dared not try to think of it out of fear that he wouldn't remember it.

It was a companionship that crumbled before he could fully understand what it was. Time on Mount Olympus would do that to a god. It passed differently than below. What could feel like an hour to a god, would be a week for a human.

This human was one he was attached to.

To her, they were perhaps the same age. To her, he was a lost boy who eyed the carousel with wonder as it took other children around and around again. The gesture was innocent. Very much so. She took his hand and pulled him up with her. She took his hand and brought him with her. There were no horses to mount on the overcrowded ride, no vacant seats among the animals. But she told him to hold on anyway. They went around and around until he found himself laughing with her. One of the few times he ever did.

He would return to the camp. No matter how much time had passed, he knew she would be there. Growing. Changing. Her limbs longer. Her face narrower. Her hair carried an aging scent and at one point, her belly was swollen. It rested between them as they held onto the carousel. As she buried her face in his coat and her shoulders trembled with each rotation. When the ride stopped, when the horses died, the dampness of her tears on his shirt were all that remained. He never saw her again after that. The human from the gypsy camp.

That was, he felt, what truly separated humans and gods. Time. When one had so much of it, their development was slow and hindering. Humans were superior in that regard as they had no choice but to learn and to learn quickly. Like trying to stuff a thousand coins into one's pockets. Craving the value but lacking the capacity to hold it all.

He didn't want to be like the humans.

He didn't want to be his former self either—missing what could have been.

He pressed his lips against Zari's for a soft and gentle kiss. One he followed with another. And another. She tasted sweet. Either from her essence or the fruity drinks she had sipped throughout the tour. His hands went to her waist where he nudged her closer to him. Where he pressed their bodies firmly together and allowed her to lean onto his sturdy shoulders. His arms keeping her as close as possible.

He lifted her chin, taking their kiss deeper. She whimpered as her fingers squeezed and released the sleeves of his shirt. Like a kitten kneading. She wanted to explore him. Her touch shifting and taking inventory of his body. Her lips learning, and to his surprise, still remembering, their first lesson in the study. His kiss moved to the softness of her neck. Her fingers rested in his hair. He kissed her with hunger. He kissed her madly. Until they were both breathless and trembling. Until her head rested on his shoulder. He held her close. He held her close as the carousel kept going.

Chapter 19

Hera

She was smitten. Gods knew it wasn't love. Just lust. Just infatuation for someone who gave her the attention she craved as a young ichor. Hera was once like that. It was how she was able to call upon her patience when it came to Zari's increasing amount of buoyancy.

Hera remembered a time when she had butterflies in her stomach. When Zeus used to praise her intelligence, beauty and competence when it came to ruling. Their marriage was not a love match but in time, she had felt it could have been. He was kind. Arrogant of course, but he was the Godking. A step above the rest. As his Queen, she was well studied and well versed. She was prepared to give him anything he asked, including a legacy.

Their children, little ruptures of lightning, would come into the world riding the sun. She had pictured them leaving the mountain to conquer and rule lands of their own. The universe was vast outside of Gaia's Earth. Mount Olympus, as Zari had mentioned when she had been trying to wrap her head around it all, was a single door in an endless hallway of doors. A land that touched others but in essence, was its own. Olympus was a small part of a bigger puzzle. One she imagined her children exploring and laying claim to.

It wasn't Hera's fault that Gaia was *uninspired*. She looked at the two of them, Hera and her husband, furrowed her brow and sighed as she ran her meaty fingers through her hair. She couldn't picture it, she had said. She couldn't knead the clay to form something that was harmonious between them. Although she approved of the match, she could not see their future. It was *uncraftable*.

Her hopes of expanding her family were gone. As was her husband.

But was he?

Looking to Zari, her mind churned with questions. Zari's hair was the same shade of her husband. As was her skin. Russet and smooth. Her eyes contained his thunder, and her power would one day be unmatched. But the resemblance stopped there. Only on the surface. Zari's personality was like nothing Hera had ever experienced in Zeus. The girl's spirit resembled that of a human's, living each day to the fullest. Adventurous. A bit mischievous. She almost reminded her of—*come now, don't be ridiculous.*

Suddenly, she wanted to shake Hades and ask what was the delay in locating Zeus. Or answers. Perhaps he would be more productive if he weren't flirting with Persephone, or telling Hera how to raise Zari—*Raise?* She shook her head again. *Handle* was what she meant. And, it was more fitting. Hera wasn't nurturing anyone, simply advising. But even that was becoming bothersome with Zari's afflux of her own distractions. Poseidon, for a start.

Hera took a breath, reminding herself that it wasn't love. It couldn't be.

Zari was already short of discipline, so morning calls from the residents of Olympus were accompanied with her need to fidget in her seat. She was also questioning every decision Hera made. It was unlike her to have doubt in Hera's verdicts.

"Why must we place a railroad here?"

Hera sighed. "It is the only plausible place. Going through the valley would cut the commute in half, therefore it would shorten travel time when it comes to importing and exporting goods."

"But...it would go through the Monakis' farm and the Petrols."

"Yes."

"Would it not displace them?"

"They would still have land Zari, just not as much as before."

"Then it would cut into their production. Would we lower their rent or grant them proceeds from the rails because of it?"

Hera blinked. The receiving room was empty now. The tenants in question had left when they came to inquire about the rumors of a railway parting the earth. The two ichor, coupled with servants and a guard, sat in thrones on a slightly raised platform. Zari was too small for her seat. The seat only Zeus' ego could fill. "Why would we do that? You're speaking as if the land belongs to them and it does not."

"But they've farmed it. And now they have no say in how it is managed."

"Zari, the land belongs to the crown."

The girl frowned, failing to comprehend the simplicity of it. The clothes on her back, the roof over her head, the safety they provided to their tenants was not free. This was built. Over centuries. Gaia didn't sculpt the palace out of clay, nor did she invent wealth. It was Hera and her husband who took their seats when they divided the realms and assigned the positions. It was Hera who governed alongside Zeus. It was Hera who huddled herself over decrees, laws and constitutions. Back when she and Zeus were a team.

As much as she was fond of Zari, the girl was proving that she was unable to see past her emotions to rule fairly. She had a long way to go and sometimes, Hera felt as though the distance was ever growing.

"If that's the case," Zari smiled, "Perhaps we could revisit the idea of modern farming equipment. It would reduce labor and increase—"

"And how would the tenants pay for it?"

"We would. And the tenants could share." At Hera's silence, Zari added, "Or we could provide a loan. It would be different from the plow and scythe and Demeter's picky harvests and I know you don't like loans, but we could see it as an investment of the people, rather than a piece of machinery. As if we were encouraging a continuing education."

"I advocate for education, you know that, but—" she massaged her temple, feeling the onset of a migraine. Zari placed a hand on hers and leaned over.

"I do not mean to be difficult. I am only learning by asking questions. It's just...I've been speaking with Poseidon—"

"No." Hera replied sharply. "Oceanus is not Olympus. If he is giving you advice, it is not from the perspective of ruling the mountain nor the skies. Oceanus is a castle under the sea. Olympus is a kingdom among the clouds."

As Hera predicted, Poseidon had been dipping his finger into areas it did not belong. How was it possible that between their midnight rendezvous and his pressing her into shadowed corners for a kiss, that they had had time to discuss politics? But, since Zari had plenty of time for leisure on her hands, perhaps Hera should increase the girl's studies. If she truly wanted to combat her then she might as well arm her with the proper tools to do so.

"He's knowledgeable and smart..." Zari said softly. "He listens to his people. As does Hades—"

"Are you implying that I do not?"

"No, not at all," Zari said quickly. Hera knew she didn't mean any harm by it, but she also knew Zari was speaking of Poseidon's *join-them* style of leadership. Hera ruled differently. Her methods garnered the results she wanted.

"And before you ask, Zari, we will not be giving him the islands." Another visitor was awaiting them, but Hera waved her hand at the guard, signaling he keep the doors closed while she put an end to the discussion.

"He manages them already," Zari said softly.

"He oversees them."

"But—"

"Zari. Have you studied the maps? Have you seen what would happen if we handed over those islands? Poseidon would have control over the fishing markets, the timber, the shipping ports. We would have to pay for things that were once ours. It makes no sense. It wouldn't benefit us. It wouldn't benefit Olympus."

"But...he's doing the work—"

"Then remind him that he does not have to." Hera rose a brow. Zari's pestering had earned her the challenge. "Tell him to stop overseeing the island cluster. He can remain in Oceanus and not burden himself with it. Of course, that would mean he would have to seek his timber elsewhere." It was a trade that Poseidon obviously had not mentioned to Zari, otherwise, Zari would not have looked so perplexed. As if she were in fact teetering on both sides of the narrative. One only did that when they were given new information to consider. "And before you speak about those damned ships, at the time, we all acknowledged Zeus as the *Godking*. All ichor, including Poseidon, answered to him. They still do. After the war, Zeus had been lenient when it came to their realms. They have more freedom than they ever had before. Just because you are fond of Poseidon, does not give your senses permission to leave you. Senses that you were only recently born with."

"I…"

"And how would it work?"

"Pardon?"

"How would you and Poseidon actually work?" Zari blinked. Hera placed both hands in her lap, releasing Zari's hold. Her crown made shadows on the floor and her chest rose and fell with a set of heavy pearls. Heavy pearls, that were getting heavier. A crown that was somehow suffocating. "Poseidon is an Ocean King. You are the Godking. Your place is here and his is there."

"I haven't thought—"

There was the problem. Zari wasn't thinking at all. Hera had tolerated the liberties Poseidon had taken with the girl—sneaking her away from Hera's sight and claiming her without the necessary discussion they all needed to have. But not only was he a distraction, he was a poor influence. She wished she would have gotten involved sooner. She should have ignored Hades and put an end to it.

Hera lowered her lashes and considered for a moment: What if Poseidon was doing exactly as she expected, using Zari to get what he wanted? Poseidon and love did not go hand and hand. The ichor had a way about him, one that often led to broken hearts and bewilderment at his ease of detachment.

Zari could blindly give him everything he wanted. Her land. Her body. Her mind. Her heart. She could give him all that he needed to break Olympus and make Oceanus the superpower of the realms.

"Let us humor ourselves with the concept of marriage," Hera said, causing Zari's eyes to widen. The girl was stiff in her seat. "Our gender means we assume the status of our husbands. Did you consider that? You would be the Queen of Oceanus and he would remain king. Olympus would be left unprotected and without a ruler. It pains me, Zari, that you would consider me to rule alone, as I know you were about to imply. When you've said so in the past, it was flattering, I will admit. But now, it is simply an abdication of responsibility. You can't go to Hades and offer to *switch* roles. You cannot abandon the mountain. A leader, a *true* leader, rules as if the people are their children. They don't abandon their home for a passion that will only fade."

"I…"

"And let us entertain that the two of you remain lovers. You'd be separated most of the time, for however long he decides to keep you. Would that not pain you?"

"L-lovers?"

"He is an ichor with needs. They all are. *Live long, get bored.* You are young so you do not know."

Hera thought she was doing Zari a favor by not mentioning children. Where would they go? Where would they live? They would not be heirs of Olympus considering they would have their father's inheritance. Little lightning bolts, she thought, would not do well suppressed under the ocean.

Zari's expression, however, made her feel as though she had done her one favor too many. The girl looked melancholy and possibly…heartbroken? Her wide eyes were small and lifeless and for the first time, Zari was quiet.

Was this how the others felt whenever Zari was on the verge of tears? It was horrible, the clutch on Hera's heart. Absolutely horrible. Luckily, Zari was not bursting at the seams or running with her face buried within her hands. She was simply quiet. Hera had a chance to soften things.

"Zari…I'm not saying that you can't see him. I'm only asking that you try to understand that being a ruler means putting your own needs last. You must think of your realm and your people. Do you understand? If it makes you feel any better, Poseidon would say the same."

"…and Hades?"

Hera was taken aback. Why would she mention Hades? He was the Soul King. Nothing came before the Underworld. Hera swallowed and nodded. It was harder to say out loud than she expected, "He and Persephone would match well."

"Even if he does not love her?"

"It is not about love." Her heart constricted again. Her pearls... *heavier?* Her crown... *more constricting?* "He will marry her out of duty because that's what we do. Duty above all else." Hera settled in her seat and nodded towards the guard. Ready to resume their morning calls. She also needed water. "He should marry her. As the Godking you should grant Persephone her wish."

Chapter 20

Zari

After their morning calls, she retreated to her room with the excuse of a headache. Not that she had one, but she noticed it was something that was said if one needed to be alone.

"I'll have a tray prepared for you," Hera said slowly. Her sharp mind would have deduced that Zari gave, did not succumb, to headaches. Nonetheless, Hera did not press. "And some tea."

"I think I'll just rest for a bit. Is that alright?"

Hera nodded. Zari waited to be dismissed. When she was alone in her room, she couldn't remember if she had blinked in the past five minutes. Her eyes were dry, and she rubbed them vigorously. Hera's words had crashed into her like a surprise exam. Only this time, the questions were tougher than usual. Perhaps, the hardest she had ever been asked. Sitting on the edge of her bed, her hands gripping the sheets and her eyes to the floor, she was expecting to see little puddles of tears on the marble. But there was nothing. Everything was numb and grey.

She was falling for Poseidon, but now she questioned her heart. Hera was the smartest of all the ichor. Intuitive and wise. She was right about everything she had said regarding her lessons and advice. How could she be wrong about him? If he were in possession of a secret motive—even one where he simply wanted her for his bed— she would never have known. That, and she felt it was too soon to speak of love or marriage.

Zari's fingers twitched from frustration. She didn't know how to explain to Hera that she did not believe that Poseidon was heartless and cruel. He was knowledgeable and experienced and only gave her advice if she asked. She could have argued that Ares was more trouble. She enjoyed him immensely, but like the rest of the ichor, Ares was quick to offer his opinions on how she should exercise her power. Like Aphrodite. Like Persephone. Like Iris. Like Hephaestus. Each had a way of meddling that tickled her enthusiasm. Each believed that their way, their methods, were the only solutions. She adored them for it. She appreciated what made them, them. But now she wondered if, like Poseidon, she had failed to see things clearly. If she had failed to see *them* clearly.

She had allowed her heart to get in the way of all things which Hera considered important. The ichor who sheltered her. The ichor who gave her a purpose. Zari's emotions had always been her weakness. They caused destruction and distraction and she felt horrible for tasking Hera with the responsibility of having to remind her of it. She wished she could be better.

The sky was dark now. She had ignored the tray that was accompanied by Hera's voice from the other side of the door. Hera said she would leave it. She had also snuck a small serving of ambrosia under the saucer. But Zari only lowered her brow. The treat sounded revolting. It represented everything that was wrong with her. Her complete lack of self-control and immaturity. She turned her gaze away, towards the window. Caelus flew by and she went to open it. When she extended her arm, the heavy eagle perched on her. Only at this moment did she wish he were a dog. Something she could squeeze. She had to settle with his nuzzling of her cheek, communicating that she was not alone. After a few strokes to his feathers, she lifted her arm and encouraged him to fly back into the stars.

She climbed out the window and jumped.

The fall did not hurt her. She knew that it would not, thanks to Poseidon's gentler training methods. If anything, the shock sent a rush of energy through her body that made her appear to be surrounded by an assortment of luminescent halos. When the energy died out, she lifted her skirts to step over the flower bushes that bordered the curtain drawn windows of a small painting room. No one was about at this hour. A perfect time to take an uninterrupted walk.

She found herself heading towards the tree line of the forest. Past the pools, past the topiaries, past the beginning stages of the garden party's construction. She should have been excited for the festivities, but she could not see past today.

"Zari?"

Her smile came first. She knew that voice from anywhere.

Adonis had ventured to the forest. His basket was over his arm and his body was mostly hidden by his shawl as he rested on a boulder. He looked...different. He was unfavorably pale, and his skin was blotchy. As if he were made of dough and fingerprints were forever branded on him in vibrant, rose-colored circles. Concaving his once beautifully full cheeks. When she approached, he gave her a tight hug. One she returned. One neither of them ended in the respectable amount of time. Both in desperate need of affection and friendship.

"I haven't seen you in weeks, my friend." Zari lowered her brow. When they parted, she held onto his arms. He gave a sad nod. "Not since I almost killed you."

His chuckle was heavy as he gave her a pat on the shoulder. "It is a long story. One I've just gotten around to seeing clearly."

"Please tell me. Tell me everything."

She sat beside him on the boulder and listened to his tale. It didn't take long for her horror to turn to anger. An emotion she was unaccustomed to. An emotion she feared and did her best to stifle. Perhaps her ichor weren't worthy of her admiration. Keeping Adonis trapped under lock and key. Keeping him from doing what he loved. How selfish of them.

"Sounds as though you are going through something similar," he countered. "The almighty Zeus, the Godking, feeling tamed and insecure. Like a broken stallion."

"Only I want to be broken, I think." If it meant re-visiting the pleasant memories of her, Hera and Hades at his dinner table, she would shatter. She would do anything Hera asked to be a part of a family. To no longer be discarded in darkness.

And then, that flash of anger returned, long enough for her to wonder why she should give a damn. As if scrutinizing one of Hera's mathematical equations, Zari was beginning to see the formula. She could spot the trends. Her ichor were all selfish. Greedy bastards. It was difficult for any of them to realize there was something they could not have. And when they did, they did everything in their power to lay claim. They called it conquering, she called it controlling. Zari did not want to believe the stories she had read about Hera. Someone she had grown to care for deeply. But, as if she had never known love or happiness, the Queen had ripped it all away from Zari. She did it so easily that Zari felt as if her feelings or their time together meant nothing.

In the corner of her eye, something gold was being handed to her. Adonis, with a reassuring and sympathetic smile, was extending a chrysanthemum towards her. Zari took it. The gesture was medicine for her pain.

"You mustn't be too hard on them. They've been alive for so long, they are set in their ways. Immortality is not their fault." He had a point. One she admitted to the petals of the frenzied looking flower. "What are you going to do?" he asked. "I want to help, in any way that I—"

Adonis peered over Zari's shoulder, a bit further down the tree line. When she craned her neck, she saw someone standing near the edge and kicking pebbles with a bony foot. Just...standing there. Just...kicking pebbles.

"Death?" she called. He lifted his head at his name, truly surprised to see them there. He then pointed to himself when she gestured for him to join them. He pointed to himself again, just to be sure. "What are you doing here?"

"For me, perhaps?" Adonis asked lightly.

"No. Not yet. I was simply taking a walk." After a pause between them he turned his neck at Adonis. "How did you get out?"

"I was scheduled to be in the care of Persephone this evening. I told Demeter of my situation, of my time coming, and she was more than happy to free me if it meant my end would quicken and that I was no longer staying within her home."

"I must apologize," Death sighed. "Your final days have been uncomfortable because of me."

It was Death's turn to explain the role he had played in Adonis' unfortunate arc, but Adonis was quick to forgive. He asked if there were flowers in the Underworld and Death shook his head, which once again spoiled Adonis' mood.

The anguish among them was too much. They sat on a rock near the forest, bonding over ineffectuality and stolen joy. It was strange. When she had spotted Death, Zari was about to ask if he was there for her. She wondered if her time had come and everything would go back to normal for her ichor. That everyone would be content again since she wasn't there to dismantle.

"I wish I knew who I was…" she mumbled. "I just need answers."

"They've discovered nothing?" Adonis asked.

"No Zeus. And I don't believe Iris has located Gaia."

"How is she?" Adonis asked with an expression Zari had never seen before. "Is she…well? Taking care of herself?"

"Iris? I…I'm not sure. I haven't seen her in a while. Hera didn't like me going down there too often but…" Zari paused. She blinked. It was an expression she had never seen on *Adonis* before, but it was one she had seen elsewhere. "Adonis…Adonis!" She gasped as he chuckled and ran his fingers through his hair. The intensity of his blush smoothed out his discoloration. If only for a moment. "Does she know? Has she returned your feelings?"

"Why would she? I am a human and she is a god. A lovely, smart…different…" he chuckled again. "I don't have the courage to tell her and she's not eager to be within my company, like the others. She understands that there is nothing special about me, which makes me want to be special for her. I cannot explain."

It did explain, however, why he always dropped his mail off personally. Or why he was always looking for an excuse to go downstairs. Why he was excited to be paired with her during Zari's first dinner.

"You should tell her. Especially considering…" her voice trailed off. He didn't appear to have much time left, and she wouldn't ask Death for specifics considering she didn't want to abuse their friendship.

Death was appreciative that she did not. He was appreciative of a lot of things—Zari's kindness, her respect for his work, her protection from the bullies and the fact that because of her, he might be getting vacation days and sick time. The least he could do was perhaps the most he could do.

"I am sorry that I can't be of much help to you, Adonis, but I might be able to...to help you, Zari." Zari and Adonis turned to Death. Puzzlement sat between them. "I might know someone..."

They gasped. For once in his career, he didn't mind leaking a bit of confidential information. Something he had yet to relay to Hades or his coworkers. Complications would arise because of it, that he knew.

"Someone who has the answers for my existence? Is it Gaia?"

Adonis nodded. "It would help you, yes? To speak to the mother herself? Might I go with you?"

"Of course," Zari smiled. "The more the merrier, right Death?"

"I...I suppose. But it's not—"

"Great! The three of us, we will make a wonderful team!"

Death shook his head. Once again, he was pointing to himself. "The three of us? Oh," he looked to the sky, "You, Adonis and Caelus."

"No," she chuckled. "Me, Adonis and you. Oh, I didn't even consider your schedule. I am sorry, I should have asked."

"You mean...you want *me* to come along as well?"

"I would like for you to join us." She placed her fingers under her chin as if she had a plan. "Caelus should stay behind. If he leaves, everyone will know that I have gone, and I don't want anyone stopping me or convincing me not to visit Gaia. I want to speak to her for my benefit. To get answers. To ask the questions that I need answers to."

Death agreed so quickly that he felt a little embarrassed, but he could barely contain himself at the thought of finally being a part of a group. Inclusion was a powerful thing.

Zari decided she was going to stop by Hephaestus shop, sneak in and steal some armor. She imagined they would encounter dragons, cyclops, ogres and nymphs. All of her training would be put to the test as she led them headfirst into battle. Adonis would throw the pointy ends of flowers with accuracy. Death would write names on his clipboard. They would be an unstoppable team. The three of them. Three unlikely heroes.

"I am so happy to be coming with you," Death said. "It will be a nice trip."

"Should we begin? Get a head start on our quest?"

"Well, it will take a matter of moments. We can use my travel credits."

"Oh…" She slumped her shoulders. "So...not a quest…"

Death attempted to sigh. It was his task to be the diminisher of enthusiasm. Zari was expecting an epic adventure complete with magic and monsters when in reality the trip would take minutes, at most.

"Alright!" she said with a firm nod. The switching of her emotions once again proving to be expeditious. "Shall we go first thing in the morning? Have breakfast beforehand?"

"Maybe at a restaurant," Adonis added. "There's a lovely spot near Lord Ares' club?"

"That will give me some time to run some errands," Death said hopefully. Yes, he was still included.

"And I can change into something more comfortable, instead of my morning dress."

"Yeah, so we—"

"Yeah, and then we could—"

"Alright, I'll see you—"

Talking over one another, they went their separate ways. They all agreed to meet back up tomorrow, fresh and rested for their quest.

Chapter 21

Poseidon

In preparation for their travels, Ares reserved the upper floor of his club for his ichor. His barber had made shop in the space, scattering his tools into neat and organized rows along the tables. Wine, whiskey, and cigars were served on silver trays. Gentle maidens with strong fingers massaged the flesh of the gods who lounged in chairs. Afterwards, they would head across the seas to watch the races on the English island. They would be gone for the few days leading up to the Olympus Garden Party and Floral Ball. No women or lady ichor had been invited.

"I must say, I like this new you," Hades mumbled as the scent of lavender water from the nail bath tickled their noses. The barber's assistant was tending to Hades while Poseidon was finishing up a shave. "You know, the one that gives a damn."

"I've always given a damn."

"Have you now?"

"I choose to focus my attentions mostly on my work, unlike the rest of you."

"If you did so in the beginning, statues of you wouldn't depict a homely looking fellow with a beard that housed a cluster of sea minions and hair that was matted like a poodle." Poseidon carefully turned his chin to leer at Hades. The artist had caught him at a bad time. After a feud with Atlantis. "Does Zari have anything to do with this change?"

Poseidon said nothing. Hades already knew the answer and was baiting him for a purpose he did not know. Zari was the reason behind many things. Including his presence on this trip. It had been awhile since he joined his ichor on an excursion.

"I am asking you, politely," Hades spoke again, "to speak with Hera regarding your intentions. To court Zari for a respectable amount of time before you ever consider marriage."

Well, that got his attention. Luckily, his face was getting wiped with a fresh cloth, hiding his mixed expression. It wasn't as if he hadn't thought about a future with Zari. He wanted her, more than anything. But he understood a relationship with her would be difficult. If not Hera to consider, his realm. There was an entirely different world beneath the waves. One he had yet to introduce her to for obvious reasons.

"She's never been to Oceanus," Poseidon stated as the towel was being removed from his skin.

"Are you not planning on giving her a tour?"

Poseidon blinked, awaiting the moment Hades would remember his own dilemma. Something about a hole in the middle of his home. In Oceanus, oxygen-filled structures housed thousands. A breach in the barriers would do more than cause a draft. He was going to invite her, but that was a conversation to be had further down the line.

"Oh, right." Hades eventually caught up to him. "Even so. Speak with Hera."

Hera. Poseidon refrained from scoffing. He also refrained from reminding Hades that Hera could not force Zari in or out of relationships. Hera could not force them apart.

"My intentions are my own and are none of Hera's concern."

"But that is what I am trying to tell you, they are."

"So then, you're asking more for your sake than mine." Poseidon watched his ichor carefully as he dried his hands and examined the tips of his fingers. As he stood to his feet with a calmness about him. With a certain mystery about him that was neither entertaining nor brilliant. Time with Hera had changed him indefinitely, but there was something else. Something different about Hades.

It was as if Hades was taking a breath of fresh air, one that was causing the rest of them to suffocate. Poseidon, as intuitive as he was, had always felt but never expressed. That Hades was hiding something. That he had been ever since Zeus disappeared.

The Soul King would have not gone this long without answers. Nor would he have been so willing to accept a stranger to the throne. Hades was speaking so frequently of second chances, Poseidon understood he wasn't only referring to Hera and his infatuation with her. Hades knew what had happened to Zeus. Poseidon could feel it in his core.

As Hades hovered over a table with an assortment of drink, Poseidon joined him unhurriedly. His mind, however, took note of Hades' expression. Of his lax shoulders. Of his hidden smirk.

"Anything you would like to tell me?" Poseidon tested. "Anything I should know?"

"Such as?" His ichor was encased in his task of choosing the correct drink. He sniffed the rims of each of their contents until he settled on one. He poured a glass and handed it to Poseidon. When the offering lingered much longer than expected, Hades finally turned to him. "Let me guess," he sighed, "you also question my composure."

"I'd be a fool not to." Or in this case, simply tardy.

Hades released a grunt that was lacking in humor. As if he was truly exhausted from having to defend himself. "Honestly, you and Hera are like...well, *you and Hera*. Always with the need to be in control. Why not simply enjoy life? Let things happen without an explanation."

"Did you just compare me to the Queen?"

"It's no wonder the two of you dislike one another. You're too similar. Equally difficult," he mumbled into his wine glass just loud enough to where Poseidon could hear him. "Perhaps Zari should join me in the Underworld. The brooding lot can stay up here."

Poseidon leaned his back on the wall and folded his arms. He still had not taken the wine that Hades made a show of drinking himself. With another glass in him, Hades pouted and felt the need to ramble.

"I allow my people to live as they choose, and in doing so, their drive and ambition and ingenuity continue well after death. Too much structure, too much hesitation, it prevents a person from crossing the road. It delays them from reaching the beauty on the other side. I'm tired of waiting..." As his voice trailed off, so did his curtness. He took a breath, filled another glass, and extended it to Poseidon passively. Poseidon took this one. "Zari has not been here for very long but already she's softened Hera, brought me from the Underworld and brought you from Oceanus. The three of us, it's been some time since we were a united front."

As Poseidon sipped, he inhaled his agreement. Never had he spent so long on Olympus and didn't mind the time. In fact, he couldn't wait for the races to be over and the palace celebrations to begin. All so he could see Zari. So that he could tell her, if she hadn't' deduced already, that he planned to court her properly. But now he was thinking of marriage and wondering what it would be like to take her to wife. To have her with him for eternity. In his home. With their children. Laughing over the dinner table and taking walks on the beach. Domestication wasn't fitting of the Ocean King. But it was fitting of an ichor who was falling rapidly in love.

Chapter 22

Hera & Hades

She could understand dinner, maybe even skipping breakfast, but when the second offering of ambrosia prompted no response, the silence unnerved her. Although she wasn't the strongest of the gods, physically, a piece of metal would never be impediment. She twisted the handle and gently forced open the door. She poked her head through the gap, expecting to see Zari in bed or fiddling with the gowns in her wardrobe. Or perhaps, at her dressing table, ignoring Hera's intrusion with a shunned silence. Hera would speak first as Zari attempted to prove her independence by braiding her own hair. Zari would argue back. Hera wouldn't have minded as much. She knew that she deserved the distance Zari was wedging between them. However, it was time to come together again and Hera needed to hear her voice. Even if it would be full of bitterness.

The room was empty.

The bed was made and there was no sign of Zari.

The clock on her mantle read late afternoon.

In her hands, Hera had a box. A gift. Something she was going to give to Zari just before the ball, but hoped that by giving it to her now, it would weaken the tension between them. But there was no Zari to give it to. No one in the woodland creatures bedroom that had been empty for so long. She didn't want to picture it empty again. Setting the box on Zari's dressing table, she rang the bell for Zari's handmaid.

"Yes, My Queen?"

"Have you seen Zari?"

"Not since yesterday."

"Yesterday?"

"Aye, yesterday morning. When she retired, she did not ring for me to undress her. And today, she has not rung for me to comb her hair. I knocked on the door to see if she needed some medicine and a tray but there was no reply. I assumed she was still sleeping."

"You mean...she hasn't been here since yesterday?"

"Perhaps she is in another part of the house? Or exploring? Or visiting one of your relatives? It is not like her to remain cooped up for very long."

All reasonable explanations. After their exchange, she imagined Zari would want to step away from the palace for a bit. She also imagined her finding solace in the arms of Poseidon and telling her how cruel Hera had been. Or crying into the sleeves of Hades and refusing to return to Olympus. Zari would only relay what they had already known—that she was a cold and heartless Queen. None of them would ever consider that she had spoken to Zari from a place of knowledge and affection. That she didn't mean to sound so callous and uncaring.

"Caelus?"

"In his home, My Queen. It will be feeding time for him soon."

This relaxed her. Knowing that the bird was nearby meant that Zari was as well. Although, there was that one time she told him to remain at the palace. That day she nearly drowned in the ocean. Hera closed her eyes and composed herself. She was jumping to conclusions and worrying too much. Zari was safe, wherever she was, and would return by the end of the day. She was sure of it.

***

The end of the day had come. And it had left Zari behind. The dinner gong had rung and there was no sound of hurried footsteps or shuffling skirts. The chair where Zari usually slumped after eating was cold and without her imprint. The fire was going and there was no one there to be warmed by it. There was no music filling the halls as Hera had no one to tutor on the piano.

Hera ate alone that night. Only she didn't remember taking a bite of food. Maybe one or two spoonfuls to prove that she was stable. But after that, she retired to her bedchamber with a book in hand. Only, she never turned the page. She had been staring at the parchment, unaware of what she was reading. Which was a book on rabbits.

Why did she own a single book on rabbits?

Setting it aside, she went to the study. She paced as the anger within her began to fester. Her fingers tapped relentlessly in anticipation for Zari's punishment. For the girl disappearing without notice. The most strenuous mathematics equation Hera could muster, she scribbled with heavy penmanship. She took the opportunity to create a history exam. And a language recital. All of which would be waiting for Zari when she returned. She should be back by morning. Just before breakfast.

Morning came.

It too left Zari behind.

At the table, Hera flipped through the pages searching for random disasters. Maybe there was a wildlife habitat where monkeys were spiraling within a tornado. Perhaps an electrical storm had ruined a hot air balloon festival. Anything to signify a mishap by Zari's hand.

The papers were silent.

As silent as the palace.

Hera took a breath and reminded herself to be patient. It was all she could do. By nightfall however, she was transitioning into a simmering state of fretfulness. Under the moon, everything seemed still. Motionless. Without feeling. Even the wind was on leave. The trees did not rustle, and the flowers did not shift from their stems. One more night, she told herself. Tomorrow, she would have a chat with Poseidon, who she deduced was keeping Zari to himself. She did not go to him directly, considering she knew the more she pushed, the more she would push Zari away. Further into his arms. She was hoping that Zari would return and that they would have a chat about it, and all would be well again. Hera simply needed to make it through one more night.

She gave up on reading. She had a servant rekindle the fire in the drawing room so that she could knit. She had found a beautiful, heavy, yarn the shade of a canary's breast. Hera had been braiding it and threading it together to have a scarf and mittens ready for Zari for the holidays. It was barely spring, but her aimless roaming about the halls had her happen across the closet of decorations that were being sorted as part of an annual deep cleaning. Hera was assaulted with the pleasant smell of stale cinnamon. Baubles, ornaments, lights, candles, garlands, toys, figurines, tinsel, displays.

She imagined Zari and her first snow. She would show Zari how to pick a proper tree, which they would decorate together. Hera imagined that by then Zari would be ready to plan the dinner for the ichor. The menu, the seating arrangements, the wine. It would be a test of her schooling and a benchmark for how prepared Zari was when it came to running a home. After, when they were alone, she would present Zari with a mound of beautifully wrapped presents underneath the tree. There was so much the girl needed, and Hera had been making a list. Pearls. New slippers. New gowns. A shawl. Scented sprays. Hair ornaments. Books. Watercolors. A music box. Board games. Hera grinned at the thought of gifting her a pegasus only if it wouldn't make Caelus jealous.

Resting her progress on her lap, she gazed out the window. She rang for a servant, one woken from slumber, to ask if Zari had returned. Perhaps she had entered from downstairs. The butler shook his head and answered before she could complete her sentence.

"No, My Queen," he said as if he had been asked more times than she could recall.

Hera dismissed him. She leaned her head on her windowsill and stayed there. At the peak of the sun, her eyes sprung open as she realized something she had overlooked. Zari wouldn't have been with Poseidon. The ichor had been gone for days to the English races and only just returned. Which meant that she wouldn't have been with Hades either. Hurrying to the pen where her peacocks were allowed to roam, she entered the open birdcage that housed Caelus. She pushed past the servants who were cleaning his quarters and gently placed her hands on his collapsed wings. She searched his body, his movement, his eyes for the answer. Caelus released a soft mumble, followed by a meager and depressing howl. He was confirming what she should have assumed long ago. Zari was gone.

***

Hades was surprised to receive her call. Ever since the trip to the luxury ship, Hera had been ignoring him. A few days on the other side of Europe was what he needed to distract him. A few days at the races surrounded by a bit of gambling and stiff drink. After they returned, he remained with Poseidon for a night before transitioning back to his realm. He needed to sleep off his vices in preparation for spring. All he needed was one, full night's rest and—

"Your Grace," his cookmaid said with a sigh. He had just gotten out of the bath. A difficult task to not let the warm water seduce him into slumber. He had dawdled into his hazardous home, bypassing the misplaced furniture and workers. The hammering and drilling was...*rude*. After the spring festivities, he would seek temporary accommodations for himself and his staff.

"Your Grace," his cookmaid said again. When he raised his head to make eye contact, she was quick to tell him that the rotary had been actively ringing. She then gave him a pithy stare. Ever since Persephone and Hera's impromptu visits, and Caelus, he wanted to make sure that he was the only one answering it. Receiving calls were no longer among her duties and she marginally scolded him for it. He dragged his feet down the hall, down the stairs and to the parlor. When he lifted the receiver, he was caught off guard by the frantic and worried voice on the other end.

"Is Zari with you?"

It didn't take long for him to come to. Hera in distress snapped him upright. "What?"

"Zari? Is she with you?"

As he considered the question, he had to refrain from chuckling. How many ichor was Hera going to misplace?

"No," he said softly. "And if she was, you know I would have called you."

"I...I know...which is why..." Hera paused, and he could hear her chest rising and falling. "Caelus isn't hunting and...she's...she's not here...I went downstairs and she's not..."

This was not the tone of an ichor whose sloth of a husband had disappeared after throwing lightning bolts at her feet. This was not the tone of an ichor who wouldn't be caught dead venturing below stairs for anything. This was the sound of an ichor who had lost something important. Someone important. He needed only to bark Iris' name before he felt himself being materialized. He was without his coat and shoes again. Only this time, it was out of urgency.

He came to her in two strides. She looked dreadful and tired. Her eyes were red at the corners. Her body fidgeted as if she didn't know what to do with herself. The tip of her nose was glossy, and her cheeks had thin, dry paths that began under her lashes and ended at her chin. She had been crying. Or up all night. Or both.

He ushered her to the bay window. The glass overlooked the darkness of the gardens. He rang for water. As well as tea. The water came first, and he encouraged her to drink it. She obliged. She took a breath and clutched the glass so tightly that he had to pry it from her fingers.

"Hera..." he brushed the hair from her forehead. Most of the time it was kept tidy, every strand securely in place. This evening, she had left it loose. Her curls, soft and full, fell just past her shoulders. There was a knitting basket at her feet. Books as well. In that seat near the window, Hera looked as though she were awaiting a lover's return. Or awaiting the view of silver locks from the horizon. "Tell me what happened. Start at the beginning."

"I said such awful things to her."

"I don't believe that."

She glared at him. "Do not speak as if I am incapable."

"I did not say that." He used his thumb to secure more of her hair behind her ear. "I am simply reminding you that you cannot be cruel to Zari. You care too much for her."

At his words, she hid her face in her hands and began to sob. It was a sight that startled the butler as he returned with a tray of tea. Hera could always disguise her sadness, but this evening she was unhinged. She mumbled into her fingers, asking if Zari was with Poseidon. Almost begging him to tell her that that was the case.

But Poseidon had been with him, practically up until morning. Their drinks were their only witnesses to their sloppy rambles of emotions. Emotions regarding two ichor who resided in a crystal palace in the clouds.

"Are you sure he was with you, the entire time?"

Hades nodded with confidence.

He and Poseidon, and the rest of the ichor in fact, had sat with their racing tickets in hand while women gazed at them under their elaborate sun hats, wondering who the tourists were. Afterward, they would have dinner in a nice restaurant and see a play. The next morning, perhaps they would go to a museum or a club and a few dirty pubs. Ares had memberships everywhere, and no place in London was off limits to those who paid in gold. What delayed them was that they stopped in Italy before returning. Dionysus was tasting a new brand of wine.

Even so. He got to his feet and decided to call Poseidon. No one picked up on the other end, as Hera told him would happen. He imagined the Ocean King had a few of his own correspondences to deal with, considering that he had been away from his realm much longer than Hades from the Underworld.

"I am still hoping that they decided to run away together," she said between broken breaths.

Hades shook his head. Not only had he just seen Poseidon, he had just spoken to him about courting Zari properly. And he knew his ichor. Poseidon would not do anything to hurt Zari or damage her reputation. Or to cause her more pain. Keeping her from Hera was not something Poseidon would encourage if he knew how much Zari cared for her. Without her needing to say or ask, she brought out the affable and domesticated side of him. A side he was only beginning to realize he had. One Hades had watched unfold since the two came face to face in the amphitheater.

"This is all my fault," she said as he resumed his place beside her. He held her, bringing her in close.

"Whatever it was, I am sure she has long forgiven you."

"Then why hasn't she come home?"

"I…" Suddenly, the phone rang. It was a dash to the receiver, but he allowed Hera to answer. Judging by her tone, it was Poseidon. Hera was quick to ask him if Zari was with him. "Are you sure…is she…if you're lying—"

Hades braced himself for Poseidon who suddenly appeared through the rotary. "How long has she been missing?" he demanded. His height over her did not make her wither. Not in the slightest.

Hera grunted like a child whose parents returned from a trip without sweets, thereby rendering them useless. Hades answered, "about four days, it seems."

"Are you sure?" Poseidon was still wearing the clothes they had arrived in. His trousers, shoes, open sack jacket with a button-down shirt. His eyes leapt between the two of them as Hades did his best to explain. Hera retook her place near the window. She filled in the blanks with simple answers.

"I told her that I would see her today..." Poseidon said, and it made Hades bite his lip. Zari would have made sure she was here to receive him. And he was late. Which meant that she was never around to begin with. "And you've asked everyone? You've checked under volcanoes and overturned food carts. You've looked between the sheets of an avalanche?"

Hades would have told them to give it more time but judging by Hera's state, she had given her enough. Zari could have been taking a break from life at the palace. She could be returning within moments. But it went unsaid. There was a feeling among them that was beginning to seep into their skin. A feeling similar to when Zeus had disappeared from this world. One he assumed Hera felt first and hardest.

"What of Caelus?" Poseidon asked. "He could find her—"

"I've encouraged him out already," Hera said somberly. "He left his cage for a brisk circle and came straight back. He...he can't find her..."

Poseidon, whose tension was building rapidly, caused the liquid tea in the kettle to expand. The porcelain shattered into a spray of shiny pieces. It wedged between the fibers of the ornamental rugs and sprinkled onto the nearby lounge chair. Hera scowled at him.

"Was that truly necessary? Try doing something that actually helps the situation."

"The *situation*?" he snapped back. "The one where you've managed to run off not one, but *two* ichor!"

"Sai." Hades extended his arm, attempting to calm Poseidon.

"Maybe Zeus isn't dead." Poseidon shrugged. "Maybe he's only pretending, so that he could get away from you. Did you ever think of that, *My Queen?*"

Hera stood tall on her feet. Her back straight. Her sadness was replaced with anger and Hades suddenly feared for them. Feared for the vicinity. In the privacy of the three kings, they nicknamed her *Earthshaker*. Her migraines, as she called them, were tremors that swayed the world below the mountains. Tremors that caused the ground to split and the streets to flood. Their egos would bring an end to the humans. Just like the dinosaurs. Hades liked the dinosaurs.

"Please, let us calm ourselves—" he attempted. But Hera snapped at Poseidon, closing the gap between them.

"You would like that, wouldn't you? To take her just as you want to take Olympus."

"What the hell are you talking about? Why the hell would I want to take Olympus?"

"You've been filling her head with ideas on how to rule. On how to combat me. You don't even live here. What gives you the right? I won't let you have Olympus. I won't let you have her."

"*Let me?*" he chuckled so loudly that Hades could hear the wind shift. "If I want Zari, I don't need your permission."

"Of course not! That's all you do is take and take and take! Leaving everyone else to pick up the pieces of your complete disregard!"

"What are you talking about?"

Hades' chin whipped between them. He knew Hera held no hatred towards Poseidon. That this was years, centuries of pent up anger for her past. Things she never said to Zeus. But only he knew that. Just as Hades understood habits about Poseidon he doubted his ichor could identify. But now wasn't the time to expose rights and wrongs. Neither of his ichor were backing down. He needed to put a stop to this.

"When you break her heart, who will be there for her?" Hera's lip trembled. "Not you!"

"I won't break her heart."

"Yes, you will! You inconsiderate bastard!"

"You don't know anything about me! You conniving bi—"

Poseidon stopped at the abrupt flash of light, followed by the collapse of Hera into his arms. Hades took her from him instantly, gently, lifting her in his hold and carrying her upstairs. He took them one at a time, handling her as if she were worth every jewel in the world. He didn't know where her room was, but he did remember where she had brought Zari when she first arrived. So, he carried her there. To the woodland themed bedchamber. He approached the bed and lowered her on the covers. He pulled a nearby blanket to her chin.

Her pale skin was still. One would think she was dead until a slight breath escaped her dehydrated lips. Her eyes remained closed. Her fingers rest at her side. One hand brushed a few curls from her forehead, the other held his pocket watch. A gold, intricate looking timepiece with a ruby center. It was glowing with the soul of Hera resting inside.

When he closed the door to the bedchamber, Poseidon was leaning on the wall with his arms folded. He looked Hades in the eye, his demeanor calm but serious.

"Are you ready to have that talk now?" he asked. "And a drink?"

Hades knew it was time. He massaged his face with his hands and nodded.

Chapter 23

Poseidon

He certainly didn't want to stick around for what would happen next. When Hera finally woke, and Hades would be forced to reveal his hand. Poseidon couldn't believe what he had heard. It was all so outlandish, he needed to see it for himself. But he promised Hades to allow Hera the opportunity. To give her the chance to come face to face with the secret he had been trying to conceal. If it were any other time, he might have found the situation amusing. For now, he would shake himself from his shock and turn his attention to the other side of the coin. The more important side, which was finding Zari.

Unfortunately, Hades' confession did not leave him with any clue of where she might be. With mutual agreement, Poseidon began the tasks of organizing a search party and diving deep within their resources. He reached out to Iris first. He needed to summon each of their primary ichor. By phone, by message, by raven—whatever means necessary. He needed Ares at the palace. More short-tempered than Poseidon, they could use a bit of brashness right now. He also needed to get word to any and everyone on the Mountain of Olympus. To be searching for her. To relay any information of where she could have gone.

Caelus wasn't being much help. As Hera had informed him, the bird simply flew around in disheartened circles and returned to his post. It was as if he had given up. Poseidon wouldn't. It wasn't in his nature to step aside and accept things for how they were. He would find her. He would search the edges of his seas until he did.

He sent word to Oceanus. Perhaps Zari did come looking for him. Maybe after her row with Hera she was looking for refuge. But he told her about the annual tradition of visiting the races. She knew he was going to be traveling. At first, he wasn't going to go. He wanted to spend that time with her, but she encouraged him to join his ichor. She didn't want him to furlough what she believed to be an exciting trip and she surprised him by saying they needed some distance. Briefly. She was falling behind on her studies. He tickled her when she said it, accepting himself as the distraction she adorably tried to avoid. Hiding in bushes. Giggling behind statues. He would chase her. Catch her. Kiss her. His solution was to help her with her studies which led to her questioning the laws and regulations Olympus had enforced. He wasn't *taking* Olympus by means of seduction. He didn't give a damn about this place.

After the ball, after the festivities, he did plan to make his next excursion with Zari. To take her to London and use Ares' connections to gain access to prestigious balls and opera boxes. After, he would continue showing her the world—Paris, New York, The Arctic, Egypt. They would sail aboard his favorite ship. Kissing on the open water. Touching each other. Exploring each other. Falling asleep with the gentle rocking of the seas. Once they'd seen everything this world had to offer, he would take her further. To Asgard. To Valhalla. To Atlantis. And even further after that.

Hera could believe whatever she wanted. He wasn't going to break Zari's heart. She would break his with the hold she had on him. Unrelenting and unexpected, he found himself thinking of her during every waking moment. She was the new standard that made anyone else appear dim and uninspiring. Each gaze into her eyes was like the beginning of a new day.

He cursed Hades. He had agreed to court Zari for the proper amount of time and according to palace etiquette. It was equivalent to a mourning period. One year and one day. And, with Hera's blessing. Although it was Zari's decision, he knew she wouldn't marry him if it would make Hera dreadfully unhappy. He cursed Hera as well. He had no choice but to remain patient on the matter.

"Sai?" He peered up from a missive he was scribbling on the annoyingly scented paper at the writing desk. This was the most important missive he would write. He needed help from the forest. Not even the breathing cluster of trees were off limits to his search.

Hecate had interrupted him however, appearing frustrated and surly as usual. The butler was behind her, eyeing the grime on her steel-toed boots. Her spurs sang from her heels. Scraping across the floor, scratching the delicate marble beneath them without a care for the finer things. Or anyone else's things for that matter.

"What is it?" He shrugged indifferently. She needed to say what she wanted so he could continue his task. He had a few royal guards, inconspicuously going door to door. Had Zari been taken, which he didn't think was likely, he didn't want her captor getting wind that they were searching. Nor did he want Zari trying to distance herself further.

"Where is Hades?" she asked briskly. Her pistols at her ribs, hanging tightly in her holsters. The butler dismissed himself.

"Hades is…" Poseidon's eyes went to the ceiling, in the direction of Zari's bedroom. "Busy."

He was going to leave it there, but she was leering at him. He grunted, "What do you need?"

She looked taken aback. "Nothing from you, except—"

"So, something."

"Do you know where Death is?"

"Death?"

"The idiot hasn't clocked in for a shift for days and I can no longer fill in. He mentioned he was getting vacation time or something, which is absolutely ridiculous. He's Death for fuck's sake! I asked Janus and she said we didn't even have time-off forms so—"

Poseidon held up a hand. "Death is missing? For how long?"

"A few days now! Souls are piling up! I am having to work double-time to collect them since there is no one to escort them to the Underworld!"

Poseidon grunted. He didn't have time to deal with Death. Nor Hecate, who was looking at him as if he were meant to do something about it. He had asked her what her problem was, deduced it wasn't his, and resumed his missive. The scribbling quill suggesting the end of his interest.

Hecate mumbled something under her breath. Something that made him stand to dismiss her when the butler came shuffling into the room again. His face was wrinkled and distressed. His body wobbled with unsteadiness. Behind him pushed three pairs of eyes. Only one of which he summoned. Ares was peeking his head behind an inflamed Aphrodite and an irked Persephone.

"What are you doing here, Sai?" Ares said with a reliving stare. As if he found his one true comrade in the room.

"I sent for you," Poseidon said with a slow blink. He lowered his chin towards the writing desk, knowing Ares had ignored the palace correspondence as he always did. "If not for my letter, then what are you doing here?"

"Well—"

"Adonis has been missing for days thanks to her!" Aphrodite pointed to Persephone who took a seat on a chair. Her rear was to the edge and her hands in her lap. She looked tired. Almost as much as Hera. But she was still presentable in a pale pink gown that matched the hue of her lips.

"As I've said, Demeter released him without my knowledge."

"Either way, he should have been back by now! He was taken! Perhaps by you!" She turned to Ares who held out his hands to Poseidon as if to display what he had been dealing with. Aphrodite could have easily blamed Ares, who everyone knew loathed Adonis.

Hecate chuckled and shrugged. "You can't hide him forever, Ares."

"I'd present him to you if I could!"

"So...he's not dead." Persephone angled her chin. She curled her lips to Aphrodite who seemed to relax a bit. "If Hecate doesn't have him, he's still alive. You can calm yourself now."

"But he's still missing! Imagine him, lost for days with no one to feed him or cloth him or put him to bed—"

"Wait!" Poseidon stopped her. He lifted his gaze to the four ichor. "How long has he been missing?"

"Days!" Aphrodite stomped. She eyed the room for the nearest settee and collapsed into it.

"First Zari...Death...and now Adonis—"

"What?" Ares lowered his brow. There was no need for secrets between this group, who all shared a common dilemma. Without the details of why or how, he explained that Zari and Death had been gone for the same extension of time as Adonis.

"The three of them were close...each of them, walking disasters in their own right..." Hecate said slowly. "This is not a coincidence."

"Close?" The room echoed.

"Death was fond of her and she and Adonis were fast friends. Death was looking for Adonis, eventually, so is it truly impossible for their paths to all have crossed? For each of them to get into some sort of trouble? Misfortune is the thread that binds them."

Hecate had a point and Poseidon didn't know what to believe beyond that. What could have caused all three of them to disappear? Had Hera been that cruel and made Zari flee into the night? Had Death gotten sick of being the most hated deity in the universe? And Adonis, perhaps he was tired of being sheltered and smothered by Aphrodite and Persephone. But was life so bad that they felt the need to run away? Perhaps. Listing their dilemmas, Poseidon could admit, it sounded like a nightmare.

"Well, that explains it," Ares said with conviction. "Death resigned without notice and Zari ran away with Adonis." An abrupt, synchronized gasp filled the room. Eyes were like spears towards Ares' throat. "It's true. Death got sick of his post, the first logical thing he has done since...well, anything. Adonis saw Zari in the vulnerable and depressed state at Poseidon's discard of her. They took his basket, filled it with wine, cheese and bread and flowers and a blanket and lyre and some books and skipped off. They're probably on a train heading to China. Or worse, seeking employment. Bowls of soup between their fingers. Poverty nipping at their heels. I suppose Zari could get a position as a lightbulb. Adonis, well, he would sell to a housewife for a decent sum."

Poseidon's growl was so low, so menacing, he felt the desk trembling underneath the weight of his fingers. "They did not run away together," he managed to say without eruption. "And I did not discard her." The discord of his ichor was neutral and binding, gluing them together like the strongest cement. "Well?" he snapped to them. "Something you want to say?"

197

"It was only a matter of time," Ares shrugged and placed his hand behind his head, massaging his hair. "It's not as though you would recognize it...if...when it happens." Poseidon's threatening silence made Ares respire heavily. He looked like an ichor who was about to tell a wife her cooking was passable, at best. This conversation was not going to go well. "Sai...we all know how you are."

"And how is that, exactly?" For not only Ares, and the exchanged glances among his ichor before him, but Hades and Hera had implied there was a *thing* about him that he was somehow oblivious. A *thing* that resulted in broken hearts. Absurd, he thought. For his heart had never been broken.

"Women flock to you. Of course, you're handsome! Abundant! Good stock, as the English say! But..." Ares' voice got higher as he passed an unsure grin. "...but..."

"You're a schizoid," Aphrodite stated bluntly. She was still lounging on the settee and examining a strand of her hair before allowing her arm to rest on her forehead. She mumbled her affirmations.

"What!?"

Ares lowered his hands in small waves. "What she means is...you can be...emotionally detached when it comes to...a significant other." Ares gave him a warm smile and attempted to pat Sai on the arm. Poseidon's response to the gesture made Ares withdraw immediately and continue in a huff. "You entertain them for a bit. You know, provocatively and all. And then you move on. In a blink it feels like. As if nothing ever happened."

Ares was speaking nonsense. As usual. And Poseidon had fallen into the trap of entertaining him. But the room was uncomfortably silent. He looked to Aphrodite, the honest type, who nodded. Persephone, always polite, blinked. Hecate scoffed and folded her arms.

"Sai," Ares leaned in and whispered, delivering his evidence, "At least each of them..." he gestured to their ichor, "...had eyes for you at some point. You had them each believing they had a chance." Dramatically, Ares placed his hand on his friend's shoulder and hung his head. "It was as if their feelings were as invisible as glass."

His blue eyes fluttered. He didn't see how that was possible. Had each of his ichor, at one point or another, thought he was.....*interested?*

Persephone used to bake him dessert. Often. She made beautiful cakes and biscuits that she had gifted to him personally. It was long ago of course. Before she was suggested for Hades. She was young and finding her footing among them. She also liked to cook. He thought he was being friendly by accepting her offerings with courtesy.

Aphrodite used to sunbathe on his beaches, regularly. But she liked the attention. She liked laying naked under the sun and passing him flirtatious smiles, as she did with anyone. She would touch his arm, as she did with anyone. If they kissed it was because they could. Nothing was ever...meaningful between them. She had told him. But...she could have simply told him that to put on a brave face.

And then there was Hecate. Maybe they exchanged a kiss or two on a few drunken nights. She wore trousers and spoke like a pirate. He liked pirates. He thought that was as far as their interests went. Apparently, he was wrong, which explained why she never seemed to respect him after. Why she was so quick to flee to the Underworld and remain. All to avoid him.

And this was just them. According to Ares, this was his habit.

"I thought you were playing hard to get," Aphrodite smirked at him, answering the thoughts that were running through his mind. "Challenge accepted."

"Or..." Persephone lifted a brow, "that you were being a gentleman. Which was why you were delayed in your advances."

"Or an asshole," Hecate finished. "You were simply being an asshole."

Advances?

He didn't even know he was making them or that harmless acts of familiarity were more detrimental than he could ever realize. He looked to the side. Not at anything in particular. He wondered if Ares was right. If he had pushed Zari away. Hera's frustration was understandable now. If he had a habit of breaking hearts and not realizing it, it made sense that Hera would want to protect Zari.

It was impossible that his feelings for Zari would be misinterpreted.

"We know you care about the lightning cub," Ares said kindly. "We understand. And we will help you find her."

"I just care about Adonis." Aphrodite wanted to make clear. "If they are together, then I suppose we are united once again."

The room turned to Hecate. "I have no choice, do I? Death needs to come back and resign *properly*. Otherwise I'll hunt him next."

Their unity should have happened when Zeus disappeared, but he was thankful to have it now. He couldn't search the world by himself and he couldn't search fast enough for his own liking. He looked to Ares who nodded with the know-how of a god who specialized in conflict and action. He removed his coat, rang for something stronger than tea, rolled up his sleeves and prepared for work.

Chapter 24

Hera & Hades

She awoke with a start. As if her life was forcibly wedged between her breasts. She gasped for air. She heaved as she clutched a hand to her heart and tried to roll over to her side for stability.

"Easy now," a soothing voice came to her.

Her eyes fluttered open. Her lashes were heavy and damp. Her body was cold and clammy. Mobility within her muscles was slowly permeating through her like water being dyed with paint, one drop at a time.

She felt a smooth surface being placed on her lips. She opened them, feeling the chilled sliver of water coating her tongue and soothing her sore throat. She took a few sips. The glass was removed. She was staring into the eyes of Hades who was sitting in a chair beside her, as if he had been watching her through the night.

"Hades…" she said harshly. "…Damn you."

"I am sorry to do that to you. I know the aftertaste is dreadful." He gestured to a small cup of strawberries and cream. She could smell the ginger. She would rather slap him than let him feed her, but she wanted the bitterness that coated her tongue to subside.

She opened her mouth as he spoon-fed her. She glared with each swallow. Hades had removed her soul from her body and trapped it within his pocket watch. She didn't remember anything after that. Just being in darkness, slightly aware of what happened without a sense of time. It was his *power*. If Zeus commanded the skies and Poseidon the seas, if Ares had his spears and Athena her strength, Hades could extract souls as if he were picking petals from a flower. If these abilities were granted to a madman, the possibilities of chaos one could design would be endless.

For now, she was mostly hopeless. And tired. And the way he was looking at her, it made her body feel unnaturally warm.

"Why are you doing that?" he asked.

"Doing what?"

"You keep looking away from me."

She didn't realize she was. If so, what did it matter to him? He was in no position to be questioning her. Arching her shoulders, trying to coax her muscles, she made sure to look at him directly.

"You stole my soul."

He was vexed. As if he wouldn't dare *steal* anything from her. "You needed to rest."

"I was fine."

"When was the last time you've eaten something? A full meal?"

She didn't have an answer. She had sipped a few cups of tea here and there but sitting at her table alone had made her appetite flee her. She didn't expect him to understand. Hades was unmarried. Alone in the Underworld with no one to share his table. She imagined him sitting in his chair in the cramped dining room. Nothing but his books to keep him company on most nights. His piano playing was horrific so his only real source of music would be her peacocks. She imagined him...she imagined him…

"Sweetheart—" he rose suddenly from his chair and sat on the bed beside her. She sank with the weight of him, nearly collapsing into his side. "What's wrong? Why are you crying?"

Was she? Oh, she was. In her crafting of his image, in her private belittling of him, she had only described herself. A painful picture of loneliness who had driven everyone else away. She was exhausted, she told herself. It was why she was allowing him to bring her closer to him. Why she was allowing herself to sink into his embrace.

He was holding her like a child. Her rear was placed on one side of his hips while her legs rested across him. He supported her back with one arm, stroking her hair while drying her face with the other. His touch was tender. His fingers were smooth. He was carrying the weight of her worry. As if everything that had ever bothered her, centuries of anger and resentment, were overflowing from her cup and he was holding out his hands to catch it.

"You've always been kind to me," she whispered. "I've never understood why." He tightened his hold on her as his chin rested on her crown. "You've always been open and honest as I've been cruel. I've said horrible things to everyone. And yet...like Zari...you...you're never short with me."

She felt the muscles of his throat as he swallowed. He was probably wanting to chastise her. If he did, she would allow every word to wound her as punishment. Zeus had been quick to put her in her place, and she realized that she had grown used to it. The affection she had received over the past few months was a dream. It was a dream of which she was undeserving.

"Hera..." he whispered. "There's something I need to—"

He paused as her fingers trailed the outline of his jaw. Strange, he had stubble. She had never seen him with it before. It was dark, unlike the silver that sprouted from his head. It made him look different enough for her to notice. She was noticing everything.

His eyes were so light around the rims. Like a disc with a hollow center. His lips were perfectly thin, and his nose was strong and regal. Her gaze followed the curve of his neck, tucked underneath his sleeping shirt. She didn't see a stray hair on his skin. He was smooth and clean.

He touched her hand with his own. He gave her fingertips a kiss. He kissed the base of her thumb and then her wrist. She spread her fingers on the shape of his jaw and brought him into her. She felt his heat on her lips, hovering for a moment as if questioning his fortune. She leaned in. He met her. Their lips came together in a wave of fever that made her release a deep and effortless breath.

His kiss was sensual and soft. His touch was not timid but careful. He was treating her like fine china. As if she were so pure that the first hint of intimacy would make her succumb to a nervous condition. It was she who pressed him. Who was firm and wanting. Until his lips parted and his velvety tongue slid into her and explored. Tasting her. Leaving nothing untouched.

She moaned as her hands wove around his neck. He was caressing her cheek, his fingers through her hair. He was holding her so close she inhaled his fresh scent. She was sure she was quite the opposite. That the scent of distress was a layer on her skin that needed to be scrubbed with heavy sandpaper. She wanted his scent on her. She wanted him on her.

"Hera…" he whispered in her ear. Kissing her there and breathing rapidly. "I…"

She didn't want to hear his logic or a joke or anything. She just wanted him to have her. She wanted him to say nothing. She kissed him again, silencing him with her body, writhing in his arms and bringing back the silence.

Nothing between them.

Just love.

Their kiss continued as he lowered her onto the softness of the duvet. They had to part but only for a moment. He spoke this promise with a brush to her temple. He was encouraging her to lay on her side. With care, he began to remove her slippers. One after the other until he sat them both on the floor. His fingers gave her toes a gentle squeeze before brushing their way up her legs, teasing the hems of her skirts and ending at her back. She took a deep breath as he relieved her of her stays. When her dress was open, he slid it down her shoulders, freeing her arms. He pulled it from her waist and over her legs. She felt him leave it on the chair he had once occupied. She felt him threading his fingers through her hair, searching for the last few pins that held bits of it in place.

Her back was to him, but his shadow danced on the walls in the pale candlelight. She heard two thuds hitting the floor. His shoes, perhaps. She saw his figure lift something over his shoulders. His shirt. She hoped. She felt the mattress sink behind her as his arms wrapped around her waist and he turned her to face him. His body hovered over hers for a moment. He was looking into her eyes. He then positioned them both on their side as if they were about to tell one another a precious secret that was dangerous and spectacular.

She ran her fingers on the soft ridges of his body. He wasn't brawny, but he was defined and comforting in his subtle edges. Beautiful. A beautiful, beautiful being. Except for a scar on his arm. A burn maybe? It was healing, but she could see the shape of uneven skin. A scar among ichor would have been something to question. But now wasn't the time for questions.

His hands stroked the silky fabrics of her chemise. They began at the curve of her stomach until they cupped her breast. When he flicked his thumb over her nipple, she gasped. He inhaled her sound with a kiss. She couldn't remember the last time she was tender there. She couldn't remember the last time a surge of heat rushed between her thighs and made her as slippery as his tongue.

He brought her leg over his own and brought her in close. They were tasting one another, holding one another, until she felt him at the opening of her undies. Laying side by side, the tip of him entered her. Her world became a sea of color as he held her firm and pressed.

The first wave came so quickly, she was a bit embarrassed. He felt so good, pulsing inside of her inch by inch. He was throbbing and hot, but also teasing and patient. As she shivered from the pleasure, she tried to tighten her hold on him with her thighs. But he was more in control than she realized. She saw the corner of his lips rise as he held her in place, demanding that she let him take the lead.

She was squirming now. Moaning. Gasping. Pleading.

The feeling was surreal, she thought she would explode if he didn't relieve her again. His teasing of her nipples and kissing of her neck only heightened her passion.

"...Damn you..." she cursed. He chuckled low and sinisterly. He clenched her rear and adjusted her leg to widen her. He gave her what she wanted. What she had been missing. A deep, hard plunder that had him burying himself within her. Her muscles gripped him with fervor.

Their coupling made Hera feel somehow complete, as if they were two halves of a heart becoming whole. Her arms wrapped around him as she whimpered with ecstasy. As he moaned her name into her flesh and pumped harder. Faster. When she threw her head back, he grunted into the delicate surface of her chest. They stayed for an immeasurable moment, clutching each other tightly as they trembled and shook. Still holding on to him, she closed her eyes and went to sleep.

***

She awoke to the tickling sensation of his fingers stroking her thigh. He had pulled down her undies, partially, to expose the arch of her hips. He was drawing invisible lines on her skin in tiny circles. He was behind her and she could feel him kissing the back of her neck and shoulders. His hand traveled up her stomach, brushing her breast, until he cupped her chin and turned her for their lips to reintroduce themselves.

"One day, we will do this properly," he said with a grin.

"Properly?"

"You without clothing. Me worshipping you first."

"Worshipping?" She couldn't help but chuckle. She couldn't remember the last time she did. Oh, yes, when Zari was here. As if the small nugget of joy was in danger of being lost, he kissed her again.

"You sleep well?" he asked, wanting to take on one matter at a time.

"I think so. How long was I—"

"It's morning. Early, but morning."

She looked past him to the curtains. They were open and it was still dark outside. She had gotten a few hours of necessary rest. She wished she had the strength for more. He must have been up for far longer, for when he lifted himself from the bed, she could see a tray behind him on the table near the window. He brought it over to her, waiting for her to get comfortable. Her chest was partially bare and colored from their heat. She didn't mind. Nor did he.

He watched her as she nibbled on toast and fruit. He wanted to make sure she ate. She wanted to lean into his fingers when they reached for her cheek, but she couldn't allow herself to be blinded by one night of lust. No matter how much she longed for him, she knew that what they did was a moment of weakness on her behalf. He had shown restraint in the beginning. She was the one who practically demanded him.

"There will not be a next time," she said passively, although she watched his expression carefully. "We can't do this anymore."

He looked to the window and displayed nothing that would have implied that he was hurt or angry. His tone was mild as he sat in the little chair. His trousers were on. The top button of his shirt was unclasped. He leaned forward. His arms rested on his knees before he reached for his shoes. Somewhere in her slumber, or resting soul, he had retrieved proper clothing.

"Why not?" he asked without eye contact.

"Need I remind you that I am married?"

"Need you confirm to me that you are in fact married, yes."

"Hades—"

"Zeus has been missing for months. Perhaps it is time we all face facts. Your husband is gone."

"You don't know that."

Hades challenged her with a look she hadn't seen before. As if he was going to ask her to prove it. She matched him. Although her ichor could feel one another, in sporadic moments like a whisper on the wind, she did not *feel* her husband. And she did not grieve either. She was waiting for him to throw that in her face. But just because she did not miss him did not mean that she didn't deserve answers. They all did. Even Zari deserved to know who or what she was.

"Do you know what would happen if Zeus saw the two of us together?"

"He would be angry," Hades smirked. "He would try to kill me."

"And humiliate me." She brought her knees to her chest. Zeus had reprimanded her with cruel and childish punishments. She hadn't thought much of it in the past. She didn't want to think of it now. But since she was finally experiencing freedom for the first time in ages, she was realizing just how toxic her marriage was. Hades reached out to take hold of her hand, his humor diminishing.

"I wouldn't let that happen. I'd keep you with me in the Underworld where he could not get to you. Or…until *I* figured out a way to get rid of him."

She chuckled. Hades was not the type to combat another physically. He was cunning and intelligent, which made her feel a match between the two of them would be interesting and long winded. She also couldn't ignore him when he said he would keep her. She couldn't ignore it, but she acted as though she did. She reached for a piece of toast and he released a sigh.

"Hera, Zeus treated you horribly. He was unfaithful and rude, and I never liked him because of it. I've always admired the strength you had with him, I was a bit jealous actually, wishing you would turn to me more often. But I have to speak my mind now—"

"Have you not been doing that already?"

"I have always wanted you with me." She lowered her lashes and looked away. She didn't want to hear this. She tried to put distance between them, but he sat on the bed again and did his best to look into her eyes. "This is a second chance, for all of us."

"What are you saying?" She closed her eyes and awaited a confession. One she knew was coming and one she feared.

"I am saying that I love you. I am saying that a mistake was made in your union. You should be spending eternity with me."

There. He said it. She thought she could taste his affection on the tip of his tongue, on the curve of his lips. Her feelings for Hades were strong but also, new. He had had time to come to peace with his emotions. Her head was still spinning from the past few days.

"No mistakes were made, Hades. I married the ichor of my choosing."

"So, you would do it all over again." This time his voice was stern. More than she had ever heard. "Do you feel nothing for me? Do you feel everything for him?"

Her silence made him stand to his feet. For once, he seemed truly upset with her. This was the treatment she should have had from him in the beginning. It was his fault for being so nice to her when he knew that she was heartless. What they had was special and she would cherish it. But a relationship between them was unrealistic. He was the logical sort, wasn't he? It worried her that he could not see the larger picture. It made her feel insane. Was she the only one who hadn't lost her mind, or had it left her long ago?

"I love you and want to cherish you forever. Is that not what you deserve?"

"This isn't about me."

"It is. Hera, you've been given a pardon. You can have love. You can have a family."

"A pardon? Family? What are you—"

"I know you've wanted children. You told me once, long ago. I thought Zari would have reminded you of that. Has she not given you relief from that void? Isn't the hurt you feel for her what a mother would feel for a child?"

"She is a friend..."

"For fuck's sake," he said. "You know she means more to you than that! *I* mean more to you than that! Time with Zeus has made you doubt anyone who shows you affections and it's—" He stopped, realizing this wasn't his nature to yell and be combative. The silence between them was painfully heavy. Like a thick cloud of black smoke. "I don't want to fight with you..." he whispered as he tugged on his coat. The promise of next time was disappearing before her eyes.

She wished she had the strength to tell him to stay. She wanted him to stay. She wanted him in bed with her. She wanted him to take away all of her pain. When he reached for the door, he paused. He looked back at her, as if he were reading her mind. As if he wanted to come to her. But he kept his distance. His smile was heartbreaking.

"I wouldn't mind more dinners with the three of us at my home." He released a soft breath. "Finish your breakfast and take your time getting ready. I will see you downstairs. There's something we need to discuss."

Chapter 25

Artemis

On the back of her stag, she retraced her steps for the fourth time. It wasn't like them to lose a scent. To lose a trail of not one, but three different beings. One of them, human. Her skills as a huntress had made her comfortable in the woods that everyone else avoided. The tall trees, heavy pines and thick oaks were dusted in poison that could be mistaken for morning ash. The barks were lined with the most patient breed of snakes. The ground would come alive at night, as insects shimmied to the surface, ready to feed. Most impressive of all was that many of Gaia's invalids took refuge here.

There was a small colony of cyclops that rested in the caves. Even deeper than that, the hecatoncheires were getting restless. An earthquake had unsettled them. It had caused the forest to stir. But long before that, before her slow and ignorant ichor had sought her help, she knew that something was amiss. She knew the moment the young Godking had disappeared.

She would have ignored Poseidon and Ares' request for her help, but she was protective of the land in which she lived and nobody else could do what she could. Because of her cunning nature, stealth and adaptability, Zeus had allowed her to protect the forest as if it were a realm of its own. She kept the invalids happy, fed and governed. She made sure the beasts of fifty heads and one hundred arms remained dormant and lazy. She clothed those who camped with her—teaching them to hunt, garden and gather. She was a leader here. As efficient as the kings. But without Zari, without the presence of the Godking's power, it was as if the world was collapsing into itself.

A slow and steady decline had begun. With strict command, she ordered her nymphs, oceanids, warriors and amazons to spread out and search the woods. She had Zari's scent from a gown that Poseidon had brought with him. She smirked as she told him that it also carried notes of almonds and coconut. He blushed and said no more.

She could smell a lot of things in addition to adolescent infatuation. She could smell...mature infatuation. As with Hades and Hera. Whenever the Soul King was in Olympus, the scent of desire carried heavily on him. She could smell the competing nurture and jealousy rising within Persephone. Her dear sister ichor was so confused that it made Artemis shake her head with pity. She could smell compassion from Aphrodite, although the ichor tried to prove she was without it. She could smell the insecurities of Ares. An ichor who wished he possessed the knowledge of how to comfort.

She was not without her own troubles, however. At one point, Artemis had reached a dead end during her search for the Godking. Zari *had* gone into the woods, that much was clear. But eventually the scent scattered and disappeared. As if she'd suddenly vanished. Perhaps, she was dead. Obliterated like everyone assumed Zeus had been. Had she brought forth the possibility, she knew her short-tempered ichor would burn the world without delay. And for the sake of her reputation, and everyone involved, she thought it best to try again.

Without much confidence in the trail of the Godking, she would have used the scent of Adonis. However, he often spent his time outdoors and smelled of many breeds of flowers and many notes of various perfumes. All that was left, was Death.

She visited the Underworld, specifically where he worked. She gathered his travel logs from Janus, looking for any trends within his routes. She learned that Death was a connoisseur of cheese and made frequent stops at the fromagerie whenever he was gathering souls. Vendors remembered him—the hooded figure who hid his face from a questionable skin condition. What puzzled them now was the sight of Artemis and her two stag companions. A bare-foot ichor dressed in fur and hunting bows. Her stags meaty, eyes piercing.

Death's shopping list included brie, muenster, and limburger. She and her stags took no pleasure inhaling each sample they were given. Especially his most recent purchase—a Roquefort that smelled as dangerous as it looked. It was their rope she extended to the fastest fliers of her forest. Her birds carried the scent on their wings without complaint. They confirmed what she had deduced from her search, that the missing beings were not in Greece. Her birds returned from the continent, from the island, from the far east. Disappointment kneading on their shoulders like the secrets of the Soul King. Meditating beneath the trees, using her ability to see what they allowed her to see, she suddenly found herself someplace warm and bright. Where the sun assaulted the skin and the trees bore fruit. There was sand. Lots of sand. Makeshift homes, tall trees, monkeys and—*them*. Her body was tired from using her abilities in such a strenuous matter, but somehow, she had the strength to fight off a fit of laughter. One that caused a few of the women who resided in her woods to exchange dubious looks as they washed themselves near the bank of the river.

Chapter 26

Hera

After a bath and fresh clothing, Hera applied extra moisturizer to her hands, face and the delicate rings just below her eyes. Her emotions were like currents that swelled after each repeating pulse. From the settled feeling of having become so close to Zari, to the disgust in herself for pushing her away. From the daze of Hades' care to the proclamation of his love. And her rejection.

She felt her migraines returning with a scheduled rhythm. Everything had changed so rapidly that she couldn't decide which alterations were for the best. She wanted Zari. She wanted Hades. But it was her duty to suppress her wants for the sake of her position, as she tried to instill in the new Godking. As she gazed at her hopeless reflection, she was reminded of how much fight there was within the heart.

The sun was rising now. As would Zari if she were present. Early to wake, bored in less than hour, Hera had planned for Zari to become more involved with Olympus by shadowing other ichor who rose at the crack of dawn—she could get in some extra training time with Hephaestus, Athena could teach her how to ride Caelus or Demeter could teach her about crops and farming. After, they would say good morning over breakfast. Zari would stack her plate too high while Hera reminded her to tuck in her fingers when she sipped her tea.

"You look as though you are sending signals to mate," Hera once told her. The girl laughed so hard she nearly choked on a strawberry. Hera had smiled too. As she was smiling now.

There was too much to do. Too many conversations to have, banter to exchange and experiences to witness. Hera did not believe their time together was over. Gathering her drive, she opened the door and joined the others. When she arrived downstairs and into the receiving room, she saw Hades standing with Artemis. Although he was dressed, the one button that was unfastened at his collar retold the story of their morning. She blushed. Wondering if he smelled of their passion. Of her embarrassing weakness. His smile was polite but guarded. Like Zari, he was wounded by her and would approach with caution. He exchanged a few words to Artemis and glanced at Hera with a worrisome expression.

"I've already called Poseidon, who is in Oceanus," he informed Hera. "I've sent a footman out to find Ares. Do you mind seeing if Aphrodite and Persephone are awake?"

"They're here?"

"Apparently they arrived yesterday, while you and I were—"

"Right," she mumbled as she looked to the floor. Only hours ago, they were cuddled together in Zari's cold bed. He appeared to want to reach out and touch her, but she stepped away, quickly assuming the task of searching for her ichor. Artemis, who saw the exchange, appeared to think nothing of it.

They stood when Hera found them in the sunroom. They were sitting across from one another, papers spread between them, appearing to be involved.

"What is all of this?" she asked. She didn't want to stare too long. Looking at Persephone, she felt a bit flighty. Afterall, the ichor who was sharing a bed with her was the one Persephone was attempting to persuade into marriage. And Hades didn't want her—however fair and lovely she was. He made that clear.

"A manifest," Persephone said softly. "All the homes we've checked. All the ichor we've asked."

"Color coded by realm," Aphrodite sighed. "None have seen them."

So, they were involved. And in a cause that wasn't benefiting themselves—*wait*. "Did you say, 'them?'"

Persephone and Aphrodite exchanged glances that told Hera that she had missed quite a bit in the past few hours. As they took their time heading downstairs, they explained.

"And now Artemis is here." Persephone shook her head at the ichor that was a sister by Demeter's adoption of them both. Two sisters who couldn't be more different. "Not sure if that's good or not."

"With her, no news is oftentimes good news." Aphrodite tugged on her gloves.

Oddly enough, Aphrodite extended her arm to Hera, escorting her to the dining hall like a widow approaching the altar of her dead husband. How she should have felt when Zeus disappeared. This wasn't comforting, as her time of distress did not make her any softer towards *all* of her ichor. But if it made Aphrodite feel useful, she supposed she could tolerate it.

It took a few moments to gather into the dining hall, and Hera was growing impatient. Poseidon had arrived, looking aggravated and weary. They exchanged brief and mutual nods that meant that nothing was forgiven because the responsibility of the blame was accepted from both sides.

"Well?" His eagerness matched her own.

Artemis, standing adjacent to them made sure the doors were secured. "I did not come in contact with them," she said. Hera felt as though the ground was going to give way beneath her feet. Artemis, the renowned huntress, could not find Zari. Neither could Poseidon or Hades or Ares or anyone. It was Hades who took hold of Hera, allowing her to lean on him. It was Hades who instructed her to take a breath. This display of affection between them was studied by the ichor in attendance—again, Artemis paid no mind. "Not dead, simply gone," she continued. "In the sense of a holiday."

Poseidon repeated her words. As he did, his eyes widened and turned to Hades. In that moment, the three of them—the Ocean King, the Soul King and the huntress—were on the same page regarding the whereabouts of Zari and her friends. Whatever it was, Poseidon was not amused. "Hades….you said…"

"I know what I said," Hades mumbled. "I still don't know how their paths crossed. I am just as stunned as you are."

Artemis blinked, pleased that the ability to deduce information wasn't lost on all her ichor. There was hope for them yet. "It explains why no one has been able to locate them. It explains why the world has taken note of their absence, although they are very much alive."

"Pray they are not in Gaia's clutches," Ares sung, holding out his hands. "What? Has the thought not crossed our minds? We all know that if that were the case, 'gone' wouldn't be the correct word to describe their misfortune. It would be...*disintegrated*. A holiday, only if one's goal was ultimate demise."

Hera was in fact praying. To all the gods she knew. None of her ichor were strong enough to face Gaia head on. In a battle of strength, they would fail. Gaia brought them into the world as little figurines that were shaped by her fingers and imagination. They were gods, yes. But only gods with titles. Gaia was a primordial deity bred directly from Chaos. The mother of Titans. The one to be feared. In the grand scheme of things, they were pittance in her pockets. With a little bit of water and her carpenter fingers, they were nothing more than pliable parts.

"Ares—"

"Sai, I vow to you, I vow to the lightning cub, that I would not short myself as a volunteer in this endeavor. As Olympus' strongest warrior—"

"You are not the strongest warrior."

"If you're talking about Athena--"

"I'm talking about me!" Poseidon clutched his hands together. "And this isn't even important. Gaia has nothing to do with Zari."

"So you know where she is too." Hera looked from Poseidon to Hades. All eyes were on the Soul King. Even Artemis was sighing as if he needed to get on with it.

"They're...in...Mexico." Hades struggled to reveal.

"What?" Hera's revulsion for his answer, reassuring perhaps, was the support her legs needed. She pulled away from Hades and turned to Artemis, positive there must have been a mistake. "Why would they...out of all places…"

"Strong magic surrounds them. Similar to that of the dear Mother Gaia." Artemis looked to the windows, as if longing for the time when she could return to the comfort of her woods and her intelligent companions. "Similar to that of someone who doesn't want to be found. The question remains, who wouldn't want to be?"

Who wouldn't want to be found?

Who, like Gaia, would even have the power to disappear?

And why would Zari seek this someone out?

"Hades," she blinked, long and hard. "The next words out of your mouth had better be the truth. Out with it, *now.*"

When his lips mouthed the name, she did not believe she had heard him correctly. He looked at her and looked away. Shame dyed his features. A substantial, agonizing and gut-wrenching silence had followed.

"Did you say...Zeus?" Persephone was the one to break the silence. "The Godking is with...the Godking?"

"Zeus is alive?"

"Zeus has been alive this entire time?"

"What is he doing with Zari?"

The onslaught of accusations was directed at Hades who took a seat in one of the chairs. He needed a drink, desperately. But if two fingers of whiskey were enough to provide him with good health, Hera would deprive him of it. She was so angry, so hurt, so confused she didn't know where to begin. She didn't know who to put an end to first.

Artemis cleared her throat, voicing her own concerns. "As you know, this is where my services end. Although, in exchange for my help, I would like assistance when it comes to fending off the hecatoncheires. Because of the Godking's absence, they are growing bold and restless. They feel as though there is nothing here protecting Olympus. Need I explain how dire this could be?"

"I have to go to her," Hera said numbly.

"I'll go with you." Hades' eyes were pleading. As if his assistance was all he had left. But she didn't want him anywhere near her. She didn't want anything to do with him. Everything was clear. Hades did have secret intentions all along. A plan that involved her husband's disappearance. Not only did he know that Zeus was alive, but he knew where he was. He could have told her. He should have.

You've been given a pardon.

She would have dismembered him outright, had he not been the only ichor who knew where they were going. For that reason alone, she would spare him his life and spare herself the tears.

"I will go too," Poseidon said.

217

"No." Hera was adamant that he remain. Hades was a necessity to find Zari, Poseidon was necessary to protect Olympus.

"Zari is mine," Poseidon said to everyone's silence. "If Zeus gives you any trouble, I can best him. I can bring her home."

Hera, a testament to her growth and understanding, placed her hand on Poseidon's shoulder. She lowered her chin and spoke calmly to him. "I know you care for her. As do I. But it is best you stay here. There are three hecatoncheires. Between you, Athena and Ares, you will need to stick together. Go, help Artemis."

"No." He was as stubborn as she. And Ares didn't help matters when he adjusted his neckcloth and puffed out his chest.

"I can take on all three invalids." He turned to Artemis. "Me and my spears will—"

"Hephaestus will do just fine," she said. "I can make do with Poseidon's generals in his absence."

That was that. It would be the three of them. She, Hades and Poseidon would prepare to travel to Mexico and place themselves in an odd reunion. Hera bit into her lip and headed towards the hall. Hades had followed her and would have continued to do so had she not turned to him abruptly, daring him to take another step.

"Hera...I'm so sorry. I did not want to keep this from you, but Zeus and I—"

"You've known all this time."

"I didn't. Not at first. But he reached out to me…for…for…"

"For. What."

"M-money."

"You've been giving him money?"

"It's a long story—"

"One filled with false truths, no less. All you've been doing is lying to me. This entire time. Leading me to believe…" She smirked. "With him gone, what did you think would happen? You were pushing Zari into Poseidon's arms, and for what purpose? Were you expecting her to go with him to Oceanus? Were you wanting the throne free of a king so that you could simply plant yourself—"

"Don't do that," he rumbled. "Don't act as though Zeus' existence changes what we've had. What we've shared—" He reached out to her, and she evaded him like a cat avoiding capture.

"I can't believe I let you touch me." She spun on her heels and ascended the stairs without him. He felt his arm being brushed by Aphrodite, who said nothing as she swept in to take on the role of Hera's confidant. Doing what ladies did—believing the other was in desperate need of free advice and wine.

"Will you sail there?" A soft voice was behind him. Persephone was standing with her arms by her side and her demeanor small. "It is a bit of a journey to Mexico." He assumed the group had used Death's travel methods to get there. Using his own, it would only take a matter of minutes, he explained. "I see," she said. "I can prepare a small luncheon for your trip. For the three of you."

In her eyes, he saw the truth. That he had hurt not only one, but two of his ichor. Both were deserving of love and kindness. His secrets, his selfishness, had robbed them of it.

"I...I'm sorry..." he said. His apology was heartfelt and definite. For no matter the outcome, he would never stop fighting for Hera's forgiveness. Persephone came forward. Her lips trembled as they parted.

"I'm sorry too."

She bowed to him before disappearing down the hall and out of his sight. Perhaps, out of his life for a while. All that was left was Ares, who pressed his lips to the side and whistled.

"No matter, Hera still loves you."

Hades' eyes widened. "You believe so?"

"What the hell do I know? About love of all things." Ares shrugged. "I just wanted to say that to make you feel better. I mean, it's not fun being the most hated deity in the universe and you are *currently* more hated than Death. And that doesn't feel good does it? To be more hated than Death? Now, even for a moment, I've made you feel better, yes?"

Ares gave him a firm pat on the shoulder and met Artemis in the foyer. The two of them exchanged a brief word before he followed her out the door.

Chapter 27

Zeus?

He left his wife for a taco stand.

He left his throne in a palace made of glass and crystal for a four-by-four shack on a stretch of beach in Tulum. He swapped his saucers for the flat discs of lime and corn tortillas. The only gold to grace his tables were the cubes of pineapple and fresh oranges. Shreds of tassels were replaced by thinly sliced greens. Harmonic whistles of colorful jays did not pierce his brain like the cries of those dreadful peacocks. The people fished on planks of wood. There were parties on Wednesdays and clothing was optional. The freeing of one's skin was not limited to baths, bedtime, and the seasons. And here, the weather never doubted itself.

No neck cloths.

No ichor.

No responsibilities.

Flesh and fresh air were everywhere.

Zack's Taco Shack was wedged between a water closet, a cluster of trees occupied by spider monkeys and a path that led to a temple resort that was built by a tribe of handymen and women. The residents were a small and private community, who also didn't mind the business of tourists. Cozumel, Cuba, Florida—there was no end to the variety of human beach advocates. Individuals who were seeking themselves and new discovery. On holiday. Escaping with mistresses. And in need of tacos.

His morning consisted of fishing for his ingredients. Mahi-mahi, grouper, snapper, barracuda. It was easy, being a former Godking. His powers had dwindled but they had not left him completely, so as he would wade out into the water, he swung his toes through the waves and emitted a tiny pulse of electricity. The fish would rise to the surface, either stunned or deceased. He would lift them into his fishing basket, always surprised by the contents of his catch.

He would proceed into the forest with his knapsack. Twirling small bolts between his fingers, he would flick them at the stem of raised fruit and the monkeys who tried to beat him to his harvest. Every now and again, if he were in a giving mood, he would shake a tree or two to leave coconuts for the wild boar. He often considered catching said boar and keeping him as a boxing companion.

By noon he would be back in his shack. It had an upper level where a cot rested on the floor, and above him a ceiling board that was misplaced so that he could gaze into the sky at night. Below was the kitchen and living area, which consisted of an array of makeshift furniture. Counters that were formally old shipping crates, stuffed wicker baskets and vibrant pottery with cracks along the rim. He had a long counter that was covered in pressed banana leaves and palm. Beyond that were a few tables on an uneven floor for dining in case the weather was a bit damp. The walls were open to his shack. More tables and crates for chairs were shoved into the sand and facing the ocean. Fishermen and explorers were the only ones out at the moment.

Soon, the crowds would begin to gather. Peddlers sold services of four sticks and a hammock. They would fan those who were willing to pay for relief. They would bring drinks and food to earn their wages. Glaring at the equally dilapidated shack a few rows down—between a fabric weaver and a painter—the strumming of a vihuela and coos of an ocarina came from *Hector's Tostadas*. The worthiest adversary he had had in centuries. They took a moment to leer at one another.

The high sun was bright enough to illuminate his space. Although he always had the advantage of a hidden supply of electricity if he needed, he preferred to not rely on his powers too much. He also had to be conservative as to not draw attention to himself. The veil that shrouded his island protected him from the outside world. It prevented the powers of other ichor and deities from locating him. But whatever came in, could witness a miracle performed by the former Godking. For secrecy's sake, much had to be done by hand. Which he enjoyed.

His cooking was done on a central grill that was coated in old skin and burned flakes of homemade seasoning. His mind eyed his ingredients as he thought of the day's special. What would drive customers to Zack's instead of Hector's? A slow grin spread across his face as he reached for a nearly petrified paint brush out of a bucket of black ink. He found an old piece of cardboard and wrote:

Delisuse Eel! Raw. Fresh. Kookeded. Eatible. And drink! Approved by the GODS!

The words were slanted and crammed into one another. He went outside his shack and wedged it between the posts that upheld the roof. He went to his storage and found a cluster of eels that were swimming among the dead corpses of soggy fish that were the catch of the day—two days ago. At the eruption of sunlight, they tried to shock him when he stuck his hand in. He laughed at their futile attempts.

Above him were an assortment of butcher knives and machetes. His meaty hands were not built for the small blades of a human, so he had no choice but to hang the more domineering weapons above his head for efficiency. He then wondered if he should remove the head of the eel? Lobster was boiled alive and tasty. One only removed the tails after the cooking. This, he thought, would be his only dilemma for the day.

The eel tried to wrap around his arm in defense. He ignored it as he decided to work on his sides and sauces. Since he had not cleaned the grill for the past few days, diners would have no choice but to accept the seasoning of old salmon residue. If the skin was the best part, then he had plenty of it that would stick to the eel once it simmered. He could make a pineapple reduction with a bit of chopped shrimp that he had around here, somewhere. He only needed to follow the smell until he found it. He also had a bit of dark chocolate he found from a vendor. Dark chocolate mixed with chili. Rare in some parts of the world. That settled it—his masterpiece!

Eel coated in seasoned salmon and reduced in aged shrimp, mystery chili, bitter chocolate and pineapple juice. And of course, fresh tortillas. His own recipe he made from corn he had bought from a woman who sold jewelry. Corn which he pounded into submission with his bare hands and brute strength and bound together by a bit of whipped grouper.

If his food was horrible, his earnings spoke otherwise. Women, especially, would fill his shack to get a taste of him, especially at work. His muscles worked tirelessly from the labor of his creativity. From his genius. He was being worshipped and praised in an entirely new way. More often than not, he had to catch them when they swooned after a sip of his Strawberry and Salmon Smoothie. Each was spiked with spirits befitting of a god's consumption.

He was that generous.

That perfect.

That skilled.

People fell to his feet from the ecstasy of his creations. They were so pleased with his food, they convulsed at the mouth with soapy foam. Some even died. His food was so delicious, people chose him as their last meal.

He went to the back, wondering if he should double the quantity of eel for his special. And in search of the lost shrimp. He found them wrapped in an old cloth that was next to the water closet. He must have been relieving himself one evening before leaving it there. Lucky he found it.

Whistling to himself, his tattered sandals kicked dirt as he made his way inside. His joy diminished, as well as the hope for an agreeable morning, when he stopped at the sight of three pairs of eyes. And they had not come for the food.

Poseidon.

Hades.

And Hera. *Fuck.*

Thinking quickly, he beamed. Wide and welcoming.

"Welcome to Zack's," he said. "My name is Zack and always has been. I am a native, I am and always...has been. I have always lived here and nowhere else. In this lovely, distinguished, award-winning-potential restaurant that I—"

Hades shook his head from behind the two ichor. A case for memory loss would not work here. He scowled. He did not need one of Hera's earthquakes putting an end to *Zack's Taco Shack*. He held up a hand, the squirming eel wrapped around it and took a bite of his finger.

"Now, before you get upset—" The eel squeezed harder. Zeus gave the creature a firm shake. "Allow me to explain by you first explaining what it is you're doing here. Or perhaps you've heard of my famous tacos." The eel was digging into his flesh. A small trickle of golden blood fell down his finger. Zeus shook his hand again, trying to disarm the creature. "The special of the day is eel," he scowled. He shook the creature again. "Eel, charred in—" When he gave his hand one aggressive tug, the fish flew off his arm and whirled past Hera's chin and into the sandy beaches behind them. Zeus held up a finger and smiled, "Allow me to fetch that."

Chapter 28

Hades

"Perhaps we should take a seat?" Hades motioned.

His two ichor looked at him before lifting their brows to their surroundings. The place was offensive. A complete assailment of things they held dear as gods. Cleanliness for one thing. And for the sake of their eyes, an elementary sense of color theory.

There was sticky on the floor. Sticky. In a variety of densities. There were knives hanging from the ceilings and everything was *peeling*. The paint, the fruit, the skin of the fish on Zeus' prep station. The smell was so strong, he knew that Poseidon, King of the Oceans, was not being dramatic when he released a heavy breath that let them know he had been holding it. He looked pale and sick. Hades didn't know if he could catch both of them, Poseidon and Hera, if they decided to pass out.

"Perhaps, a seat outside? In the fresh air?"

"No air is fresh within two feet of this place," Poseidon grunted. He looked like an ichor in pain. "Need to get away..."

Hades took hold of his shoulders to steady him. "For Zari." He nodded until Poseidon's eyes, hazed liked a wounded soldier losing the will to go on, flickered with understanding. He was trying. He was desperately trying to keep a hold of himself, but the unskilled butchering of his beautiful sea creatures, the unsanitary conditions of live and dead meat sharing the same confinement, the dreadful decor and now, the sight of Zeus. It was all overwhelming.

From behind his counter, coming back into his shack, Hera gasped as if all the air had left the atmosphere. "What...What the *shit* are you wearing!?"

Zeus, the dirty eel in hand, glanced down at himself. His ichor was still attractive, even underneath his white, unkempt beard and russet skin. But even that was underneath a layer of sticky. Sticky. A coat of dark-colored grime was on his elbows. His shirt, or what she thought was a shirt, was cut in odd places and without sleeves. Who made shirts without sleeves? He also wore a pair of vibrant colored trousers that were too small for him, they appeared to be shorts. On his feet were sandals. Not the elegant bindings of Roman leather or lace, but a rough slapdash of twigs and leaves. The state of his fingernails was sickening. His dirty toes looked like sausages wedged between sausages.

"What are these colors!?" she growled. "What is this place!? Why do you smell like a donkey's ass and what is that!?"

She pointed to a small canister on a nearby surface. It was stacked with dirty paper. Paper that was assaulting them now as a gust of wind entered the shack and disturbed the odor.

"That is what you call, a *napkin dispenser.*"

"What?"

"You use the cloth to wipe your hands."

"Wipe your hands with paper!? Who are you!? And what have you done with Zeus!?"

Hades saw the opportunity in Zeus' eyes. An opportunity his ichor had to once again play the part of someone who had lost their memory. Someone beside himself. But Hades calmed the room with quick order. He asked for Zeus to join them outside. He attempted to pat Hera on her shoulders, but she shoved him and left. Poseidon walked behind her as if he were in a daze. Zeus' chuckle filled the tiny space.

"None of this is funny," Hades replied simply.

Zeus removed one of his machetes and threw the eel onto the prep space. As if to remind Hades that this was what he wanted. That a lifetime with Hera would never be unaccompanied by her temper.

"You are more than welcome to stay with me in my shack," Zeus said with a whack. "That is, if she doesn't murder you first."

***

"Tacos," she growled behind clenched teeth. "Tacos."

"Gourmet tacos," Zeus clarified when he joined them. "Eccentric. Eclectic. Gastronomical."

"Tacos."

"Of course, you were never happy with anything. I am a successful entrepreneur. A businessman."

"You are the King of Gods who left his position for a ruined shack and the name Zack! You've been alive this entire time! What happened? I need answers, now!"

"And Zari." Poseidon took deep breaths. He was slowly returning to himself. "We are looking for—"

"Yes, the whimpering creature who also abandoned her post. She is fine."

"Where?"

"One thing at a time. As much as I would love to veer this conversation, and your disruption of my hours of operation, elsewhere, my new lifestyle has brought upon a change in me. A change that brings with it understanding, patience and cooperation. You could do with a bit of relaxation, Hera. I can tell that you are considering in which order you plan to murder myself and Hades. Your head is throbbing with the most creative, slowest, painful, agonizing punishment you can think of." He placed a hand gently on the table. "It is warranted."

A pop from the shack made him stand to his feet. He was gone long enough for the three of them to take note of the bead of sweat at each other's brow. It was hot. Unbearably hot. But they would rather sit there and bake than spend one more minute in the shack.

If Hades were bold enough, he would offer his lap to Hera who was sitting on a wooden shipping box, afraid to touch anything. She could touch him. She could use him as a shield between herself and their foul surroundings. But in her eyes, at that moment, he was no better than the gunk that stuck to the bottom of his shoes. Poseidon crossed his arms, color returning to his cheeks.

This part of Mexico was covered in magic. Strong like Gaia's defenses of her studio. Hades assumed that Zeus had gotten the know-how from the last time they had spoken, in an effort to keep himself hidden. Zeus had often commented how he would leave it all if he could. When the opportunity presented itself, Zeus presented himself with an opportunity. He would have remained hidden had he not reached out to Hades for traveling help. Or for money to fund this endeavor.

It was a laughable idea, one that Hades did not think would bring him happiness. But seeing his ichor now, he was a bit lighter on his feet. He even smiled. His movement was slow and meaningless. Time away had done him well.

"We need to find Zari and get the hell out of here," Poseidon said.

"He said she's alright. I believe him."

"Do you know that?" Hera scowled. "How do you know he didn't hurt her or try to—" Before Hera could speak the damnable thing, before she could put images into Poseidon's mind that would make him conjure a storm that would drown the world, she finished, "Feed her."

Poseidon relaxed. A bit.

Just then, a thud of simmering food was being placed before them. Hera braced herself onto Poseidon's arm.

"The special," Zeus said proudly. "With a bit of extra. Brandy soaked pineapples, candied oranges, cabbage, slaw, cherry powder and oyster excretion. The tiny dot there, the little pearl, is a single caviar. And the dandelions are edible. Go on. Indulge."

Hera said nothing. She could barely swallow. Hades bit his lip and did his best to sound casual. "No...utensils?"

"Eat with your hands!" Zeus laughed and held out his own. An aroma came from them. One that made them each feel as though the world was tilting.

"What. Has. Happened. To. You." She trembled. She also noticed there was movement on her plate. Something wasn't dead all the way. "I'm going to...going to…"

Hades had hurried to catch her. He secured his arms around her and sat her in his lap. She cowered into him, scowling, but not moving from his embrace. Nor did Zeus chastise his ichor for holding his wife.

"I shall start at the beginning." Zeus took a chair and flipped it around so that his forearms leaned on the back. Jesus often sat like that. When he sipped coffee and said things like, *Mondays*. "I didn't want to rule Olympus anymore." He ran his fingers along his beard. "Simple as that."

"It is not as *simple as that,*" Hera snapped in Hades' arms. She almost brought them both to the sand. "You disappeared! You were gone! You've been gone for months! Were you ever planning on returning?"

"No, not really."

"So, what then, you were going to sit here and stay in this...this...*shit!*" Zeus leaned back, stunned that she would insult his masterpiece. "You are Zeus—"

"Zack." He pointed to himself. "And Zack's not going back. Come now Hera, I was bored."

"Bored of being a god?"

"Precisely. I get bored of a lot of things, really. And I credit my compulsiveness to my behaviors. At least, that is what my shaman told me. And the monks when they'd choose to speak." She mouthed the word *shaman.* "I was bored of ruling. The politics. The squabbles. If not one war, then another. If not one human, then another. And for *centuries.* Centuries with no end in sight. Even for the most libertine of men, vices get old and bothersome. I was looking for a change. I was wanting something different."

"Tacos?" She clutched Hades' shirt so tightly that it was beginning to rob him of air.

"Tacos today. Maybe calisthenics tomorrow. The point is, I've felt like a king for the first time in a long time. I can actually do as I please. No responsibility. I am king of my own life."

"But what about—" *me?* Hades could see it in her eyes. As entitled as Zeus was to his opinions, he had abandoned his realm and abandoned his wife. Even if he wanted a change, he did not communicate his unhappiness to her, and worse, he didn't think to include her in his future. He included none of them.

It was as Poseidon had told him once before. Personalities came in waves. Zeus was getting to know himself again and to do that, he needed to cleave himself of his former life.

Tacos today.

"I didn't want to leave like this," he said to Hera. "I understand why you are upset. But we were never happy. Not for a while. The state of our marriage has been written on your face for so long, my dear." Poseidon exchanged glances with Hades, wondering if he should be here for this sort of talk between husband and wife. But Zeus took a playful bite of his food. His eyes rolled back with pleasure. "The girl you're looking for. She was meant to be my parting gift to you."

"Zari?" Hera blinked. And for once, there was no hostility behind her voice. "What do you mean, Zari was a gift?"

"Shall you tell her, or shall I?" Zeus' aim at Hades made Hera remove herself from him. Hades was once again in possession of the truth. Another secret. "Zari is a result of a squabble over the mixing bowl." Zeus lifted a shoulder. "She is in essence, my child. She is in essence, his child too."

Chapter 29

Hera & Poseidon

Her skirts brushed the wild that was the jungle of Tulum. A path was paved with frequent travelers who made their way to the community of stone temples. Monkeys leapt overhead and seemed all too eager to run up to them in search of food or anything shiny. Poseidon noticed one trying to withdraw a tiny parcel from his upper pocket, grabbed the animal by the tail and set him on the ground. When the monkey tried to approach again, its friends eager with support, he sent a wave of wind and chilly water in all directions, causing them to scatter.

She noticed he used two fingers to open his pocket and peer inside. When he caught her staring, he reluctantly removed a small box from the folds and held it in his hand. She stopped.

"Poseidon—"

"It's not what it looks like. Although, I wish it were. To limit strife between us, to make things

easier for Zari, I can wait."

"May I?"

Hera was beside herself. Although, she had to keep her composure. She had already destroyed *Zack's Taco Shack*. Much to some stranger's delight. A man named Hector, she recalled. She flipped open the velvet cover. In the box was one of the most beautiful rings she had ever seen.

"It's a South Sea Pearl," he said of the radiant golden jewel. It was modest in size but abundant in the number of tiny diamonds that embraced the center stone. It looked like a ring that had captured the sun.

"It matches her eyes."

"Yes." He held out his hand and she almost didn't want to give it back. A jewel like that was rare, she could feel it. She wished some thought had gone into her own. Zeus had gifted her something so large it often shifted from side to side. She had to weld it to an additional band to keep it in place, thereby making it bigger. It symbolized a proper lady. One who was meant to sit silently and have her portrait painted. Not one that would push quills on parchment or wield a sword.

He looked at it for a moment before securing it into his pocket.

"You don't need to explain your feelings for her to me," she began, "as you have been the most transparent. Especially after all of this. I just hope you understand that I want Zari to have an opportunity to truly find her place here. Among the rest of us. I know now...assuming what she wants and forcing her into place, would be a mistake on my part. I know now that she should be given the opportunity to make more...mistakes."

The fear was the same between them. She couldn't belong to either of them. Not currently. There was a world out there she needed to explore. At the very least, she needed to tour other realms and meet other deities. She couldn't do that with the responsibility of being Poseidon's wife or the weight of being the Godking without more training. They needed to share her, not only between themselves, but with the universe.

***

A mixing bowl, apparently, was what stood between Zeus and Hades one day in a makeshift studio. There was a trapdoor in the floor of his bedchamber. One that was reserved for the cowardly if the palace were ever under siege and one needed to escape. "As if I would ever need to flee," Zeus would scoff. Therefore, the space went mostly unused. The tunnel led to a small room that was disguised as a shop. A shop within the mountain. It had a small window for light, a table on which rested a mound of clay and a large pot full of dirt. And stuff...everywhere. When Hades saw it for the first time, Zeus was pulling him inside and barking orders at him to be quick about it.

"Quick about what?"

"Your pocket watch. I need you to capture a soul before it—
damn." Zeus grunted over a mixing bowl that was pale and striped.
A flicker of light had illuminated and fizzled from its contents. He
began rummaging through a stockpile of materials—the room was
in the same condition as his taco shack—and was attempting to
pour, mix and sort. The only things that were kept from harm's reach
was a shelf that contained wads of earth. Hades furrowed his brow
as he approached the assortment of... *somethings*... that rested upon
it.

"You like them?" Zeus had said with a smirk. He was proud of
whatever *them* was. "Sculptures. Bodies. I used my own two hands
to make them."

"I think I would have deduced as much..." Hades turned back
to the forms. There were large fingerprints imprinted into the clay.
Uneven, wobbly orbs where a head must have been. And hair that
was made by sticking thin pieces into the skull to make for some sort
of shape. Uneven arms. Uneven legs. He would have feared what
would have become of them had they been given the opportunity to
live. Cruel as it may have sounded, Gaia's invalids were not for the
faint of heart.

Looking to the floor, among the sea of clutter, Hades spotted
a small basket of models that were far more appealing. Compared to
Zeus' clumps, these were perfect. Gaia's discards. A bit unfinished,
but not shy of being beautiful. He picked one up and looked into
the blank face of a woman. He blinked and sat it down again.

"Zeus, what are you doing?"

"How could Gaia not be inspired by *me*? It's unbelievable." He
responded so easily his tasks were uninterrupted. "Therefore, I am
making a child."

Hades thought his ears had betrayed him. "Why?"

Zeus had often complained of boredom. Even back then, when
his troubles were not serious ones. It was an ongoing thread during
their meetings. One that Hades and Poseidon had no choice but to
ignore. Maybe he had mentioned that he wanted an heir. Someone
to hand Olympus over to, eventually. To rid himself of it. But Zeus
was often self-loathing. He would pick himself back up again after a
stiff drink and a strong woman.

In an assortment of jumbled minutes, Zeus explained how Gaia's comment was more like an insult than an observation. And that he took it upon himself to craft his own child. His own heir. This wasn't a project of affection and good intentions. He wasn't doing this to prove his love for his wife. It was merely an egotistical exercise, which irritated Hades.

"The soul is too weak," Zeus mumbled to himself as he overlooked the mixing bowl. "I have the strongest essence known to anyone. I should require nothing more."

"A child of just you…" Hades slowly turned to the wall of clay models. "In a body like that…are you trying to kill us?"

"This child will be perfect. It's simply so strong it's diminishing itself. Too strong for stability."

"It's so strong…it's…unstable…?"

"So, when the soul ignites, I need you to capture it. Then, I will put it in my mold and plant it. I will have the perfect babe." Zeus was giving him orders. Hades almost wanted to follow them. He almost wanted to see the spawn of Zeus, so hideous and disgusting it devoured its own father. He wanted Zeus' worst traits to be reflected in the eyes of what only he could create. But this would be Hera's child too. She deserved more than two imperious ichor.

No matter. It wasn't how his powers worked. A soul needed to come into full ignition for it to become a soul. A flicker was nothing. A failed match to phosphorus or a brief flick of the flint.

When Zeus tried again, Hades pretended to be too slow with his watch.

When Zeus tried again, Hades had let the soul escape before Zeus could retrieve a mold.

It wasn't long before Zeus mumbled that Hades was being incompetent on purpose. That he was wasting his time and his molds. Zeus didn't care for rules and explanations as he lunged for the pocket watch. Hades evaded him. Zeus was fast but Hades was lithe. They had played keep-away many times when they were younger. This space was just as small as the childhood bedroom he, Zeus and Poseidon once shared.

Words were exchanged. Insults propelled. Until Hades cursed him and played the best prank he could while Zeus' back was turned.

He began to tilt the bowl of Zeus' work on its side. Preparing to spill the contents to the floor. A child of only one, it was time to put an end to this.

He heaved.

Everything was a blur after that.

Zeus trying to save it. Hades' arm being burned by the liquid in the process. The two of them were intertwined as Zeus was preparing to throttle him. Hades wasn't a fighter, but he could take a punch. Or two. Even from the Godking who he knew would never hit him with full power anyway. But as Zeus pulled back his fist, a vibrant glow came from the bit of essence that had fallen into a whiskey glass that was somehow on the floor. Among the junk.

The most beautiful light Hades had ever seen. Or perhaps, the foul surroundings made it appear so.

"It's...it's..." Zeus stumbled as they leaned over the glass. They eyed the floor as if it were metamorphosing into something new. "Trash!"

Zeus' anger had caused him to erupt from the tiny space, slamming the door open and huffing away furiously. Hades was left with the glow in the dirty whiskey glass. He picked it up, knowing the best thing to do was to destroy it. Only, there was something different with the life he held in his hands. A tug in his heart to offset the burn in his arm. An unfamiliar feeling. One of parental instincts that was difficult to experience as a god.

Hades clutched the whiskey glass closer to him. *Trash* was so unfair to the innocent life that was beating between his fingers, it made him shiver for the unborn's behalf. Had his mind been slower, like the majority of his ichor, his actions would have taken too long, and the light would have died. But the tingling in his arm, the tickle in his heart, and his naturally curious nature had won.

What was the worst that could happen?

He reached for one of Zeus' molds, chuckled to himself and reached for one of Gaia's discards instead. In a sense, this little life was made of abandonment. Of Zeus' neglect and Gaia's castaways. Where was the harm? Examining Gaia's attempts, he noticed they were all male, as Zeus had requested. Only one was a girl. He chose that one.

He wasn't a fine seamster, but he had feigned interest in Hera's knitting long enough to pick up on a technique or two. And he was in the mountain—on the shopkeeper's side. There was a haberdashery close by. He easily obtained some needle and thread. In the safety of Zeus' panic room, under the soft glow of candlelight, he poured the liquid onto the mold and began to sew the thin sheets of essence that were blanketing it. It was a shit job. He didn't need a tutor to tell him so. He found the makeshift pot of Gaia's soil, dug a hole, and placed the mold inside. Zeus had obtained some of Gaia's milk. He truly had thought of everything. Hades poured it. Unsure of the amount so he began with a little. When the soil drank it all he poured a little more. And a little more. And then...nothing.

A little sprout of green should have made its way to the surface by now. But nothing happened. Nothing happened to signify life.

"There, there little one," he said to the earth. It remained still and cold, Gaia's milk no longer providing warmth. "Come now, it's alright."

At the silence of the room, he had given up. The sequence of events that played out in his head made him laugh at his own foolishness. A replacement for Zeus. A girl. Hera had mentioned she wanted a daughter. He would give that to her, and she would have a new family. One without Zeus. She would be happy again and he would be happy with her. Shielding her and her infant in the Underworld. Together. Keeping each other indefinitely.

It was a fantasy. One he was embarrassed to ever think possible.

Leaving the shop, he assumed Zeus would deal with the mess. His ichor had always been untidy, and he imagined the evidence sitting there like buried treasure. But Zeus must have forgotten about it. As did Hades. For buried in that pot of soil, they had left behind a smothered soul.

Dark, it must have been.

A bit of noise from the halls of the mountain's shops might have filtered through. Sounds of doors slamming and holiday shopping. He imagined Zari being unaware and scared of the world that was causing her little discarded pot to tremble and shake.

And then, Hera had called. Zeus pierced himself in the heart with a lightning bolt. The Godking was meant to materialize but his energy had filtered through the vault and seeped into the escape room hidden beneath his bedchamber. The catalyst for Zari to join the world. Hades imagined her soul and form like that of a freed spirit. Rising to the top. The girl's aura had wandered until it found its way through the floor and into Zeus' room. Emerging from underneath his bed. From the trapdoor.

Zeus recalled peeking his head through the door to see them all huddled together. Perhaps, mourning over him. His neck twisted as he tried to hear their despair. He imagined them bawling at his absence. He was about to return to the surface, but Hera had unleashed Robin. Zari casted thunder and he felt it in his heart. She was his ichor and his replacement. She was the daughter he never wanted. She was what set him free. Using the door disguised as a shop entrance within the mountain, he stole some clothes, put on a disguise and ran. He left Olympus and never came back.

Well, he did contact Hades for money a short time after. And for a book on franchising, in regard to *Zack's Taco Shack*. Zeus made sure to look Poseidon in the eye when he repeated the word, *franchise*. The shack was ready to take its endeavors out to sea, "you know...in a certain pleasure ship…"

***

The story was ridiculous.

For Hera, it came down to the fact that Zeus' ego and a prank from Hades had gone too far. Zeus was no more creative than the idea of her slippers being functional after leaving the shack. She had disposed of them and left Hades behind on the beach with Zeus. Zari was a discrepancy after all. A cross-reference. A tangled thread. A manifestation of selfishness and vanity. And yet, none of those things. She was the opposite of those who offered their essence as her life.

After the story, Hera needed a walk. She found Poseidon along the way, his pocket stuffed with Zeus' business plan, and the two joined one another's side as they rounded the path and headed back towards the beach. Despite the past few days of panic, he overall appeared younger. His face had a healthy color and his body seemed lighter. Beneath it all, however, she knew he was anxious. They were simply waiting. Digesting everything until sunset. When Zeus said Zari would be in attendance—preparing for an appointment the two of them usually kept.

When they approached the temples, she felt a nudge on her arm. Poseidon was gesturing towards a cliff that housed a waterfall and overlooked the stretch of sand and water. There, on the edge, sat a small frame in a heavy red robe. Silver hair was secured to the top of her head and her chin was resting on the back of one hand as the other extracted blades of grass thoughtlessly. Her chest rose and fell for a heavy exhale. Hera looked at Poseidon who gave her a brief nod. He would allow her to go first.

Timidly, Hera approached.

Chapter 30

Zari

"Are you real?" the girl mouthed.

Hera nodded. At the extension of her hand, Zari's slow rise to her feet changed into a mad dash into Hera's open arms. She inhaled the scent of her ichor, vibrant and soft. Zari could feel her own electricity, pulsing through their clothing and making tiny scratching sounds as Hera chuckled lightly. Hera ran her fingers through Zari's hair, which was secured with a ribbon. And a tad shorter. Fresh fringe and loose strands shaped her face.

She had cut it. She admitted that at one point she'd been completely bald.

It was part of her training with the monks who'd relieved her of their company after she broke all the rules. She'd spoken during a vow of silence when she spoke of her ichor. When she'd reminisce about her and Poseidon she spoke of kissing and temptations of the flesh. She drank most nights—spirit was one of the few edible things at Zeus' shack. And she'd been clumsy to a fault. It hadn't taken long for the monks to betray their own vow of silence and usher her to the door.

Hera continued playing with her hair. Separating the strands and then allowing them to fall into place again. Zari had her nose in Hera's chest. Her arms were tight around her waist. A tear or two rolled down her cheek as Hera dried them with a steady laugh.

"It's alright, sweeting."

"I didn't think I'd see you again," Zari sniffled.

"Whatever would make you say that?"

"Because I ran away." Zari dried her eyes. The veil around Zeus' perimeter prevented the grimace of a heavy rain. "I was quite awful. The moment I did it, the moment I left, I knew I shouldn't have gone without telling you. But...the longer I stayed...the harder it was for me to come back. I've been gone forever."

Hera asked carefully. "How long do you think you've been absent, exactly?"

Zari was aware that time passed differently. What could seem like days to a god could be weeks to a human.

"An eternity," she sighed. "Six months. Maybe a year."

"Oh...Zari...it has only been six days."

"Only days!?" She was shocked. She felt as though she had been there forever. Choking on water as she sat firmly under waterfalls. Running from the bears she was supposed to fight. Building her own little shack out of wood and leaves only to have it overrun by monkeys.

"Six days too long. But, why did you come here?" Hera moved a loose strand of hair from Zari's face.

"I thought that if I knew who I was I would know how to be better. And to be honest, I thought we were going to see Gaia."

It was a good thing that was not the case, otherwise Zari would have been nothing more than particles of Earth. Gaia was always striving for perfection in her creations and if she knew that one of her missed opportunities had returned to her, she would have disposed of Zari like an artist ripping a page from a sketchbook. She would have taken her within her fingers and unraveled her thread by thread.

"Zeus says I was a mistake. And then he said, 'not really.' I suppose it is because without me he would not have his tacos. The only good thing I've done is bring about tacos and they're not even good." She wiped her eyes. "It's as if I got the worst parts. I'm not as strong as Zeus or as smart as Hades."

Hera held her again, much to Zari's surprise. "You are the best parts of them, believe me."

Zari couldn't help but breathe into Hera's dress, which was a bit damp from being warmed on the beach. And Hera was without shoes. It made Zari smile. Her embrace was so comforting, Zari could have fallen asleep then and there.

"Gather your things and let us be off."

"I can't return to Olympus. I made a promise to myself that I cannot break."

When Zari arrived at Tulum, when Zeus told her the story over a meal that made her skin crawl, he was far less comforting than Hera was now. He was admittingly embarrassed by her. Bluntly, he told her that if she had been a boy and shaped from his fingers, she would be perfect. Strong. That it was Hades who made her soft and weak. His foul mouthing of her ichor made her furious. She had never been furious before. It worsened as he chuckled and laughed, getting a rise out of her that made him straighten himself in his seat and issue a challenge. A challenge for her to try to lay a finger on him.

To her own surprise, to the surprise of Death and Adonis, she leapt across the table. He twirled the end of his beard and laughed as he dodged her assault. She lunged again. Until she grew tired and weary and determined.

"Olympus can't help but crumble with you at the helm," he had pointed to her. "Maybe I should hand you to Gaia. A defect."

"I'll show you," she had said. "I'll prove you wrong!"

"Do that, *sparkles*, and I will give you my sword. And, unlimited tacos!"

She vowed to beat him. Not for the tacos. Not even for the sword. She had told herself that she wouldn't return to Olympus until she defeated Zeus in combat. This was something she wanted to do. For her, this was the proper way to earn the throne. That, and Death had underestimated how much travel allowance he would consume at the transport of three beings across the oceans. They had no plan to get back.

Hera looked as if she didn't know what had gotten into Zari and Zari was more than happy to repeat each and every word, in case Hera had missed a few. Hera held up a finger to stop her. She then quickly, anxiously waved her hand behind her. She was summoning Poseidon, whose smile undid her.

Tall, sturdy, warm and comforting. His touch was different from Hera's, but all the same welcoming. It was one that would make her crumble into a thousand pieces if she wasn't careful. His kisses. He took to her mouth instantly, reminding her of where she belonged.

From above her head, Poseidon looked to Hera.

"Zari does not want to come back."

He held onto her arms but separated them so he could look into her eyes. "Why not?"

"I need to defeat Zeus in combat."

Zari could see her past exhibitions in his worry. She wasn't the most skilled fighter on Olympus. But she wasn't the worst either. Her style resembled Hera's but it was still raw and unkempt. She even had a bit of a hop in her stance, from her restless amount of energy and eagerness to fight. She did not fear Zeus. She only feared failing.

"Let's just go home." Poseidon lowered his forehead to hers. She missed him terribly.

"I know you don't think I can do it—"

"Of course, you can…"

"Ares taught me how to lie," she giggled. "Better yet, he taught me how to spot one." She gave him a brief kiss to his lips, knowing that once she allowed it to linger, she would have changed her mind and retreated back to the comforts of his arms and the palace. With Hera watching over her. Getting her out of trouble. But no more. "I have to do this. It's the one thing I've truly set my mind to—" she cleared her throat when Hera lifted a brow to her. "I mean…the one *self-starting* thing I've set my mind to."

Already, she saw the proof in her increasing fortitude. If neither Hera nor Poseidon could sway her, she was growing more and more resilient. Something she would need when she left this island. The sun was setting, and it was time for her nightly appointment with Zeus. Losing her robe, she revealed the small sword and shield that was on her back. The training pair that had been given to her—that she had taken—from Hephaestus' shop. She handed her cloak to Hera who took it with a hesitant smile.

She proceeded towards their spot on the beach. Zeus was already waiting.

***

"You know what to expect when we return?" Hades' narrow eyes and statuesque posture shook him. To say his employer was angry, well, words could not describe. He had brought Zari here without his knowledge and, despite having a perfectly functioning pocket watch, had lost track of time. And travel credits. But not all hope was lost as his friends instantly fell into new traditions. Zari was determined to defeat the former Godking, Adonis was seduced by the locals and the new breeds of flowers and as for himself, well...aside from having the sand crystalize between his joints and being without a respectable variety of cheeses, the island life had welcomed him.

In the culture of the humans in this land, Death was...in a way...celebrated. So much in fact, that his very skull was painted in beautiful colors and the children, instead of throwing stones at him, danced with him. He was invited to dinner parties. He was praised and prayed to. Never feared.

"A bath..." Death said carefully, testing his employer's humor. Magenta flowers and curls of ice blue paint on his facade made him look lively and capable of banter if Hades wanted to do that. Instead, Hades did not flinch, nor move. Death wondered if his lordship was breathing. "And...a performance evaluation."

Death wondered if a compliment would help. He could mention Hades' lack of coat due to the heat, his wind-swept hair that was speckled with bits of sand or the sweat along his brow. No, perhaps a compliment wasn't the way. Death knew, there was only one way to atone for his mistake. He hung his head. His master had the words *exit interview* written all over him.

"I will hand in my notice—"

"And save you from Janus and Hecate and all the rubbish you've caused for everyone for the past few days..." Hades grinned with a sadism that could only belong to the Soul King. He said nothing after that. And for once, Death resented his job security.

***

She was happy but nervous to see Hades. Although they were ichor, gods without relation, she felt that he was closer to her than soil. As if they were...family. Paired with her natural ability to forgive, she held no resentment to the ichor who had given her a chance and welcomed her into his home. She gave him a small wave, a bend of her fingers. He returned the gesture, recapping their meeting day. She also tried to smile at Death whose skeletal structure looked so helpless she could only imagine the level of trouble he was in. She made a note to try to smooth things over in time. It wasn't Death's fault. He was simply trying to help. She never would have found her answers without him.

Parting the heavy leaves, Adonis was being followed by a court of islanders. Women and men and children trailed behind him like a massive cape made of people. He took his place beside the ichor and smiled at Hera, attempting to hand her a flower.

"Just so we're clear," Hera said to him, "None of us came for either of you two."

He and Death exchanged glances. They then stood shoulder to shoulder as if they had only each other to lean on.

Zari took her place before Zeus. He looked irritated. Rumor was that his taco shack had an unfortunate mishap. Structural issues, perhaps. It was poorly built so it was only a matter of time before the shed came crashing down. She hoped his distress would be to her advantage. She tapped her sword and shield together and prayed to her confidence. *I need you today. Please give me strength.*

She was parallel to the ocean. Everyone else was positioned along the tree line. Zeus grunted as he conjured his sword. A large, heavy Claymore with a golden hilt and diamond tip.

"Let's get this over with," he said from behind his thick beard.

She nodded.

She lunged first.

Purposely, she shortened her attack, making his parry ineffective. She did a sidestep to his right and gave her sword a horizontal swipe at his ribs. She missed. His sandals dug into the sand as he slashed his blade through the air. It made contact with the ground, but the force of his power shook her anyway.

Neither bounce nor balance would have prevented her from stumbling. Planting her feet firmly and absorbing the shock, she found that worked better than trying to avoid it. The electricity funneled through her body and fed off her own. She sent a pulse through the earth, trying to unsteady him this time.

He chuckled, low and cumbersome as he countered with a more powerful wave.

"Clever," he said as they reset. "But not enough."

"I'm not finished yet."

He lurched.

She knew it would be to her disadvantage if their blades ever made contact. Zeus was simply heavier. More power was behind his swing. And his sword was massive. Enough to make quick work of her if she didn't keep moving. She ducked. She dodged. Her movements were swift but if she didn't figure out a way to go on the offensive she would tire.

The race to dismantle one another would stretch for days.

Ever since she challenged him, she hadn't come close to being victorious. She didn't have the heart to tell her ichor that they would be waiting for quite a while for her return. She thought it best they saw it for themselves. Just how unsuitable she was to be the Godking.

"You're getting better at running away," Zeus taunted her evasiveness. "Why not accept that about yourself?"

"I'm still here," she wavered.

"And wasting my time."

This time, when Zeus thrusted his blade in her direction, he used his lightning as an extension of his reach. She held up her shield and found herself stunned by the impact. Constricting electricity made her bones feel like stone. He had her now, his sword pressed against her blade. She did her best to push against him, but he was too large. Too powerful. He was burrowing her into the ground with pounding pulses of energy.

One, after another.

After another.

The sand and dirt hugged her. Her ankles, her knees, her waist. Until she was buried to her chest. Her arms holding onto her weapons.

"You are at home, girl. In the dirt from which you came. You're no heir of mine."

Zari could hear Hera's cursing of him. She could see Poseidon readying himself to intervene. She didn't want her ichor coming to her rescue. She called out to them, demanding they not assist her.

"Zari, end this nonsense!" Hera called.

Zari shook her head. She still had her blade in hand, so she wasn't disarmed. Not yet. There was still some fight in her. She simply had to get free. She began churning her electricity around her, shifting the sand away from her body. It was considerably difficult. Useless, even. Zeus was pushing her back into the ground the more she tried to come up from it.

"I am Zeus," he bellowed huskily. "You are but a measly thread of me. Weak and feeble. The power of the skies is within me!"

It was in her too. As well as...

She turned to Hades. She had not one but *two* ichor's essence strengthening her golden blood. Zeus' power had come front and center. As pretentious and unforgiving as he. But Hades' power was also within. Subtle. But just as strong. She needed only to *feel* it. To coax it into coming to the surface.

As if reading the invisible thread that bound them, Hades smiled at her and nodded.

Suddenly, the ground began to tremble. And not from their electricity. Something large and heavy was moving beneath her. Something caused a wave to fold towards them from the ocean. It wasn't Poseidon. It wasn't one of Hera's notorious earthquakes. It was something else. Something big and powerful was making its way from the water to the beach. Below her feet. Lifting her. Supporting her.

High. High. Higher she went. Until Zeus was small beneath her. Zari crouched and placed her hand on the back of a whale. The whale who had performed tricks for her and Death when they released him in the Underworld.

She thanked him for his help.

It released a howl at her appreciation.

It dissipated and she landed on her feet. Using her electricity to tighten the grip of her sword, she did not waste time with unnecessary gloating. She lunged at Zeus. As quickly as she could. Meeting him head on.

"Nice trick," he cursed. A smile was hidden in the corner of his lips. "But it won't help you."

She wasn't done. Nor was she expecting to beat him like this. *He* should have known that. The sound of a large cat came from behind him. Zeus lowered his brow at the sight of a charging panther. *The* panther. The ghost of the cat she had accidentally tossed at Adonis was emerging from the tree line and pouncing on Zeus from behind. It released a growl and sunk its teeth into his skin. Zeus tried to reach for it, but the animal was a spirit. Its body was pure energy. Only his electricity would work and even so, the panther would materialize and lunge again.

Zari noticed two things.

First, Zeus did not like animals. Especially peacocks.

When Zari summoned Robin, the bird morphed at her feet with a visible attitude. As if he could not be bothered. But as much as Robin did not like being disrupted or commanded by none other than Hera, he loathed Zeus. Robin watched the fumbling ichor as he continued to combat the cat. The peacock's eyes shrunk into tiny, blood lusting slits. As if he had been training for this day, he charged. Pecking. Biting. Nipping at Zeus' heels. No part of the former Godking's body was safe. Hera was overjoyed. Zari understood Zeus' pain.

But then she noticed the second thing.

The animals were attacking the spirit of Zeus. She could see it. His celestial form was being tugged and pulled from his physical body. The effect slowed him. It made him weaker. She had a chance.

With her sword, she dodged and rolled for a few strikes before their blades crossed again. This time, she leaned in, dropping her sword and keeping her shield up. She reached out her hand and took hold of him. With her *feeling*, with the power she knew she had, she clutched her fingers around his soul and pulled.

The spirits of the animals disappeared. They took refuge, back into the Underworld, allowing her to send one final jolt of electricity to draw Zeus' stubborn spirit from his flesh. When she had him, when his body went still and stiff, she dropped her shield, opened her hands which were pulsing with electricity and called forth her sword. The blade filled her grasp and she twisted her body to swipe his blade from his hands. She released his spirit, which fell eagerly into his body. When Zeus blinked, he realized he was on the floor. His hands freed of his weapon. Zari was standing over him. Panting. Proud. A tear filled her eye and she promised herself she wouldn't cry. But she couldn't help it. She was so happy that she could not help but weep.

Zeus was on his back.

Zeus was disarmed.

She did it. She defeated the Godking.

Chapter 31

Zari & Hera

Zari examined herself in the mirror. She liked her look for Spring, even though it was a bit provocative. Her dress was made of sheer fabric studded in jewels and gold embroidery. Without the silk overlay, she would have appeared naked and dusted in riches. Her peplos was trimmed in gold. The top draped over one of her shoulders, gathered at her waist and cascaded into elaborate folds down to her ankles. A leather strophion lifted her bosom and her arms were wrapped in weaving gold cuffs. On her feet were thin gold sandals that wove around her legs. It was the first time she looked in the mirror and felt like a god.

Her handmaiden was inserting the final pins in her hair. It was parted down the middle, aside from her growing fringe and was woven into two chunky braids that intertwined into a knot that was held in place with ribbons. The rest of the hair was allowed to fall down her back. Delicate earrings no bigger than a coin hung from ears.

She smiled at her reflection but more so at the gift that had arrived that morning. It was from Poseidon. A beautiful Russian Faberge egg smothered in sapphires and gold trimmings glimmered from every angle. Gold eagle wings protruded from the top. Pressing the diamond clasp, the egg parted vertically. When it did, it became a music box, playing the carousel song *Nani Nani* from a mechanism under its cushioned interior. And there, in the center, was a glass figurine. A replica of the precious bay horse that was wrapped in a wreath of gold ivy and grapes.

"Well, don't you look darling." Hera smiled when she entered her room. But if she was *darling,* Hera was a dream. Her white dress featured a plunging neckline with cutouts across the length of her body. The openings were lined in gold that cascaded down her skirts and ended at her ankles. On her shoulders was a modern cape that was not shy of gold beading. Her hair was traditionally styled—thick curls and gold cords held it in place. In her hands was a box.

When Zari turned in her seat, her handmaiden, still struggling to insert the last pin, withheld a playful sigh at her inability to sit still. Hera took the pin from the handmaiden and dismissed her so that she and Zari could have the room to themselves.

"Do you truly think I'm alright?" Zari asked. "It's a bit breezy."

"Others will be wearing quite less." Hera adjusted a strand of Zari's hair. She then secured the box before her, waiting for Zari to take a seat on the settee before her bed. *Her* bed. This was Zari's room now, officially.

"What is it? Is it a present?" Hera chuckled at her impatience and handed the box to her. Zari's fingers were delicate but eager as she untied the ribbon and opened the lid. She held a hand to her mouth, and the box almost fell from her lap. "I...I don't know...is it for me?"

"I was going to give it to you for last year's ball, as a coming out present."

"You said I wasn't going to get one unless I did something grand. Or...got married."

Hera did say that. And when she intended to give it to Zari, the girl hadn't done anything spectacular. It was a gift to ease her guilty conscience for being so short with her and dampening her spirits. But circumstances had changed.

"I would say you've earned it, yes? You defeated the Godking."

Zari beamed. "I did do that." And she had a magnificent sword because of it. It functioned well as a floor mirror.

"And, you've been more disciplined when it comes to your studies."

"I have...tried..." Now, she had a coronet. As perfect as Hera's. It had two small vines of petrified beech leaves and cypress. Instead of a diamond center, it was a sapphire. A beautiful blue stone that reflected specks of gold.

Hera asked for Zari to turn around in her seat. The girl clutched her hands together, keeping them in her lap and out of reach of anything she would stun from her visible excitement. Anything, except for Hera. The moment her ichor lowered the coronet to Zari's hair, the electricity tickled her fingertips.

"Careful Zari, or I might not need the pins to keep it in place." As she finished, she nodded at Zari to meet her reflection. Hera couldn't deny, it fit her perfectly.

"It's so beautiful." Zari twirled before her mirror. "Thank you so much, I love it!"

"I am glad."

Zari took Hera's hand and guided her to the side of her bed. The two of them sat comfortably close.

"You've done so much for me." Zari squeezed her hand. "I want to do something for you."

"I don't need anything." In fact, Hera looked a bit nervous. And not in the way one would expect from a surprise. Being notoriously picky, Hera wasn't a fan of them.

"You do." Zari's certainty made her smirk. "You need my advice."

"Advice?"

"Because you know I would say or do nothing that would cause you harm. Ever. Which is why I think, no, it's why I *believe* you need to speak to Hades." Hera sighed. "Please, please talk to him. He's so miserable without you and it makes me sad. It makes my heart feel as if it's going to burst into pieces. He loves you. He told me he told you."

"Honestly." Hera was appalled that the two of them had spoken about her in confidence, but Zari had been spending so much time in the Underworld and Oceanus, it appeared that the three kings had a camaraderie that had never been stronger. It was quite nice. Although, a bit annoying when they compared policies.

It had been a year since their time in Tulum. When they came back to Olympus, the Garden Party and Spring Ball were so behind schedule—practically over— that they settled for a small celebration instead. Everyone dove into their work and the aftermath caused by the hecatoncheires. Most upset, however, was Cerberus. The poor girl, robbed of her time to dress up and be photographed, made sure to give the invalids a piece of her mind when she was unleashed from the Underworld in order to help defend the realm.

This year, they were making up for lost time. The gardens were overflowing with roses, hydrangeas, tulips and water lilies. And a dozen other flowers that she would have to turn to Adonis to identify—she could do that, considering. After she spoke to Hades on Death's behalf, asking for forgiveness and his mercy, Death returned the favor by seeking ways to spare Adonis. The reluctant Soul King, not wanting to deal with any more of Zari's tears for that day, might have mumbled that the quill could have been mistaken. For now, Adonis' demise was furloughed. A happy ending, Zari thought, for he could tell Iris how much he cared for her. Even if the feeling was not mutual.

For the past few days, they had been mingling with the residents of Olympus. Persephone brought a few baked goods to distribute and Dionysus debuted his new flavor of wine. Ares and Athena nearly flattened the mountain during their chariot race. Which didn't matter really, considering that Poseidon won. He made sure that he was going to be the only one bestowing the winner's kiss to the Queen, which allowed him to break tradition and kiss the King instead.

Tonight, the ball.

But Zari couldn't be happy knowing that Hades was still heartbroken. She needed Hera to forgive him.

"He lied, Zari. He lied about who you were and what happened to Zeus."

"Was that worse than what Zeus has ever done to you?"

"Maybe not. But I *expect* those things from Zeus. I didn't...not Hades…"

Zari smiled, when she truly wanted nothing more than to shake her. "He's waited lifetimes to have you. And he'd do anything not to lose you. A love like that, it's so beautiful. You deserve something beautiful."

Hera patted Zari's hand. "I have you."

Zari's groan made Hera laugh. She tilted her head back and looked to her painted ceilings. She mumbled, so low Hera could barely hear her. "This was never about me."

"What?" Hera lowered her brow.

Zari shook her head and stood to her feet. Her outstretched hand acknowledged that the conversation was over. There would be no more mention of Hades. Not now, anyway. The two of them interlocked their arms and proceeded down the halls giggling as if it were their first Season. They paused at the top of the stairs before descending together. Music could be heard from the gardens. Zari squeezed Hera's arm as they stepped outside. Everyone cheered for the King and Queen.

***

Of course, the moment Zari exited the palace, Poseidon closed the gap quicker than Hera could blink. If Hera wanted Zari to experience other possibilities, neither of them were giving the other the opportunity. Hera had feared Poseidon smothering Zari. But, from what Hera could see, Zari commanded him in equal measures. He was an ichor who would have wanted nothing more.

When Poseidon offered his hand for a dance, he swept her away among the sea of soft, white fabrics and gold jewelry. Everyone was happy. Everyone was in good spirits. Hera, who took her place on her throne, overlooking the dancing guests, lowered her lashes. Zari's words tinged her heart.

A love like that, it's so beautiful. You deserve something beautiful.

She was tired of people telling her what she deserved. It only reminded her of what she didn't have. She wanted love. She simply did not want to be hurt by it. She knew that love could not exist without pain, but it suited her to avoid the trials altogether. Love might have been beautiful, being alone was easier.

But even so, her nights were full of fits as Hades invaded her dreams. She thought the ichor had developed a second power. A power that made her think of him so much it unnerved her. His touch. His kiss. The way he made love to her so sweetly. Had he truly been miserable, as Zari had relayed? Compared to her, she didn't think he knew what *misery* meant.

Her fingers needed the company of a drink.

But, speak of the devil—

"My Queen." Hades stood before her, just before the first step that led to the platform where her and Zari's thrones were placed. It would be the first time they had spoken today. For the past week in fact. The year consisted of brief conversations that she tried to end even faster. And mostly, him asking if she had received his letters. He knew where to hit her, when he began sending her correspondence from the point of view of Robin.

Apparently, Robin missed her terribly.

Apparently, Robin wondered why she never came to visit.

Robin wanted to know if she would come over for dinner.

Robin said that Hades got better at playing *Watch My Cow*.

Those letters had made her smile, even though she did her best to conceal it. She looked away from him. Wanting to ignore him. However, he was clearing his throat and extending his hand. She examined him as if he had lost his senses.

No one asked the Queen to dance. Ever. Zeus would have thrown a fit in the past, and for a moment she wished he were there to dissuade Hades. Oh, it would be difficult to tell him no. He was so handsome, her breath nearly left her. He was wearing his draped trousers—loose around the leg but fitted around his hips and ankles. Over his shoulders was an open chiton with the cords of his rank. His chest was partially bare. His skin teased her behind a partially buttoned vest.

Her answer was in her silence. And he would have accepted it, had not her body done the opposite and nearly leapt into his arms.

"My word!" she gasped. Her backside felt as though it was on fire. "Zari!"

The girl shrugged from behind Hera's throne, as if she had forgotten something...behind Hera's seat. She had given Hera's chair a bit of a charge for Hades' liking. He mouthed his appreciation as he held onto her, whose trip would have been embarrassing had he not been there to catch her. *No,* her trip would not have happened had Hades not been there. Had the two not been conspiring with one another to get her attention.

"Found it," Zari said of nothing as she took a seat in the Godking's chair. Hera pushed away from Hades, but he did not release his hold on her.

"Let go—"

"I want to dance with you," he said into her ear. "Please."

"No." She wanted to go back to her place, but Zari shook her head. She held out a finger to the vacant throne, threatening Hera with another shock that made her wonder what happened to her kind, pleasant, angelic—

"Just a turn," he pleaded with those large puppy dog eyes. Ones that rivalled Cerberus.

She couldn't. She wouldn't. She...couldn't go back to her seat. If there was any question of whether or not they were cut from the same cloth—she sighed.

"One dance," she grumbled.

"I will cherish it until next year."

"You are hopeful."

He took her hand, much to everyone's surprise at the changing tides. The Queen was dancing. Dancing with the King of the Underworld. His hand rested on the nape of her back. He pulled her in closer and she complied, wishing he would maintain the distance of respectable dance partners. She took a breath. He took a step. He led her as he did during their lovemaking.

Lovemaking.

She could call it that because she had experienced everything but. Hades had introduced her to parts of her heart that were submerged in uncharted waters. Stone was softening. The darkness was residing. She didn't want to be upset with him. She missed his company and even in her snubbing of him, his smiles in her direction melted her problems for the day.

Why did she have to be so stubborn?

Why was he once again being so patient with her?

"I love you," he said, as if he could read her mind. When she lifted her chin, still surprised that he could declare such a thing after she had treated him unkindly, he was smiling. Warm and affectionate. "I am still in love with you. I will be. For eternity." Her cheeks must have turned the shade of roses for he pulled her in closer to him.

A love like that, it's so beautiful. You deserve something beautiful.

"But I don't deserve you," she said out loud. He nearly mis-stepped. Something Hades never did.

"Why would you say that? Have I ever given you a reason to believe otherwise? Darling, we could compare our inadequacies until the world came to an end, but would that not waste *more* time? As much as you don't believe in how wonderful you are, I will happily remind you, every day, that you are wonderful."

Her blush deepened. "You have always been tenacious…"

He chuckled lightly. "I will need something to do in between having you in my bed. Worshipping you would be a better use of my time, don't you agree?"

"Goodness…" Her face grew hot.

"I will worship you every day, every morning, every—"

"Hades." Her knees began to tremble. His hold tightened. She blinked and wondered why the room was spinning. Or, on the contrary, why it was not. The music had stopped. Long ago. The floor was clear, and it was just them.

"Tell me you love me." His fingers brushed the underside of her chin. "Tell me."

"I…"

"Or don't you? Are you…still angry at me—"

"I will always be angry with you," she said, wondering when a tear escaped her. One he was catching with his finger. "I will always be angry with *something*. But…" She took a breath. She imagined her past. One with a loathsome husband who abandoned her and empty rooms. Now, she had…more. She had Zari. She could have Hades. Both of them reminded her that she could have something… *beautiful.*

"I would want more children," she admitted. She was embarrassed by her outburst, and even more so, by her easy inclusion of Zari. Admitting that the girl was her child. He nuzzled his nose to her own in tiny, tender strokes.

"Ten, maybe twenty?" He whispered. "I can make them myself. I would say, I'm a bit of an expert."

256

She laughed, too loud for her reputation. "Perhaps we could start with one or two." She raised her chin towards him, looking deep into his silver eyes. She couldn't hold it anymore. She could afford to take a break. A break from pushing him away. If it meant that they could finally come together. "I love you, Hades. Gods, I can't believe I've said it—"

He pressed his lips to her, as if she would change her mind if given the opportunity. And in that moment, everything became warm. Everything became hazier. Her future was uncertain, their titles, their realms. However, she was certain of her love for him. She wanted him, more than anything. Nothing between them. Just love.

For all eternity.

ABOUT THE AUTHOR

Chantel Grayson was born in Dallas, Texas where she went to school for Journalism. She enjoys drawing, playing video games and re-organizing her art studio for the hundredth time.

COMING SOON

FROM CHANTEL GRAYSON

Will You Be My Hero

Paige Waters has worked hard to become the most infamous supervillain in the world. But when her fame and fortune is jeopardized after her arch nemesis and renowned hero unexpectedly retires, she learns his secret identity in order to convince him to return to the limelight to combat her. To her surprise, Paige finds out that he is none other than her high school crush, Jay Alexander.

Visit www.chantelgraysonbooks.com for updates and excerpts.

Made in the USA
Coppell, TX
03 September 2020

36473513R00148